**"Time for me to step up and make a fresh start."**

"Really?"

I saw the expression of doubt on my sister's face. "Really," I assured her. "As a matter of fact, after dinner I'm going to browse the Internet and see if I can find a place to stay for . . . well, I'm not quite sure how long. But longer than a week."

Her expression of doubt now changed to concern. "Geez, Chloe. I don't want you to think I'm pushing you to leave. Can you afford to rent a place over there for an extended period of time?"

That thought had been floating around my head, too, and a solution had occurred to me. "Yes, I can. God knows when this house will sell. But don't forget, Aunt Maude also left each of us fifty thousand dollars, and remember what she said in her will?"

Grace laughed. "I do. She said to be sure not to spend the money on something practical. To use the money on frivolous things."

I nodded. "Because she wanted us to remember her and smile whenever we spent any of that money. She wanted us to enjoy the moments and have fun with it."

"Exactly. I have to agree with you, Chloe. Aunt Maude would love for you to take some of that money, rent a place in Ormond Beach and give yourself a chance to start over."

And I knew my sister was right.

**Also by Terri DuLong**

*Spinning Forward*
"A Cedar Key Christmas" in *Holiday Magic*
*Casting About*
*Sunrise on Cedar Key*
*Secrets on Cedar Key*
*Postcards from Cedar Key*
*Farewell to Cedar Key*

# Patterns of Change

Terri DuLong

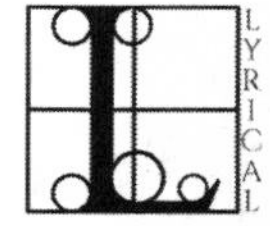


LYRICAL PRESS
Kensington Publishing Corp.
www.kensingtonbooks.com

LYRICAL PRESS BOOKS are published by

Kensington Publishing Corp.
119 West 40th Street
New York, NY 10018



All Kensington titles, imprints, and distributed lines are available at special quantity discounts for bulk purchases for sales promotion, premiums, fund-raising, educational, or institutional use.

Special book excerpts or customized printings can also be created to fit specific needs. For details, write or phone the office of the Kensington Sales Manager: Kensington Publishing Corp., 119 West 40th Street, New York, NY 10018. Attn. Sales Department. Phone: 1-800-221-2647.



First Electronic Edition: November 2015
eISBN-13: 978-1-60183-551-2
eISBN-10: 1-60183-551-5

First Print Edition: November 2015
ISBN-13: 978-1-60183-552-9
ISBN-10: 1-60183-552-3

Printed in the United States of America

*With love for my BFF, Alice Jordan*
*Thank you for helping me to keep my dream alive*

ACKNOWLEDGMENTS

A huge thank you to Pauline Oilowski and Sandi Van Epps, owners of The Ball of Yarn in Ormond Beach, for hosting many of my book signings, but most of all for welcoming me into the community when I relocated to your town. I deeply appreciate how you shared the history of the area with me and answered all my questions. Your shop became the inspiration for my fictional Dreamweaver Yarn Shop.

Thank you to Mary Ann Sines for being my "Maddie" and for driving me around the area and showing me important places in my new adopted hometown.

To Melba Hayden, my very good new friend. Thank you for so many things . . . for making me feel so welcome in the community, for taking me on the tour at the Casements, for including me in your YaYa group and especially for introducing me to the Stetson Mansion. What began as author and fan has evolved into a fun and loving friendship. I'm so glad that our paths have crossed!

To the YaYa's . . . Thank you so much to Shirley Marquez, Patty Calender, Gail Dockery, Celenia Saunders, and Joyce Johnson for allowing this Yankee gal to join your group.

Another huge thank you to JT Thompson and Michael Solari, owners of the Stetson Mansion in DeLand, Florida. Thank you, JT, for doing the personal tour with Melba and me and for sharing your uplifting philosophy of dreaming big. Thank you to both of you for the major renovation and love you put into the house so the rest of us can now enjoy it. The mansion was my inspiration for Koi House . . . because I truly do believe that houses have souls. And thank you to Debbie Pixley for all you do to welcome the many guests to the Mansion.

To the Daytona Diva Red Hatters . . . you gals are so much fun! A writer needs fun time in between the isolation of penning a novel so a huge thank you to our Queen Mum, Alice House, for the outstanding job you do organizing and planning all the fun things for us to do.

To the Ormond Beach Historical Society, thank you for providing lectures, information, and tours that enabled me to get to know the history of my new town.

A big thank you to another new friend and fellow knitter, Madonna Reda. You were certainly one of those friends I just immediately clicked with. Thank you for the fun outings we've had and for all the ones that are yet to come.

To Alicia Condon, my editor. Thank you for giving my new series a chance, in addition to being the ideal editor to work with.

And to my readers and Facebook friends . . . I hope you know how much I appreciate your support. Thank you so much for your feedback and love for my stories and characters. You have been with me through the ups and downs. You have encouraged me, shared with me, and made me laugh on days I really needed a chuckle. I'm very grateful to have you in my life . . . both the real and the fictional.

# Chapter 1

Sitting on Aunt Maude's porch watching the April sun brighten the sky wasn't where I thought I'd be ten months ago. Having experienced two major losses, I found myself still in the small fishing village of Cedar Key . . . and like the boats in the gulf, I was drifting with no sense of purpose or direction.

Life had proved to me once again that it can change in the blink of an eye. I certainly found that out four years ago when my husband, Parker, left me for a trophy wife. But eventually I pulled myself together and made my way from Savannah to this small town on the west coast of Florida. Straight to the shelter and love of my aunt. At the time, I'd been estranged from my sister, Grace, for many years, but eventually Grace and I renewed our bond and now we were closer than we'd ever been.

The ring tone on my cell phone began playing and I knew without looking at the caller ID that it was Gabe's daughter, Isabelle—she was the only person who called me before eight in the morning.

"Hey," I said. "How're you doing?"

A deep sigh came across the line. "Okay. I just had another battle with Haley about going to school, but I managed to get her out the door. How about you?"

"Yeah, okay here too. Just finishing up my coffee and then I'll be heading to the yarn shop to help out."

I wasn't even gainfully employed anymore because I'd given up my partnership with Dora in the local yarn shop when I thought I was relocating to the east coast of Florida . . . with Gabe. And now Gabe was gone.

Another sigh came across the line. "It's funny. I didn't see Dad all that much, but I knew he was *there*. Do you know what I mean?"

"I do. Sometimes I think we just take it for granted that those we love will always be with us."

Losing Gabe in the blink of an eye was a heartbreaking reminder of the fact that life was indeed fragile. We had made great plans for a bright new future together. When he arrived in Cedar Key to spend the winter months, he had signed up to take some men's knitting classes at the yarn shop. I knew immediately that I liked him, and the feeling was mutual. Eight months later we'd made a commitment to relocate together to Ormond Beach on the east coast. Gabe was also an expert knitter and we had put a deposit on a lovely home just outside the city limits, where he would tend to the alpacas we'd raise and we'd both run a yarn shop downtown. But that wasn't to be.

"Exactly," Isabelle said. "And poor Dad didn't even make it to Philly to sell his condo. This might sound selfish, but if I had to lose him, I'm glad it happened right here at my house." I heard a sniffle across the phone line. "At least I was with him at the end."

We both were. Gabe had wanted to make a stop outside Atlanta on our way to Philly to visit his daughter and granddaughter. But on the third day of our stay, sitting on Isabelle's patio after dinner, a grimace covered Gabe's face, he clutched his chest and he was gone. I jumped up to perform CPR while Isabelle called 911 but by the time the paramedics arrived, it was too late. A massive coronary had claimed his life. Just like that.

"No, it's not selfish at all," I said. "I'm glad I was with him too."

"We've both had a time of it, haven't we? I lose Dad and then two months later, Roger decides he doesn't love me anymore."

It was actually the breakup of Isabelle's marriage that had brought the two of us closer. While she had been civil to me when we'd first met the previous June, she had been a bit cool. I remembered how she had emphatically informed me that she wasn't called Izzy or Belle. "It's *Isabelle*," she'd said.

I chalked it up to father-daughter jealousy on her part. Although she wasn't at all close to her mother, who had taken off to Oregon years ago after her divorce from Gabe, I had a feeling that Isabelle didn't want another woman in her father's life. But when her husband up and left her, I was the first person she called. Sobbing on the phone, she related that she was experiencing the same thing that had happened to me—her husband had fallen out of love with her. Common troubles have a way of uniting women.

"Any further word on the divorce settlement?" I asked.

"Yes, that's why I'm calling. It's been decided that I will get the house. At least until Haley is eighteen, so that gives me five years to figure out what I'm doing. And when we sell it, we each get half."

"That sounds fair enough."

"Yeah, except that Haley is so unhappy here. Between the loss of her grandfather and her father leaving, it's been a difficult time for her. And to make matters worse, things at school aren't going well either."

I knew Haley was a bright girl and a good student, so I was surprised to hear this. "What's going on?"

"Well," she said, and I heard hesitation in her tone. "In the ten months since you've seen her, Haley has really packed on some pounds. Unfortunately, I think she's taking comfort in food. And you know how cruel kids can be. Especially thirteen-year-old girls."

"Oh, no." I didn't know Haley well, but when I met her for the first time we immediately clicked. Unlike her mother, she didn't display any frostiness toward me. Quite the opposite. She seemed to genuinely like me and I liked her. "What a shame. Gosh, I know kids have always been mean but today, from what I hear, they seem to have taken it to a new level."

"You have no idea. Hey, how's Basil doing?"

I smiled and glanced down at the twenty-pound dog sleeping inches from my foot. I guess you could say that Basil was my legacy from Gabe. I had gotten to know the dog well during the months that Gabe was on the island, and we had taken an instant liking to each other. When Gabe passed away, there was the question of what to do with Basil. Although I know that Haley would have loved to keep him, Isabelle had insisted that wasn't possible and even hinted that perhaps he should go to the pound. That was when I stepped in and offered to give Basil a home. I think gratefulness has a lot to do with loyalty, because Basil hasn't left my side since we flew back to Florida from Atlanta. Basil in his carrier, in the cabin with me, of course.

"Oh, he's great. I'm so glad I took him. He's a great little dog and sure keeps me company."

"That's good. Well, give him a pat from Haley and me. Any decision yet on what you're doing? Do you think you'll stay in Cedar Key?"

"I honestly don't know, Isabelle. I'm no closer to a decision now than I was after Aunt Maude died two months ago. And Grace has been hinting that she and Lucas might want to move to Paris permanently."

My sister had married a wonderful fellow four years before. Lucas owned the book café in town, but he was originally from Paris, and it was beginning to sound like he wanted to bring his family back to his roots in France. Which included my sister and three-year-old niece, Solange.

"Oh, gee, and where would that leave you? Would you put your aunt's house up for sale?"

"I just don't know. I think Grace is trying to go easy with me right now. She doesn't want to add any more pressure, but it's not fair of me to hold them back if that's what they want. Besides, in this economy, property just isn't selling on the island. My building downtown has been on the market for ten months."

"Yeah, true. Well, listen, Chloe, I need to get going here. You take care and keep in touch."

"Will do, and give Haley a hug from me."

I disconnected and looked down at Basil, who had his head on his paws but was looking up at me with his sweet brown eyes.

"Well, fellow, time for us to get moving too."

He jumped up, tail wagging, ready for whatever I suggested.

I headed into the house for a shower and breakfast before we opened the yarn shop at ten.

Dora and I took turns opening the shop, and today she wouldn't be in till noon.

"Come on, Basil. Time for coffee first," I said, unclipping his leash and heading to the coffeemaker.

Dora had her own dog, Oliver, who was now elderly and didn't come to the shop with her anymore, so she was more than happy to have Basil with us during work hours. He was a good boy and enjoyed greeting customers, and I think he was a hit with them as well.

Very well mannered, he had just turned two years old. Gabe had gotten him as a puppy from a rescue group. His ancestry was of unknown origin, but he strongly resembled a cross between a Scottish terrier and a poodle. When designer dogs became popular and Gabe was questioned on Basil's breed, he'd jokingly refer to him as a Scottiepoo.

I had just poured the water into the coffeemaker when the door chimes tinkled and I turned around to see Shelby Sullivan enter the shop.

"Hey, Shelby. Just in time for coffee. It'll be ready shortly."

"Great. I found a nice pattern to make Orli a sweater, so I need to get some yarn."

Shelby Sullivan was a best-selling romance author, born and raised on Cedar Key, and an addicted knitter, especially when she was between novels.

"How're Josie and Orli doing? I imagine they appreciate the sweaters to keep them warm in the Boston area."

Shelby laughed as she fingered some yummy lavender alpaca yarn. "They're doing great and they seem to have survived their first winter up there and all the snow. Although I'm told it's not unusual to get some even in April."

Shelby's daughter, Josie Sullivan Cooper, had married the love of her life and the father of her daughter, Orli, the previous October. The wedding had been the event of the year on the island and thanks to Shelby's expert guidance, it had been on par with many celebrity weddings. Josie's husband, Grant, was an attorney in Boston and the three of them resided on the North Shore of the city.

"I saw on the national weather that the temps are still pretty chilly up there," I said, handing her a mug of coffee. "I'm sure it's quite a change from the tropical climate they're used to."

Shelby nodded. "Thanks. Yeah, but they both seem to love being in Boston and that's what matters."

I smiled as I recalled the control freak that Shelby used to be. But a scare with uterine cancer the year before had put life in perspective for her. She truly did seem to be less stressed and more understanding of Josie, allowing their mother-daughter relationship to strengthen.

"How about you?" she asked. "How are *you* doing?"

I let out a sigh. "I'm doing okay. As well as can be expected, I guess, but I'm beginning to feel like my life is on hold. In limbo."

"Two major losses in your life within eight months will certainly do that. When the time is right, you'll know which direction to take."

"I hope so," I said and took a sip of coffee. "I feel fortunate that we had Aunt Maude these extra years. We knew her heart was bad. The house is just so empty without her around."

Shelby placed eight skeins of alpaca on the counter and patted my arm. "I'm sure it is. Maybe you should still consider going over to

Ormond Beach. You know . . . something different. New beginnings and all that."

"It just wouldn't be the same without Gabe. All of our plans are gone."

"Yes, they are, but that's part of life. It constantly changes whether we want it to or not. Believe me, I found that out last year. But, Chloe, that doesn't have to be a bad thing. Life is always full of surprises, and some of them can be quite wonderful. If we pay attention. Maybe you should go over there for a visit. Allow yourself to chill out and renew your energy."

"Alone? You mean go to Ormond Beach alone?"

Shelby laughed. "First of all, you wouldn't be alone. You'd have Basil with you. But yeah, find a nice place to stay for a while. No pressure. No commitments. I don't think women do this nearly enough. It's good to be alone sometimes. It allows us to reconnect with ourselves. Especially during times of change or confusion."

"Hmm," I said, slowly beginning to warm to the idea. "Maybe you're right. Maybe a change is what I need for a while."

"Give it some thought, Chloe. We just never know what's around that next corner," she said, passing me her credit card to pay for her purchase.

# Chapter 2

When Dora arrived at the shop, I could tell right away that something was wrong. Normally she was very chatty, but for the past hour she'd replied to my attempts at conversation with only brief answers. Although she was now in her late seventies, she'd always been in excellent health. However, I wondered if perhaps she wasn't feeling well.

It had been another very slow afternoon. The weakness of the economy over the past few years had hit Cedar Key especially hard. Restaurants had closed. Some gift shops and galleries had either closed or cut back their hours. Even Lucas had said recently that sales were way down at both the bookshop and café.

When I had first moved to Cedar Key, restaurants and shops might close, but it wasn't long before a new owner was taking over. That simply wasn't happening now. And without choices for restaurants or shops, tourists were not as likely to visit either.

"I'm sorry I haven't been very chatty today," I heard Dora say.

I looked up from the yarn I'd been pricing. "Are you feeling okay?"

She let out a deep sigh. "Physically, yes. But I guess it's time we have a talk."

I nodded and walked over to the coffeemaker, where Dora had just filled two mugs, and we sat down.

"I'm not sure where to begin," she said. "As you know, business has really slacked off during the past year."

"Right. We're not getting as many knitters from out of town."

"Yes, and I know local knitters are finding it more difficult to afford the cost of good yarn. I bumped into Flora and Corabeth last week at Walmart. I'm not sure who was more embarrassed, me or them. They each had a basket filled with yarn. I think they felt disloyal not purchasing it from me, but hey, I certainly understand. They can get it much cheaper than our prices. And if it's a toss-up between high-priced, quality yarn and putting food on the table . . . well, who can blame them?"

I nodded. "Yeah, Lucas pretty much said the same thing about books. He said at first he thought maybe people were buying ebooks simply as a matter of taste, but since the price of a print book can be much higher, he realized some of it has to do with the economy. With many ebooks either free or at such low prices, they become much more appealing to readers with financial problems."

"Exactly." Dora let out another sigh. "And so . . . I've been giving some serious thought to closing the shop."

I wasn't surprised, but to actually hear the words spoken out loud broke my heart. The yarn shop had initially been opened under the name of Spinning Forward by Dora's niece, Sydney Webster. After a couple of years, Sydney had sold the shop to her daughter, Monica, who changed the name to Yarning Together. When Monica gave birth to triplets four years ago, the shop still remained in the family when Dora Foster fulfilled her dream and took over as owner. And now . . . it appeared that the demise of the shop was in the near future.

I reached over to give Dora's hand a squeeze. "I'm so sorry. I know how much this shop has meant to you, and I love being a part of it."

She nodded and I saw her gaze taking in the display tables of yarn, the cubbyholes along the wall filled with alpaca, cotton, and all the various fibers that knitters were drawn to.

"Yes, I have enjoyed every single day of owning this shop, but sometimes . . . we just have to let go. I think at my age I'm simply grateful for being given the chance to do something I've loved for the past four years."

"Does Marin know yet?"

"I think she has a pretty good idea. I thought expanding the shop with needlepoint last year might help to boost sales but unfortunately, that didn't happen. I know Marin enjoyed running that part of the shop, but to be honest, I think she'd be fine with not working here, closing up her house, and permanently moving into Worth's home in Ocala. With Fiona graduating from UF in June, she'll be busy working at Shands as a nurse and being a mom to Andrea. Besides, I hear she and Greg are planning to be married in the fall. So Marin's life is also changing, and I think she's welcoming more time with Worth."

"And what about you?" I asked. "What will you do?"

A smile crossed Dora's face and she patted my hand. "Oh, Chloe, I'll be just fine. I've lived here all of my life and I can't see myself leaving. At least not permanently. All of my friends are here and even without a yarn shop, we'll still meet at each other's houses to knit and gossip. Just like we always did before the island had a yarn shop. It's sad to lose this place, but I think it might be the best decision. Now, what about you? I know you've only been working part-time these past months, but . . . at least it was some income for you. So I feel bad about that."

"No, no. Don't be silly. I'll be just fine too." I managed to force a smile to my lips. But would I?

I had left Basil at home after lunch and when I returned at five he was eagerly waiting for me. We always had dogs when the boys were growing up, but they had been more family dogs, not just mine. Basil was different. He showed excitement when he saw me, followed me everywhere, and slept at the foot of my bed every night. He was my pal and my companion. Plus, he made Gabe seem a little bit closer.

"Hey, fella," I said, bending down to give him a pat. "I think after the news of this afternoon, I've earned a glass of wine."

That was another benefit of having Basil around: I didn't feel foolish for talking out loud. I headed to the fridge, grabbed a wineglass, and poured some pinot grigio.

"Let's go on the back porch so you can sniff around the yard."

He dutifully followed me outside, ran over to a bush, and promptly lifted his leg.

I took a sip of wine and thought, *Now what*? I hadn't been completely honest with Dora about my financial situation. I certainly wasn't destitute, but I also wasn't on Easy Street.

"Oh, that wine looks good."

I looked up to see my sister and niece coming in the gate.

"Auntie Chloe, look what I painted at school today."

Solange ran up the steps and handed me a piece of paper filled with bright colors, but I wasn't able to discern exactly what the drawing was. "It's gorgeous," I told her, glancing up at Grace for assistance.

"Doesn't she do a great job with scenery? I love the park and all the flowers."

"Beautiful," I said, still not able to see much beyond a splash of colors. "Help yourself to a glass of wine, Grace, and there's lemonade in the fridge for Solange."

My niece crawled up on my lap, still clutching her paper.

"So did you have a good day at school?" I asked her.

"Yeah, but it's not big girl school. Mama says I can't go there for three more years. That's not fair, is it?"

I laughed and kissed the top of her head. Better she find out at a young age that life isn't always fair.

"Here ya go," Grace said, coming back out and passing a plastic glass to Solange. "Now be a good girl and let Mommy and Aunt Chloe have a chat."

"Okay," she said, jumping off my lap. "I'll go play with Basil."

A smile crossed my face. "Kids are so easily entertained and satisfied, aren't they?"

Grace laughed. "Not always. What's up? You're looking a little glum."

I took a sip of wine and nodded. "Well, I can't say this was one of my better days. Dora had to give me the sad news that she's going to be closing the yarn shop."

"Oh, no. I've been hearing rumors to that effect. The economy and lack of sales?"

"Yup, and I think she's been struggling to hold on for a while now. She finally made her decision and, actually, I think she's comfortable with it."

"What about you? Where does this leave you, Chloe?"

"Good question. I honestly don't know. The pay wasn't much, but it helped supplement my income. My building downtown has been on the market almost a year and zip. Nothing is really moving with real estate right now."

"Yeah, Lucas is finding the same thing with the book café. He's not losing money, but he's not making much either. I guess the good thing for us is that he leases the space now. He was fortunate to sell the building last year to an investor."

"I sure wish an investor would come along and buy mine. But I guess I'm lucky to at least be renting my apartment. The rental income is a plus, and I'm living here at Aunt Maude's rent free. And of course I have the rent from Berkley for both her chocolate shop and her apartment. But it's a scary situation for a woman alone in her early fifties. I was stupid enough to listen to Parker all the years I was married to him. Telling me I didn't have to work. Financially, I didn't, but here I am now with no pension to fall back on, no retirement fund. The smartest thing I did was take the divorce settlement money and put a hefty down payment on the building I purchased. At least my mortgage is low enough that I can handle it without fear of foreclosure like so many other people."

Grace nodded. "That was a very smart decision on your part, but . . . you're still not sure what you want to do long term, huh?"

I let out a deep sigh. "Not really. Although Shelby mentioned today that I should still consider going to Ormond Beach. At least for a visit. Alone."

Grace swung around in her chair to face me. "Oh, Chloe, I think that's a great idea. I know I suggested this to you at the beginning of the year, but then Aunt Maude died and it didn't seem right bringing up the subject again. But I really do think a change would do you a lot of good."

"Hmm, yeah, maybe. Just for a week or so."

"Don't be silly. Give yourself more time than that. You'll just be getting used to the area and finding your way around when it'll be time to come back. Who knows . . . you might find yourself loving the town and the people, and you'll want to settle there permanently."

I seriously doubted that would happen; then it hit me that Grace's encouragement might not be all about me. "You and Lucas want to move to Paris, don't you?"

She began fiddling with the stem of her wineglass. "Well . . . ah . . . yeah. Someday."

I definitely didn't want to be the old maid sister she felt responsible for. Grace was more than entitled to her own life and I began to feel guilty for possibly holding them back these past few months.

"You know what," I said, forcing a smile to my face. "I think you and Shelby are right. Time for me to step up and make a fresh start."

"Really?"

I saw the expression of doubt on my sister's face. "Really," I assured her. "As a matter of fact, after dinner I'm going to browse the Internet and see if I can find a place to stay for . . . well, I'm not quite sure how long. But longer than a week."

Her expression of doubt now changed to concern. "Geez, Chloe. I don't want you to think I'm pushing you to leave. Can you afford to rent a place over there for an extended period of time?"

That thought had been floating around my head, too, and a solution had occurred to me. "Yes, I can. God knows when this house will sell. But don't forget, Aunt Maude also left each of us fifty thousand dollars, and remember what she said in her will?"

Grace laughed. "I do. She said to be sure not to spend the money on something practical. To use the money on frivolous things."

I nodded. "Because she wanted us to remember her and smile whenever we spent any of that money. She wanted us to enjoy the moments and have fun with it."

"Exactly. I have to agree with you, Chloe. Aunt Maude would love for you to take some of that money, rent a place in Ormond Beach, and give yourself a chance to start over."

And I knew my sister was right.

# Chapter 3

I cleaned up after dinner, made myself a cup of herbal tea, and settled down at the computer to do some searches for vacation rental properties in Ormond Beach.

The first few listings I found were either too high priced, too large, or they didn't accept dogs. After more than an hour of browsing, I was about to give up when a particular listing caught my eye.

*1200 sq. ft. spacious condo. One bedroom, one bath. Balcony overlooking beach. Parking. Security. Elevator.*

It didn't say they accepted dogs. But it didn't say they didn't either. This one looked promising. I clicked the link to check out the photos. Very nice. Very nice indeed. The furniture looked stylish and comfortable. The view from the balcony was breathtaking.

What did I have to lose? I read further and saw that interested renters could call Henry. I reached for my phone and dialed the number listed. A male voice answered.

"Hi," I said. "I saw your rental on the Internet and I'm calling for some information. Is this Henry?"

"It is," I heard him say. "Well, my listing is fairly descriptive. I'm not sure when you'd like to rent, but there is a one month minimum. Would that be a problem?"

"No, not at all," I told him, although I had been thinking more along the lines of a couple weeks. "That would be fine. I was considering possibly the month of May?"

"Yes, that would work for me quite well, actually. Because I have plans to be down there myself mid-June. Are you familiar with Ormond Beach at all? Have you been there before?"

"I visited a few times last year," I said and recalled my trips with Gabe. "But I'm looking forward to getting to know it better."

"It's a wonderful little town. Well, not too little with a population just over thirty-eight thousand. Would you be flying or driving?"

"I live on the west coast of Florida. Actually, directly across the state from Ormond Beach, about an hour west of Gainesville. So I'll be driving over."

"Great. Well, the condo is available and if you're interested, I can book it for you whenever you'd like."

I hadn't actually intended to make a commitment immediately. I had only thought I'd browse and see what was available, but my intuition kicked in and told me to just do it.

"One last question," I said. "Do you accept dogs in the condo?"

I heard his laughter come across the line. "Well, that depends. How many do you have?"

A smile crossed my face. "Only one and he's a good boy. Basil is around twenty pounds and very well mannered."

"I'm sure he is and yes, it isn't a problem at all. I have a dog myself and she always comes with me when I spend time down there."

"Oh, how nice. What kind do you have?"

"Delilah is a Golden and my best pal. By the way, nothing compares to walking your dog on the beach, and of course, it's right out the door of the building. The condo is on the third floor, but you probably read there's an elevator, so it's convenient."

"Wonderful. Well, then I definitely want to book for the month of May. Do you also live in Florida?"

"No, not permanently. I'm retired and I spend some time up here in Vermont. I dabble a bit in photography so I have the best of both worlds with scenery. Will it just be you renting the condo?"

I had a feeling that was a roundabout way of asking if I had a spouse. "Right, just me and Basil."

"That's great. I think you'll both be comfortable there. If you'll give me your mailing address, I'll mail you some information about the condo, along with directions and the keys. The building has a code and you can access the pad both from the underground garage and the front door."

"Excellent," I said and proceeded to give him my address. "Do you want a check for the full amount or a credit card?"

He stated that a check was fine and gave me his address.

"Okay," I said. "Then I think I'm all set. I'll get that into the mail for you tomorrow and I'll plan to arrive on May first."

"Would it be possible to have your cell number, just in case any questions or problems arise? And I'll give you mine."

"Of course," I said. "Oh, and who do I make the check out to?"

"Henry Wagner, and your name is?"

"I'm Chloe Radcliffe, and thank you so much."

"It's been my pleasure, Chloe. If you have any further questions about the condo or the town, don't hesitate to give me a call."

I hung up and let out a deep sigh. Well, that was that. And I felt like I'd made a good decision despite the fact that it hadn't been my intent to actually rent something this evening. But it felt right, and after conversing with Henry Wagner, it also felt like I'd been chatting with a friend.

I looked down at Basil, who had been napping near my feet. "Well, fella, you and I will be heading to the east coast in two weeks. Are you up for an adventure?"

He wagged his tail and gave a bark.

"Right, I think we both are," I said. I'd just headed to the kitchen to make another cup of tea when I heard someone knock and walk in.

"Are you busy?" Grace asked.

"Not at all. What's up? Would you like some tea?"

"That would be great," she said, sitting down at the kitchen table. "Well, Lucas and I were talking after supper, and we've decided to go to Paris for a month. As you know, we haven't been over there for a while and he'd like to visit with his family."

"I think that's a great idea because I'll also be gone for a month."

"Did you book something already?"

I laughed. "I did. I found a condo on the beach that sounds ideal, I called the owner and I'm confirmed to arrive there on May first."

"Wow, that was fast. You weren't kidding about really wanting to go. That's great, Chloe."

I refrained from telling her that booking something right away hadn't been my initial intention, but it had just kind of happened. "Here's your tea," I said, passing her a mug. "Come on, I'll show you the photos on the computer."

I clicked the link and scrolled through, showing her the rooms and the balcony.

"Gosh, that's really gorgeous," she said. "And it's pet friendly?"

"It is and that was the deciding factor. Apparently, Henry, the owner, also has a dog. He lives in Vermont but gets down here frequently. I guess he really likes Ormond Beach, both the setting and the people. I'm looking forward to spending some time there and forming my own opinion."

Grace leaned over and gave me a hug. "I just want you to be happy, Chloe. No matter where you are. You've had a difficult time these past few years."

I nodded. "Yeah, I have, but it's like when I first came here. Nothing was going to change until I took the first step to make it happen. And coming here to Cedar Key was absolutely the right thing to do. The thing is, sometimes a place is just a temporary stop on our journey . . . and then it's time for new beginnings."

"Exactly, and you won't know until you go over there and see for yourself. Is there anything I can do to help you get ready to leave?"

I laughed. "Thanks, but I think you'll be busy enough getting things together for the three of you to fly to Paris. Do you have dates yet?"

"Lucas is going to check on flights tomorrow and I'll let you know. But if we're both gone at the same time, Berkley or Marin can come to check on the house."

"Oh, I'm sure they'll be happy to. We'll give them a key. We have to put a hold on our mail delivery too. I guess I should start making a list tomorrow. Is Lucas going to keep the book café open while you're gone?"

Grace shook her head. "No, not this time. I feel bad about putting Suellen out of work while we're away, but business is so slow that it really isn't worth staying open. Lucas has been giving her hints that we might be going to Paris for a while and she actually mentioned to him today that she's thinking about moving to Gainesville. I think she's been going there to check out job possibilities."

"Gosh, I hope it all works out for her."

"Me too. Well, I need to get back upstairs. I'll talk to you tomorrow."

I got up to give her a hug. "Thanks, Gracie. Thanks for all of your encouragement and support. I love you."

"I love you back," she said before leaving.

As I drifted off to sleep that night, I thought about my trip to Ormond Beach. It wasn't really a vacation in my mind. Instead I considered it a visit to do research and check out the area. Discover if perhaps I did still want to relocate there. On my own. And for the first time in a year, I felt an emotion that had been absent in my life: excitement.

# Chapter 4

Henry Wagner had sent a packet of information as he promised, along with the keys to the condo and the security code. He had also included various brochures of restaurants, maps of the town, community events, and little notes with descriptions. And he had called me twice. The first time he said it was to make sure I'd received the packet and the second time . . . well, I'm not quite sure why he called the second time except we did end up having a nice conversation for about twenty minutes.

And with only one day remaining until I left, my excitement level continued to creep up.

I had just poured my first cup of morning coffee when I recalled a dream I'd had the night before. It was still a bit foggy in my mind but I worked to bring it to the surface. The dream had been about a house. A large, two-story, Victorian-style house. I remembered that it had a black wrought-iron fence surrounding it, set back from the sidewalk with grass in front and a driveway to the side. The image got a little clearer and I recalled a turret on the second floor, but the most striking part of the dream was the fact that my mother had been standing in the doorway, waving to me with a huge smile on her face and beckoning me to enter. That was when I woke up.

I shook my head. Dreams could be so confusing and most of the time made no sense. My mother had passed away almost thirty years ago. It wasn't like I'd been thinking of her or talking about her the day before. It was then that I remembered Grace's experience shortly before she married Lucas. She claimed the spirit of our mother had appeared to her, wearing the exact wedding gown that Grace ended up wearing after Aunt Maude gave it to her, telling us it had belonged to our mother.

Grace and Aunt Maude had always claimed to have a gift of sight in relation to dreams and visions. I humored them but never for a moment believed in any of it. Although my dream had felt real, I chalked it up to the fact that I'd been researching various vacation rentals and house images were in my subconscious.

I turned around as I heard Grace's voice and a knock on the kitchen door.

"Are you up, Chloe?"

"Yeah, come on in," I hollered.

"I just dropped Solange at the day care center, and I wanted to let you know that Lucas finally got our flights arranged."

"Oh, good. Coffee?" I held up the pot.

"That would be great. We'll be leaving May sixteenth and fly back June sixteenth."

"So you'll be here for a couple weeks after I leave."

"Right, and you'll be back a couple weeks before we are. And I spoke to Berkley and Marin yesterday and they each offered to take turns checking on the house during the two weeks it's empty."

"Sounds like we're moving right along."

"Are you all packed and ready to leave in the morning?"

I nodded. "Pretty much. I thought I'd start loading up the car this afternoon. I really don't need that much staying in a fully equipped condo. But I do know one thing . . . I have to stick to a diet when I get over there. I could barely fit into some of my clothes when I began packing."

Grace laughed. "A diet on vacation? Unheard of."

"Yeah, well, when a woman gets to be a certain age, the pounds creep up out of nowhere and I have a good ten to lose."

"Oh, I just realized. We leave for Paris the day after your birthday, and we won't be together to celebrate it. I feel bad about that."

I waved a hand in the air. "Don't be silly. Turning fifty-two isn't a momentous occasion. Just another day."

"No, it's not and I want you to promise me that you'll do something fun and nice. A good dinner and wine. Who knows, you'll be there two weeks by then—maybe you'll have made some friends to celebrate with."

I seriously doubted that. "I'll celebrate with Basil. Hey, Grace . . . do you still read your tarot cards?"

Grace laughed. "I thought you hated those things and had no belief in them."

"Well . . . I really don't. But I remember you did read them once and a lot of that information was correct."

"Hmm, yeah, they can be pretty accurate, but to answer your question, no. I gave them up shortly before Lucas and I married."

"And you never dabble anymore? You were always the one who said it was part of our heritage, passed down through generations of women."

"True, but what's the sudden urge to have your cards read? What's going on?"

I shrugged. "Nothing. It's just that I had a dream last night."

Grace sat up straighter in her chair. "Oh, now dreams . . . that's an entirely different matter. I still pay attention to my dreams. And visions. They have to be taken seriously. With the cards, I really don't want to know what's ahead. I just want to *live* it. But with dreams . . . well, those are messages. Sometimes from your subconscious, sometimes from beyond."

"Like from spirits?"

"Exactly. What was your dream about?"

I explained about the house, gave a good description of it, and then mentioned our mother standing in the doorway, wanting me to go inside.

"Interesting."

"What's that mean?"

"Do you remember anything else? Was the house here in Cedar Key?"

I pulled back into my brain for a moment and then shook my head. "No, it wasn't here. I know that, but . . . I do remember water across the street from the house."

"Well, all of it could mean a number of things. Your subconscious knows you're going to a new area, so it could have to do with that. As for Mom being in the dream . . . you said she wanted you to go inside the house?"

I nodded.

"It sounds to me like she's telling you there's change ahead for you, which isn't so surprising either. You're going away for a month, but there could be more to it. Wish I could be more help, but just pay attention, because you're the only one who will be able to figure out any meaning."

"It's probably nothing. Just an overactive imagination on my part." I glanced at the clock over the fridge. "Well, I need to jump in the shower. I want to go downtown and say bye to Berkley and stock up on some chocolate to take with me."

Grace got up and placed her mug in the sink. "I need to get moving too. Oh, before I forget, Lucas and I want to invite you to dinner tonight. He's cooking some special French dish for your going-away dinner."

I laughed. "Aw, he didn't have to do that, but I never turn down one of his great meals. I'll be there. Usual time?"

"Yup, seven is good. See you then."

I had the car pretty well packed, stocked up on my chocolate, enjoyed a delicious dinner with Grace and Lucas, and was just preparing a cup of herbal tea before settling down with a book for an hour or so when my house phone rang.

"Hey, Mom," I heard my son Eli say. "You weren't in bed yet, were you?"

I laughed. "It's only nine. No, I don't go to bed quite this early. How're you doing and how's Treva?"

"We're both great. Just super busy working."

My son had been married for four years already, and I admit that each time he called, I wondered if it was to tell me I was about to become a grandmother. Not that they were trying, as far as I knew. Living in Boston, they were both in high-pressure situations—Eli as an accountant with a prestigious company and Treva as a Columbia University grad who had recently completed her master's in health care administration. I doubted this left much time to think about planning a family. So I was quite surprised at what he said next.

"Actually, that's why I'm calling. We're both getting a bit tired of the rat race up here. Not to mention the horrible winters we've been having the past few years."

"Oh, so are you moving?"

"Yes, but not until autumn. Still, we'll be out of here before another snowfall—we're heading for the sunny south."

"Seriously?" I had never dared to hope this might happen.

Eli laughed. "Seriously. I've been offered a very nice position with a company in Jacksonville."

"Jacksonville, Florida?" Surely, he was joking.

He laughed again. "Yes, Mom, that's the place. On the east coast, and since it's north Florida, we'll be a lot closer to you. Don't forget, I grew up in Savannah, and although I've toughed out the northeast winters since college, it's not my favorite climate."

"And how about Treva? Does she have a job too?"

"Not yet, but with her credentials, I don't think she'll have a problem. That is, unless she gets pregnant first. We had always agreed that when that time came, she wouldn't work full-time."

*Grandma, here we come!* "Well, Eli, I couldn't be happier for both of you. You have an exciting time ahead."

"And how about you? All set for your solo adventure tomorrow?"

"I am." I let out a deep breath. "And actually, I'm quite excited as well."

"That's great. Well, give me a call in the next day or so after you get settled in. I love you, Mom."

"I love you too," I told him as I felt a huge smile cross my face.

I took my cup of tea and headed to bed to read a little before sleep. Basil promptly jumped up next to me.

"Well, Basil, it looks like there could be some good things ahead for the Radcliffe family. And tomorrow, you and I will take the first step on that journey."

# Chapter 5

Following a weepy good-bye with Grace and Solange, Basil and I headed east right on time. It was roughly a three-hour drive, depending on traffic, and I planned to arrive in Ormond Beach around noontime.

It was a beautiful, sunny May morning and I tried to push thoughts of Gabe out of my head as I drove along US 27 in Ocala. But it was hard not to remember just a year ago when Gabe and I had made this trip together, both of us filled with plans for our future.

But as I knew all too well, sometimes plans simply don't work out. I recalled my conversation with Eli the night before. Following my divorce from Parker, both of my sons had also seemed to drift away. Granted, both Mathis and Eli were busy forging their own careers, but I can't deny that it felt like rejection to me.

Mathis was now twenty-eight, two years older than Eli, and had been living and working in Paris, France, for the past three years before transferring to Atlanta the year before. He did call me now and then and had managed to fly to Florida to visit me twice, but I didn't feel like I knew very much about his life. Only what he wanted me to know.

And until Eli married Treva, he had also kept to himself. I wasn't happy when I learned that they'd had a simple civil ceremony in Manhattan with no family present, but that was their choice, and since becoming a husband, he was always in touch with me a few times a week, which I welcomed. I attributed some of this to Treva. Her mother had passed away before she married Eli and she didn't get along with her stepmother, so even her relationship with her father was strained. I always got the feeling that she liked having me in her life. And I adored her. As soon as I met her, I forgave both of them for not including me in their marriage ceremony. And now within a few months, they'd be living much closer.

Just as I turned east on SR 40, the sun disappeared behind clouds. "Damn," I said out loud. "I hope it doesn't rain before we get there."

In case it did, I thought we should stop at a McDonalds I spotted. I could let Basil out of the car to pee and I could grab a coffee to go.

As I pulled out of the McDonalds parking lot after our brief pit stop, the sky opened up and it began to pour. I turned the radio to NPR and took a sip of coffee. Maybe by the time I reached Ormond Beach, the sun would be shining again.

We had just entered the stretch of road that bordered the Ocala National Forest when I felt a thump beneath the car and the steering mechanism seemed to freeze up.

"Oh, no! I think we have a flat tire," I said, as I slowly edged the car to the side of the road.

I had no choice. I had to get out and check, and of course, my umbrella was packed in my luggage in the trunk. By now the pouring rain had turned to a deluge.

I pointed at Basil, who was sitting up in the backseat, probably wondering why we'd stopped. "You stay right there," I told him. "This might not be pretty."

I jumped out and was immediately drenched. Sure enough, the left front tire was flat. As a pancake. Shit! Now what?

I ran back inside the car, shaking my head like a wet dog. Droplets of water flew everywhere. Since Parker had left me, I'd learned to become somewhat self-sufficient. However, changing a tire was beyond me. I recalled Lucas telling me many times that I really should sign up with AAA just in case I encountered a road problem alone. And had I listened? Of course not.

I realized no traffic had even gone past since I'd pulled over. Great. Just great. Alone in the pouring rain. I guess I could call Lucas, but God. That would be a one-hour drive for him to just get here from Cedar Key and then a one-hour drive back. What the hell was I going to do? Without any warning, tears slid down my face, mingling with the rain. Maybe I never should have made plans to do this trip. Maybe I should have just stayed put on Cedar Key. Safe and sound. But that was the old me talking. Afraid to take a risk. I'd been a doormat for Parker almost all of my married life, and once I had made a decision to leave Savannah and arrived in Cedar Key, I'd become a different woman. And I wasn't about to go backward.

I swiped at my tears and saw a black BMW speed past me. *Thanks*, I thought. *Thanks so much for stopping to help me.*

I took another sip of coffee while still trying to decide what to do when I glanced up and saw the BMW had turned around and was now slowly heading back toward me. For a brief second, I felt relief, and then I realized whoever was in that car could be a serial killer.

The car slowed across the road and the driver's side window slid down. I saw it was a man alone. Yup, could definitely be a serial killer.

"Do you need any help?" he hollered across the road.

Yes, of course I did. "It seems I have a flat tire," I yelled back.

The man made a U-turn and I thought he was going to speed off again, but I looked in my rearview mirror and saw he'd pulled up behind me with his hazard lights on. He jogged to the side of my car.

"Got a spare?" he said as the rain pelted down on him.

"Yes, I think so."

"Flip your trunk," he instructed me.

This perfect stranger wasn't going to actually change my tire, was he? But I did as I was told and then jumped out to join him, getting drenched again within a matter of seconds.

I watched him push aside my luggage, remove a tire from the wheel well, and go to the front of the car.

"You should get inside," he said as he went to the front of my car with a jack in his hand. "You're getting soaked. Besides, it's not safe standing on the side of the road. Put your hazard lights on."

Again, I did as I was told and slid into the driver's seat sopping wet. After turning on my hazard lights, I peered to my left to better see him and make sure he was okay. Not that I could do anything to help. In the brief encounter we'd had, I noticed he was about my age, quite good looking and wearing a white shirt and tie that would probably end up in the trash heap before the day was over. I also noticed that although more cars were now speeding past, not one stopped to offer any assistance. This man was quickly becoming my savior.

Within a half hour he'd finished. He ran to the passenger side of my car. I was still uneasy but clicked the lock for him to jump in.

"Whew," he said, running a hand through salt-and-pepper curls. "You're all set. The spare is on but you'll need to get to a garage fairly soon. That's just a donut I've replaced your flat with. You don't happen to have a towel, do you?"

It was then that I remembered putting a stack of towels on the floor of the backseat just in case I needed them at the condo.

"I do," I said, twisting and leaning over. "I'd completely forgotten about them." I passed a bath towel to him and began drying my hair with another one.

"Thanks," he said, rubbing the towel across his face and then his hair. "Where're you headed? I saw the luggage. Are you moving or on vacation?"

"On vacation and heading to a rental condo in Ormond Beach, about another hour's drive from here. Will I be okay till I get there?"

He nodded. "Sure. Just don't go above fifty and don't do too much driving around once you get there. I live just north of there in Ormond-by-the-Sea." He reached in his pocket for a small notebook, wrote something and passed the paper to me. "Here's the name and address of a good place to get a new tire in Ormond Beach. Be sure to tell Gil that Chadwick sent you."

I wondered why he went by his last name and saw that Basil was attempting to scooch into the front seat with us.

"Hey, fella. I think you like me. Cute dog." He reached out to rub Basil between his ears the way Gabe used to.

"I just don't know how to thank you," I told him and wondered if I should offer him money. "You were a true lifesaver. Thank you so much."

"Not a problem at all," he said, reaching back into his pocket and then passing me a business card. "Maybe when you get settled in, give me a call and I'll let you buy me a drink as thanks." He got out, and then stuck his head back inside. "Oh, and you might want to consider signing up with Triple A."

I glanced at the business card and saw that Chadwick was his first name. Chadwick Price. And apparently he didn't go by the nickname of *Chad*. I also saw that he was the owner of a real estate office in Ormond-by-the-Sea.

He tooted his horn and I looked in my rearview mirror to see him waving his arm out the window, indicating that he wanted me to pull out and drive in front of him.

"Well, here we go, Basil," I said as I turned on my indicator and moved onto the road. The car felt a little strange with the donut tire on it but I was quite grateful that a stranger would stop, especially in such weather, to help me, and I trusted that he was right about the tire being safe until I got to the garage the next morning.

I kept my eye on Chadwick's car, which followed me along SR 40 all the way to Ormond Beach. I wondered if he was doing this to make sure my car was okay or if he was just going in my direction. When we got to the end of Granada, I got into the right lane to turn onto A1A and he pulled into the left as he gave a beep of the horn and leaned over to give me a wave. I waved back and smiled before taking my turn.

Farther up on the left was the condo building where Basil and I would make our home for the next month. And if Chadwick Price was any example of the friendly and helpful people in the area, I had a feeling I was going to enjoy my stay here.

I punched the code to allow me into the parking garage, found a spot near the elevator, and decided to get Basil outside first before I began unloading the car. We found a grassy area that served the purpose and headed back into the garage. I knew it was going to take quite a few trips to fully unload the car and decided to bring Basil and my rolling luggage up first. As I was getting his leash wrapped on my hand, grabbing my handbag and the piece of luggage, another car pulled into a spot beside me.

A woman who appeared to be in her midseventies got out, smiled and waved a hand toward me. "Hello, there. Looks like you could use some help with your stuff. Are you new to the building? I don't recall seeing you before."

I shot her a smile and nodded. "I am. I'm Chloe Radcliffe and I'm renting Henry Wagner's condo for the month."

She walked toward me with hand extended. "Nice to meet you. I'm Louise Blackstone and I live right next door to Henry. Nice fellow. I think you'll like his place. Here, let me give you a hand."

I was really glad that I'd listened to Henry and purchased a cart on wheels. He told me it easily folded up to keep in the trunk and would be helpful transporting shopping bags from the garage up to the condo. I filled the cart with bags of food that I'd brought along, various other bags, and put Basil's bed on top.

"Thank you so much. If you could take Basil, I can handle my piece of luggage and the cart."

Louise bent over to give Basil a pat. "Well, aren't you just the cutest little guy," she said, taking his leash. "My Ramona is going to like you. She's such a flirt."

I laughed as we walked to the elevator and Louise pushed the button for the third floor. "You have a dog?"

"Well, don't tell Ramona she's a dog. She truly thinks she's a human. Spoiled rotten. But I love her to pieces. She's a mixture of this and that, but I'm sure if she could speak, she'd tell you she was descended from royalty."

I laughed again as the doors slid open and we stepped into the corridor.

"Just down here," Louise said, turning left. "Here you go. Three oh eight. Got your key?"

She pointed to the door and I nodded as I fished for the key in my handbag. "Thank you so much for your help. Would you like to come in for a few minutes?"

She waved a hand in the air. "No, no, I'm sure you have plenty to do getting settled in. Besides, Ramona is waiting for me to take her out. And I'm sure we'll be seeing a lot more of each other." It was then that she spied one of my tote bags filled with knitting. "Oh, you knit?"

I heard the excitement in her voice that all serious knitters seem to share. "I do, and I take it you do too?"

"Oh, my yes. I've been knitting practically all my life. Except for Ramona, it's my favorite love. Well then, you'll just have to join us at Yarrow's for tea and knitting. Do you like tea?"

"I'm usually a coffee drinker but, yes, I enjoy tea now and then."

"Great. Well, my very best friend is Mavis Anne—Mavis Anne Overby—and Yarrow is her niece, who owns the tea shop downtown. A group of us meet there to knit and gossip a few times a week. You go get settled in and I'll be in touch in the next day or so."

She passed me Basil's leash and I unlocked the door. "Thanks so much, Louise, and I look forward to seeing you again."

# Chapter 6

Basil and I stepped into a small tile foyer, and the first thing I saw was the breathtaking view straight ahead. I dropped his leash and walked to the sliding doors in the living room, which led to a good-size balcony. Unlocking the doors, I stepped outside to where a table, four chairs, and potted plants had been placed. In front of me was a stretch of beach and the mighty Atlantic. I inhaled a deep breath of salt air. The Gulf was very pretty but it was placid compared to what was before me. Large waves crashed onto the shore and I smiled. Already I felt a sense of calm.

I knew Louise's condo was to my left but a brick wall separated our balconies and provided privacy.

Basil had followed me outside and was sniffing every inch of the balcony. "Come on, fella, let's go check out the rest of our new home."

The living room was spacious and open with the kitchen on the other side of a counter with two stools. Tastefully decorated in muted colors of beige, brown, and tan, it looked identical to the photos on the Internet. We walked into a good-size bedroom with king-size bed, nice furnishings, and another glass door that led out to the balcony. Off the bedroom was a modern bathroom complete with tub and separate walk-in shower.

"Very nice," I said, walking back to the foyer and pulling the cart into the kitchen. "Let's get the food unloaded first," I told Basil as he sat and watched me emptying bags.

I glanced at my watch and saw it was already going on two o'clock. No wonder I was hungry. Courtesy of Lucas, I had some nice homemade soup to warm up in the microwave. I had just settled myself on the sofa to enjoy both the view and my lunch when my cell phone rang. I answered to hear Henry Wagner's voice.

"Chloe? Sorry to bother you, but I just wanted to make sure you arrived okay and the condo is what you hoped."

I smiled. "That's so nice of you, Henry, and yes. Despite a flat tire on the way over, I managed to get here a little while ago."

"Oh, no. I'm so sorry to hear that. Did you get the tire changed?"

"Well, a nice gentleman stopped and took care of it and I'll have a permanent tire put on in the morning. Basil and I were just getting unpacked and settled in. The condo is beautiful, and I love it. This view is really something."

"I'm glad you like it and yes, I never tire of seeing that stretch of beach and ocean. Well, I won't keep you. If you need anything, just give me a call."

"I will and I'm sure I'll enjoy my stay here. I've already met your neighbor, Louise Blackstone. She was kind enough to help me upstairs with my stuff."

I heard a laugh come across the line. "Oh, yes, Louise. She's a real character and a very nice person. Okay, you take care and I'll be in touch."

I smiled as I disconnected the call and began sipping my soup. Henry was a very responsible property owner, but I had a feeling that some of his calls were due to loneliness on his part. It was too bad I wouldn't get a chance to meet him when he did get down here. From his voice during our phone chats, he seemed like a very nice person.

I finished my soup, gave Basil a biscuit, and dragged my luggage into the bedroom along with Basil's bed.

"Here ya go," I told him, placing his bed in a corner of the room. "Home sweet home. I think we're going to like it here."

After I finished unpacking my clothes, I grabbed some bath products to place in the bathroom and flipped on the light switch. That was when I saw myself in the mirror. Good God! I still looked like a drowned rat. My chin-length brunette hair hung in limp strands. My eye makeup was smeared from all the rain pelting down on me. I was a total mess. Chadwick Price instantly came to mind. After seeing what I looked like to him, it was hard to believe that he'd even bothered to give me his card and told me to call him. No doubt he was only being nice.

By the time I'd finished settling in, I realized I needed to give Grace a call.

"Hey," she said. "It's going on four. I was starting to get a little concerned. Everything okay?"

I explained about the flat tire and the delay in getting to the condo. "Then I had some of Lucas's yummy soup and got unpacked. But yes, everything is fine. I love this place. The view is to die for, both from the living room and the balcony. Basil has already settled in very well." I glanced to the end of the sofa where he was curled up, snoozing away.

"Oh, that's good. But gosh, sorry about that tire. Lucas told you to get—"

I interrupted her. "Yes, I know. Triple A. I'll definitely have it before I make the return trip to Cedar Key in a month."

"Well, you really were lucky that guy stopped. But I'm happy it seems to be going well."

"It is. I even met my neighbor. Louise Blackstone. A woman in her midseventies. I met her in the parking garage downstairs and she lives right next door. Guess what? There's a group of women here who gather at a tea shop a few times a week to knit and gossip."

Grace laughed. "That's great. I guess I'm not surprised, though. With the knitting craze continuing, most towns now have yarn shops and groups. Is there a yarn shop in town too?"

"Oh, gee, I don't know. She didn't mention that but I plan to stop by the tea shop in the next day or so and I'll find out."

"Okay. Well, get a good night's sleep and tomorrow you'll be ready to start exploring. You keep in touch. Love you, Chloe."

"Love you too."

I hung up and smiled. Although Grace didn't come right out and say it, I think she worried about me. About what would happen to me long term. I knew she really wanted to move to Paris with Lucas but she didn't want to leave me alone. Ah, well. What would be would be.

I walked to the sliders and saw the sun was now beginning to peep through the clouds over the water. It looked like the rain had stopped. I had made a promise to myself before I left Cedar Key that I'd lose the pesky ten or so pounds that had snuck up on me.

I reached for Basil's leash and my keys. "Come on, I need some exercise. Let's go walk the beach."

By the time we returned, I was surprised to see we'd walked for close to two hours. It was so tranquil walking along the shore, watching the waves roll in, and seeing how patterns of clouds above me constantly changed. It was easy to lose track of time here.

I was a little late feeding Basil his supper so I got him fed before I sat down with a heated-up casserole, also courtesy of Lucas. I had uncorked a bottle of pinot noir and filled a wineglass.

Sitting at the counter, I also had a view of the beach, ocean, and sky. I had only been here a few hours but it felt comfortable. My thoughts drifted to Gabe. I missed him and felt bad that he couldn't be here with me to enjoy the beautiful evening. But then, if he were here, we wouldn't be at this condo. We'd be on the outskirts of town in the house we'd planned to buy. Strange how things worked out—one change can lead to so many different patterns in one's life.

I had just finished filling the dishwasher when my cell rang. It was Isabelle.

"Chloe, hi. I wanted to see if you arrived in Ormond Beach okay."

"Yes, fine. A minor mishap with a flat tire but Basil and I got here safely around two. How're you and Haley doing?"

"Oh, gosh, sorry to hear about the tire. But I'm glad you're there. Yeah, we're doing okay. Things just aren't getting any better for Haley, so I'll be glad when school finishes in a couple weeks."

"Geez, I was hoping the situation would improve for her. Is there anything that can be done?"

"Well, the school is involved and it seems there are a few other girls being bullied as well. Parents have been meeting to try to find a solution, but so far, nothing. One thing I did do, and I feel bad because it seems it was more of a punishment to Haley than anything else—I took away her iPad and the Internet capacity on her cell. No getting online."

"God, that's terrible and you're right. Poor Haley has done nothing and yet she's the one being punished. So it's cyberbullying as well as in person?"

"Oh, yeah. It's both."

"I'm so sorry to hear this, Isabelle. I wish there was something I could do."

"Well, as I said, I'll be glad when school ends. At least then she'll be away from it for a while. Listen, I won't keep you. I just wanted to touch base and make sure you arrived okay. So you like the condo and everything's going well?"

"Yes, the condo is very nice with a gorgeous view, and Basil and I are settling in well."

"Well, have fun and keep in touch."

I hung up and decided to take a shower, get into my jammies, and settle down on the sofa with a glass of wine and the book I was reading.

I must have dozed off because I woke from a sound sleep and momentarily felt disoriented. I looked around and realized I was in Ormond Beach at the condo. I glanced at my watch and was shocked to see that it was three in the morning. Basil was curled up at my feet sleeping away. I began to get up to head to bed, and it was then that I recalled the dream I'd had before waking.

I saw a pond in my mind. A fishpond. Located in a beautiful area surrounded by a low brick wall, large leafy trees, and butterflies hovering above the pond. I pulled at the dream, trying to remember more, but that was it. I did remember I was standing beside the pond, looking down into the water, and it appeared that the multitude of fish were looking up at me—smiling.

I shook my head and took the last sip of wine remaining in the glass. "Come on, Basil. Let's go to bed and get a proper sleep."

# Chapter 7

I awoke the next morning feeling rested and refreshed. Glancing at the clock, I saw it was just after six. I must have dozed off around nine, woke on the sofa, and went right back to sleep in the comfortable bed, with no further dreams. But the fishpond dream was tugging at my mind. I wondered if there was a connection between it and the house dream.

I'd left the bedroom drapes open the night before and, sitting up, I could see the gorgeous ocean and sky from the glass door. Basil began stirring at the foot of the bed. Guess he'd passed on sleeping in his own bed and preferred to be with me.

"Come on, fella," I told him as I got up and threw on a pair of sweatpants and a T-shirt. "Let's hit the beach for a walk."

When we returned, I was true to my word and only had a container of yogurt and piece of fruit for breakfast. I decided that a drive around town might be in order. It would enable me to get to know the streets and the surrounding area. After I changed into cropped pants, a cotton top, and sandals, I clipped on Basil's leash and we were off to explore, making our first stop a service station to get my flat tire fixed.

The area the condo was located in was called Beachside, for obvious reasons. But if you got back onto Granada Boulevard and drove over the bridge, you ended up in the downtown area of Ormond Beach. Just before the bridge, I glanced across the street and saw the sign for the Casements, which I remembered from the brochures that Henry had sent about Rockefeller's winter home. I made a mental note to add it to the list of places I wanted to tour.

Just over the bridge, I took a left on Beach Street and discovered a row of nice parks along the river. After finding a parking spot, we got out, and Basil and I walked around for about twenty minutes enjoying the beautiful May morning. Huge, leafy trees provided shady spots and the view onto the Halifax River was a tranquil scene. Joggers and other walkers passed us, each one nodding a hello.

We got back in the car and, with no particular destination in mind, I decided to drive straight across to North Beach Street. It appeared to be a combination of both homes and small businesses. Farther up on my right I saw a sign that jutted out from a shop: Yarrow's Tea Place. I was pleased that I'd found the tea shop Louise had mentioned and decided I'd come back later in the afternoon without Basil.

I continued driving slowly down the street, admiring the beautiful old houses. That was when I saw it on my left. The house. The exact *same* house from my dream. I felt a jolt of recognition as chills crawled up my back. How could this be possible? I pulled over so as not to block traffic and stared at the huge two-story structure. Just as in my dream, the house was situated back from the sidewalk with a fair amount of grassy frontage. A brick driveway to the right, a turret on the top floor, and even the black wrought-iron fence. I couldn't believe my eyes, but there it was. It was then that I noticed an elaborately carved metal plaque hanging from the fence on a small silver chain. Maybe it was a museum or historical house and I'd seen it in a brochure. I decided to turn around and park across the street directly in front of it in order to see the plaque better.

When I pulled up, I leaned toward the passenger seat and saw that the sign read "Koi House." That certainly didn't sound like anything I remembered from Henry's information. It actually sounded more like a private home to me. I craned my neck and could just about make out a couple of outbuildings behind it. Tall sycamore trees in full leaf created privacy for whatever was back there. It just didn't seem possible that a house I had dreamed about could exist in reality. It was then I realized that even the river across the street had been in my dream. The only thing missing was my mother at the front door.

I had no explanation for what I'd just witnessed. None at all. And I was sure that if I shared it with anybody, they'd think I was nuts. I let out a deep breath and noticed my palms had been gripping the steering wheel and also noticed that Basil had been whining as he stared out the window at the house.

"No, I'm afraid not, buddy. We can't go in there, and if we don't get moving, we just might be arrested for trespassing."

His whining increased as I slowly pulled away and I saw in my rearview mirror he had jumped up on the backseat in order to better watch the departing house behind us.

"Sit down and be a good boy, Basil," I told him. "We're going to drive around a little more." I almost wondered if the next thing I'd see would be the fishpond from last night's dream.

But the rest of the morning was uneventful, and finally we headed back home.

After lunch at the condo, Basil and I took another walk on the beach, and by the time we got upstairs, I saw it was going on two. My usual time for afternoon coffee, which today I'd be replacing with tea. I closed and locked the sliders to the balcony.

"You be a good boy and take a nap," I told Basil as I picked up my knitting tote and handbag. "I'll be back in a couple hours."

I easily found a spot to park in front of the tea shop. When I walked inside, the aroma of spices filled the air. Soft classical music was playing and I heard the trickle of water from somewhere. Huge tubs of potted plants flanked the room. A cozy sitting area was in front, with a wooden counter in the back. Behind the counter, glass jars filled a huge shelf area taking up the entire wall. Two women were knitting—an older woman sat in a beige leather club chair and another, around my age, with legs tucked under her, was on the matching sofa.

"Hello," the older woman said.

"Welcome to Yarrow's Place," the other replied. "What can I get for you?"

"Hi," I said and walked toward the back as the younger woman moved behind the counter. "Gosh, I'm not sure. So many teas to choose from." I saw little printed signs attached to the glass jars—lavender, chamomile, and a variety of other flavors.

"Green tea is best in the spring," she said. "Would you like to sample a little?"

"Sure," I said as I watched her unseal one of the glass jars, pour a small scoop of leaves into a glass mug, and remove a simmering kettle from a hotplate. She poured in the boiling water and clicked a timer on the counter. "Three minutes. Tea must steep for three minutes for the perfect flavor."

I felt like I was getting a course in Tea 101. "Why is that?" I asked.

"The teas give out substances like amino acids, vitamins, and caffeine," she explained. "The concentration will reach peak value in three minutes and give the full flavor."

"Interesting," I said and turned around as I heard the older woman exclaim, "Oh, do you knit?"

I glanced down at my tote and nodded. "Yes, I do. Actually, that's why I dropped by. I met a woman yesterday, Louise Blackstone, who told me about the shop. She said her best friend's niece owned it. So you must be Yarrow?" I questioned the woman behind the counter.

Before she could reply, the older woman laughed and said, "Yes, she is, and I'm Mavis Anne Overby. Very nice to meet you."

"Same here," I told her as the timer buzzer went off. "I'm Chloe Radcliffe."

Yarrow poured the tea through a strainer and then handed me the cup. "Try this."

I took a sip and felt a burst of flavor hitting the roof of my mouth. "Oh, very nice," I said. "Yes, I'll have a cup of that, please."

"Come and have a seat," Mavis said and gestured toward the other chair. "So how do you know Louise?"

Sitting upright in the chair, knitting away, she reminded me of a southern belle entertaining guests for the afternoon. Her snow white hair was pulled away from her face in a French twist. She wore a beautiful green silk pantsuit and her wrists, fingers, and neck were adorned with what appeared to be quite expensive jewelry.

I explained that I was renting a condo next door to her friend and had just arrived in town the day before.

"How nice. Just a vacation?"

"Well, I'm actually doing research about possibly relocating here," I said and then went on to explain about Gabe and the plans that didn't work out.

She nodded. "Oh, yes, it can be very difficult losing a loved one, but you're doing the right thing, coming here to see if perhaps this is where you're meant to be now. It's been almost fifty years since I lost the love of my life." She nodded again. "And although I never have gotten over the loss of Jackson Lee Hawkins, he's always with me." She pointed to her heart.

I couldn't say that Gabe was the love of my life—actually, I had begun to think I'd just be one of those women who never had one—but I sympathized with Mavis's loss, despite the passage of time.

"Here you go," Yarrow said, passing me the glass mug, which was only partially filled. "I prepare tea the correct way here. In China tea has a lot to do with both sense and concept. Many experts believe that tea should only fill seventy percent of a cup, because the other thirty percent is space for your emotions."

I was definitely getting an education in tea, I thought as I took a sip. "Very good. How did you get such an unusual name? Isn't yarrow a plant?"

She nodded. "It is. According to the Greek myth, Achilles put it on the heels of his soldiers to stanch bleeding from wounds. The plant blooms in August and I grow it in pots at my house. Then I grind up the leaves and we have yarrow tea here at the shop. But it was my mother who chose my name. I guess you could say she was a bit of a flower child back in the sixties when she got pregnant with me."

From the look of the woman sitting across from me now, I had a feeling perhaps that hippie gene had been passed on to her daughter. Yarrow was tall and slim with a thick salt-and-pepper braid hanging down her back. She wore baggy cropped pants, a T-shirt that had "Peace" written across the front, and didn't wear an ounce of makeup.

"I like your name," I told her. "I think it suits you."

"Oh, I'm afraid my sister was more than just a flower child. She was a wild one, that girl," Mavis proclaimed. For a brief second I thought I saw annoyance cross her face, followed by a smile. "But Emmalyn meant well. The most beautiful girl in Ormond Beach. The trouble was that she knew it. And our father spoiled her rotten."

I removed my knitting and began working on the lace shawl I'd started a few days before.

Mavis leaned forward. "Oh, that's just beautiful. You certainly are a knitter."

"Thank you. That's a lovely afghan you're working on," I told her. "I see you're making socks." I glanced over to the gorgeous purple-and-rose-colored socks that Yarrow had on double-pointed needles. "Both of you are quite accomplished knitters also. By the way, is there a yarn shop in town?"

Mavis shook her head. "No, I'm afraid not," she said and I caught the expression of downturned lips she sent to Yarrow. "The closest ones are either Orlando or Cocoa Beach. I've been telling my niece to turn this place into a yarn shop. She could still have her tea, but this community needs a yarn shop."

I wasn't sure I should volunteer the information that I had been a partner at the yarn shop in Cedar Key and decided not to say anything. "That would be nice. Combining both businesses," I said.

Yarrow shook her head. "Aunt Mavis refuses to understand that this shop simply wouldn't be large enough to carry stock for knitting plus the items needed to run a tea shop. Besides, trying to juggle both businesses isn't something I'd welcome."

"Well, you know I have the perfect location for a combined yarn and tea shop, but I won't pester you." She put her knitting in her lap and removed her reading glasses as she shifted in her chair to face me. "I think you'll like our community. It has a small-town feel once you get to know it. Not a tourist town like those around Orlando."

I nodded. "That's what I've heard. Are you from here originally?"

"Oh, my, yes. Born and raised in Ormond Beach. My father was the town doctor, so we knew pretty much everybody in town. I'm the oldest of three and our mother passed away when I was fourteen. My brother, David, was twelve but Emmalyn was only eight. I think it was the hardest on her to lose her mother so young."

I nodded. "I can understand that. Do they still live here too?"

"No, I'm sorry to say that Emmalyn passed away quite young—at twenty-eight—but my brother lives next door to the house we grew up in. Which was where I lived until three months ago. I had a nasty fall, ended up in the hospital with knee surgery, and he insisted I move in with him and his partner, Clive, until I could manage the stairs. I must admit I do enjoy being waited on and having my bedroom on the main floor."

It was then that I noticed an elaborate cane propped beside her chair.

"Yarrow was only ten when she lost her mother, so David and I had her come and stay with us until she went off to college."

"Oh, how nice," I said. "And do you still live together?"

Yarrow shook her head and laughed. "Oh, Aunt Mavis would really love that, but no. I own my own house. Just a small cottage over the bridge behind the old Ormond Hotel."

"Well, that's good. At least you're still very close to both your aunt and your shop."

Mavis gave a sniff and said, "Yes, and I just rattle around in that big old childhood home of mine. All by myself. Alone. So I'm grateful to be with David for a while."

I saw the wink she tossed my way and I smiled. "Are you in the downtown area also?"

She gestured toward the door. "Oh, yes, just down the street. A very short walk from here to Koi House."

For the second time that day, I felt chills go up my back.

# Chapter 8

A few days later I found myself back at the tea shop due to an invitation from both Mavis and Yarrow. They told me that Friday afternoon many of the other women would gather for their group knitting and they urged me to stop by.

I had come to no conclusion about the connection between my dream and Mavis Anne Overby's owning the exact same house. It truly defied explanation and it was difficult not to wonder about it. Without ever having been inside her house, I knew without a doubt that she had a fishpond on her property. Hence, the name *Koi House*.

There were a lot more cars in front of the tea shop this time when I pulled up, but I managed to find a parking spot and went inside. Once again, the shop was filled with an exotic aroma and classical music was playing, but the room now had a buzz of female chatter.

Mavis saw me and waved a hand to call me over. I glanced around and saw six other women knitting, but none of them was Louise Blackstone. Yarrow was behind the counter preparing various mugs of tea.

"Have a seat," Mavis said, gesturing to the sofa. "Hey, everybody, this is Chloe Radcliffe. She's thinking about possibly relocating here."

She then proceeded to introduce everyone, though none of the names stuck in my brain. They were a mixture of women in their fifties and sixties and two of them had probably seen their eightieth birthdays. All of them were friendly and welcoming, asking questions about where I was from, where I was staying, and saying they hoped I'd like Ormond Beach. After giving them a brief bio, I headed to the counter for a cup of tea.

"I'm glad you could join us," Yarrow said. "My special today is raspberry lemon."

"Sounds good. Oh, you have baked goodies too?" The display case held assorted cookies and muffins.

She nodded as she began preparing the tea. "Yeah, nothing fancy, but the ladies like a little something to go with their afternoon tea, so I bake a few things fresh every day."

"That blueberry muffin looks great. I'll have one of those too." So much for trying to lose those ten pounds.

"I'll bring it over to you," Yarrow said and I headed back to the sofa.

"So are you here by yourself?" one of the women asked.

"Yes, just me and my dog, Basil. I'm divorced and I thought it was time for a change in my life."

"Lord knows we can all use that now and again," the woman I thought was named Barbara said and all of us chuckled.

"I came here with my husband about twenty years ago," one of the older women said. "But Mike has been gone ten years now. I can't imagine living anywhere else, especially with all my friends here."

Gatherings of women have been occurring since the beginning of time. Whether it was a sewing circle popular in the eighteen hundreds, a knitting group during the war years of the forties, a coffee klatch in the fifties and sixties—women had been drawing together to socialize and bond. It was universal and it didn't matter where the location was. Women gravitated together to form connections.

"Same here," a few of the others agreed.

"I hope you'll like Ormond Beach," said a woman whom I remembered as Maddie. "I came here alone also about five years ago. Divorced, my daughter was grown and gone, so I decided it was my turn. I'd always wanted to own a florist shop . . . so that's exactly what I did."

"Thanks," I said as Yarrow passed me a mug of tea and a muffin before sitting down to join us.

"Maddie owns the florist shop in town," Yarrow explained.

"That's really great," I said. "I guess nothing compares to fulfilling your dream."

Maddie laughed. "Well, I can't say it was easy, but . . . anything worthwhile usually isn't. It took me a couple years to save the money

I needed and then I was able to secure a small business loan, and after eighteen months . . . I'm no Donald Trump, but I'm doing pretty well."

"Good for you," I said, and we all looked toward the door as a flustered Louise Blackstone came rushing in.

"I'm here, I'm here," she announced before plopping into one of the club chairs.

I saw Mavis Anne shake her head as a grin crossed her face. "Without the drama, tell us what happened," she said.

"Whew." Louise puffed out the word. "Well, I was all set to leave and little Ramona just didn't want her mama to leave her behind. Usually I can just give her a little treat and she's content. But not today. She refused the treat and every time I headed to the door to leave, she whimpered."

Nobody said a word, waiting for her to go on.

"So I tried explaining to her that I wouldn't be gone very long. I took her outside one more time, thinking perhaps she had to piddle again. She has such a tiny bladder, you know. But nope. None of that worked. I talked to her, I cuddled her, and she continued whimpering, telling me she just didn't want me to leave."

"And who's the boss here?" I heard Maddie mumble under her breath.

"Yes, okay, Louise," said Mavis Anne, exasperation in her tone. "So . . . what did you do?"

It was then that I saw the red leather Namaste bag on her shoulder was wiggling.

"Well," Louise said, as she slowly unzipped the bag and the cutest little furry head peeped out, "I just *had* to take her with me, of course."

Yarrow threw her arms up in the air. "You're damn lucky that Sylvia isn't here today. She's allergic to dogs and she'd pitch a fit. Besides, I serve tea and food. You know it's against health regulations for her to be in here."

An apologetic expression covered Louise's face, which was now being licked by the adorable Ramona. "I know, I know and I'm sorry, but I didn't want to miss the knitting group."

Yarrow shook her head and I could see she was fighting to suppress a grin. "Does anybody have any objections to Ramona staying?"

All heads shook in a negative motion.

"Okay," Yarrow said. "But try to keep her in the bag. I don't want her running around the shop."

I couldn't help myself. "My God, she's so cute! Is she a Yorkie?"

A huge smile crossed Louise's face. "Yes, she does have a lot of Yorkie and she's such a good girl. Well . . . usually." She removed the bag from her shoulder, placed it on the floor beside her, and shook her finger. "Now, you stay right there near Mama and be a good girl."

Ramona's top hair was caught with a tiny yellow ribbon and I saw her adoring eyes never wavered from Louise's face.

"Well, Chloe, it's so nice to see you here. I'm glad you made it. Settling in okay?"

"I am. Thank you."

"Did you tend to that tire of yours?"

"Yes, I got it fixed and I'm all set." I saw the inquisitive glances from the other women and went on to explain about my flat tire mishap.

"You were really lucky somebody stopped on that stretch of road to help you."

"I know and apparently he lives in Ormond-by-the-Sea, so he followed me all the way down Granada to make sure I was okay."

Maddie laughed. "Not a bad way to meet a new guy."

I could feel a blush creeping up my neck. Damn those hot flashes. "Oh, no . . . it was really just . . ." I stammered.

Maddie nudged me playfully. "I was only kidding you. Did you exchange names, though?"

"Actually, we did. I wanted to repay him and wasn't sure what to do, so he gave me his card and said I could call him sometime and buy him a drink. Chadwick Price was his name."

The entire room went silent. I looked up from my knitting to see all faces glued to mine.

"What?" I said. "What's wrong?"

"Did you say Chadwick Price? Maybe I wasn't kidding," Maddie said.

"Why? Who is he?"

"Only the most eligible and richest bachelor in Volusia County. Maybe in all of Florida," Maddie replied, and I knew she wasn't kidding with me this time. Thoughts of Worthington Slater, the love of Marin's life, floated into my mind. I recalled that he had been reputed to be the most eligible and wealthiest bachelor in Levy County.

"Oh," was all I could say.

"Well, I always said that young man had manners," Mavis Anne said. "He was raised by a good southern mama. Just like my Jackson Lee Hawkins. Now there was a true gentleman. You don't see many like him around anymore. That was very nice of Chadwick to stop and help you."

"It was," I said. "His card said he's in real estate. So I guess he has a lucrative business?"

Maddie never lifted her eyes from the blue-and-white-striped socks she was working on. "Honey, Chadwick Price is into everything. Real estate is his main business, but he's also an investor in various projects and he's always giving back to the community. It was Chadwick who founded and funded both the domestic abuse center and the rape crisis center in town."

Mavis Anne nodded. "Yes, he's quite the philanthropist. He's a very good man."

"Not to mention pretty damn hot," Maddie said, bringing forth chuckles from the others. "He throws a fund-raiser at his home every Fourth of July. I mean to tell you it rivals any of the celebrity gatherings. Black tie all the way."

"You've been?" I asked, somewhat surprised.

"Oh, yeah. It's the highlight of my year. It's a fund-raiser for the hospital, and the guest list includes a lot of the doctors on staff, some professors from the college, but also a fair number of business owners in the community. I've been twice and wouldn't miss it for anything."

I couldn't help but wonder where I'd be in two months' time.

Mavis Anne nodded. "I have to agree. I've gone every year since he began having them about ten years ago."

"And lucky me," Louise said. "Mavis Anne always chooses me as her *date* for the evening. It's quite the lavish affair."

"It certainly sounds it," I said.

"So where are you taking him for that drink?" Maddie asked.

"Oh . . . I'm not sure I was planning to call him."

"Don't be silly," Mavis Anne said. "Of course you'll call him.

Where're your manners? It's only a drink as a thank-you for rescuing you in a downpour on a lonely stretch of road."

Well, when she put it like that. "Yeah, maybe I'll think about it . . . but I have no clue where to go around here."

"Take him to the Grind," Maddie said. "It's just around the corner from here and they have a nice tiki bar out back."

I nodded, but I'd clearly have to give this more thought.

The rest of the afternoon passed quickly as I got to know the other women, and I was surprised to find that I was the last one still there. It had been a great way to spend a few hours—in the company of other women, talking, knitting, and sipping tea.

I glanced at my watch. "Gosh, I can't believe it's going on five. I have to get home to walk Basil."

"We're so glad you joined us," Mavis Anne said. "I was wondering . . . if you're not busy on Sunday afternoon, would you like to join us for dinner? David and Clive put together quite a wonderful feast every Sunday for Yarrow and me."

"Oh, yes. Come," Yarrow said. "It's the one day of the week that I do have to dress a little more formal than usual, but it's worth it for Clive's incredible cooking."

I took in Yarrow's bib overalls, T-shirt, and sandals and wondered what the definition of "a little more formal" was.

"Gosh, are you sure? I wouldn't want to intrude on a family dinner."

Mavis Anne waved her hand in the air. "Don't be silly. David and Clive simply adore entertaining. Sometimes Louise joins us too. We always do Sunday dinner at the family home. It's just down the street here on North Beach and there's a plaque hanging from the fence that says Koi House. You can't miss it. Plan to arrive around twoish. Cocktails first, of course."

Of course.

# Chapter 9

By Sunday morning I was beginning to feel as if I'd lived in Ormond Beach much longer than only six days. I was already making friends, getting to know my way around the area, and I even had a nice dinner invitation.

When I returned from walking Basil on the beach, I bumped into Louise and Ramona outside our building.

"Hey," I said, walking over to them. "And how are you and Ramona today?"

Basil did his customary sniff and turn routine with Ramona, who seemed to welcome his attention.

"We're just fine. Oh, I think my girl likes Basil. I told you she was a flirt."

I laughed as I bent down to pat her. "She's so cute. And it's obvious that she adores you."

"Yes, and it's definitely mutual. I spoke to Mavis Anne this morning. How nice you'll be joining them for dinner. I had to decline. I've been invited to my nephew's home in Ponce Inlet, so Ramona and I are driving down there shortly. You'll have a nice time at Mavis Anne's. David and Clive are wonderful hosts."

"I'm looking forward to it. How formal should I dress?"

Louise laughed. "Oh, if Mavis Anne had her way, it would be a ball gown. But a skirt or dress will do just fine. I love her dearly but sometimes her elitist attitude is over the top."

I joined her laughter. "You have a great day and I'll see you soon," I said, heading into the building.

By one thirty I had decided on a black skirt, white silk blouse, and a black shrug that I'd knitted. I was looking forward to the dinner, but even more, I was itching to get inside that house. It had taken on an air of intrigue for me, yet I had no idea why.

I had popped by Maddie's florist shop the day before to purchase a bouquet of flowers as a thank-you, and a nice bottle of cabernet completed my offering. Picking up both from the table, I ruffled the top of Basil's head with a promise not to be too late and headed out the door.

I pulled into the brick driveway and stared at the house. Beyond its obvious beauty, I felt drawn to the house itself. And although my mother was not standing in the doorway beckoning me inside, the structure did seem to open its arms to me with a feeling of love.

I rang the doorbell and waited. I could hear chimes inside the house and a moment later the door was opened with a flourish. A man of medium height, wearing black slacks and a white shirt, bowed. I wondered if Mavis Anne had a butler.

He extended his hand and gently guided me inside. "Hello and welcome. I'm David Overby, Mavis Anne's brother. I'm so glad you could join us, Chloe."

I liked him immediately. He exuded a sincere friendliness in his demeanor, and his slightly pudgy face had an expression of joy.

"Thank you so much for inviting me," I said, as my eyes began to take in the room. Though far from ostentatious, it had a subdued grandness. A staircase to my left had an intricate carved balustrade of dark wood that matched the moldings in the room. Huge mullioned windows with panes of glass in a diamond shape flanked the front and side walls of the room. A lace swag curtain hung from the top of both windows and complemented the deep blue upholstered sofas and chairs.

"Oh, it's our pleasure," David replied. "Everybody is on the patio having an aperitif. Right this way."

I followed him through a large archway into the next room, which appeared less formal, with buttery yellow leather furniture, bookcases, a round table set up with an onyx chess set, and a large flat-screen television hanging on the inside wall.

We continued through a few small passageways toward the back of the house as I glanced at tables holding crystal bowls of fresh flowers, a walnut deacon's bench with a gorgeous beige afghan placed over the back, more antique tables holding books or a lamp. We emerged into a bright breakfast area with a large lemon yellow oval table and chairs, cornflower blue walls with a huge designer kitchen to the right.

I think by this time I let out a gasp at the beauty and luxury surrounding me.

"This is absolutely stunning," I whispered.

I saw a smile cover David's face. "Yes . . . but to us, it's simply home sweet home."

I barely knew this man but I had no doubt that he did not possess one ounce of snobbery.

"This is Marta," he said, nodding toward a woman who was carefully placing canapés onto a silver tray. "We'd be lost without Marta. She is our right and left hand both."

A very attractive woman who appeared to be in her late thirties looked up and smiled. "Mr. David is too kind. Welcome."

She was tall and thin, with a fair complexion and exceptionally blue eyes; I detected a European accent but couldn't quite place it.

"Thank you," I said. I glanced around the kitchen and knew it rivaled any that I'd seen on the cooking channel.

I followed David through French doors off the kitchen and out to a brick patio where Mavis Anne and Yarrow sat on green-and-white upholstered furniture sipping wine. Standing beside a marble bar was a tall, thin man holding a martini glass. With a receding hairline and wire-rimmed glasses, he reminded me of a professor I'd had in college. In contrast to David, his demeanor was more reserved, and as soon as David introduced us and he said hello, I heard his clipped British accent.

"Welcome, welcome," Mavis Anne said. "What can Clive get you to drink?"

I passed the flowers to her and handed the wine to David. "Just a little thank-you," I said. "Oh, a red wine would be nice." I turned toward Clive and smiled.

"A red wine it is," he said and returned my smile.

"Come and join us," Yarrow said, pointing toward an empty chair. "It's such a gorgeous day to be outside, isn't it?"

"It is," I said. "I guess we should enjoy it before the heat and humidity arrive."

I looked up to see Marta coming out with the tray. She placed it on the table in front of us along with napkins. "Would you like me to place the flowers in water?"

"Thank you," Mavis Anne said. "That would be nice."

It was then that my eye caught some movement to my left and I realized a swarm of butterflies was hovering just beyond a brick wall. I had no doubt the koi pond was inside that wall and felt a shiver go through me.

"Your home is absolutely amazing," I said.

Mavis Anne took a sip of wine and nodded. "It is, and we were fortunate to grow up here, but the house is so lonely now. A house shouldn't be lonely. I've always believed that this house has a soul and that soul needs to be nourished. During the time David, Emmalyn, and I were growing up here, there was constant activity. Not only us, with our friends, but also my father and his friends. Now . . ." She waved a hand in the air and I almost got the feeling she was speaking about a person rather than a house.

"Here you go," Clive said, passing me a wineglass.

"Thank you."

Mavis Anne raised her glass in the air. "Here's to Koi House and here's to our new friend, Chloe. Welcome to Ormond Beach and may you be so happy here you won't want to leave."

"Hear, hear," Yarrow said and I smiled.

I took a sip of wine and reached for a canapé. It was a stuffed mushroom but unlike any I'd had before. "This is delicious," I said.

Yarrow nodded. "Marta made those. She's a real treasure. We'd be lost without her."

She certainly seemed to have a special place in their hearts. "Does she work for you?" I asked.

"Yes," Mavis Anne said and took another sip of wine. "She's been with us just over ten years now. Marta came from Poland to join her sister in Palm Coast. There's a large Polish community there."

I knew Palm Coast was only about thirty minutes north of Ormond Beach. "How nice," I said. "She speaks English very well."

Mavis Anne nodded. "Her sister is my hairdresser and that's how I met Marta. She needed a job and we needed a housekeeper, somebody to help out around here. My father was still alive then and I needed a caregiver for him. He adored Marta and when he passed away a few years later, we simply couldn't part with her."

"Right," David said. "So now we share her. She cleans for Clive and me and also looks after the house here and anything else we might need."

"That's wonderful," I said. "It certainly sounds like an ideal situation. Does she have a family besides her sister?"

"She has a daughter. Krystina is now fourteen but they still live with Marta's sister and her husband."

"So how do you like Ormond Beach so far?" Clive questioned and I realized he was making an attempt to change the subject.

"I'm loving it. It already feels like home to me. Have you been here a long time?"

"Over thirty years now. David and I met in London when we were both studying interior design and we've been together ever since. We own our own business here in town, although we're not taking on many new clients. Are you retired?"

I laughed and shook my head. "No, not really. More like between jobs at the moment. I was co-owner of a yarn shop in Cedar Key but I gave up my partnership last year when I had plans to move here with my significant other. We had made arrangements to purchase a home, raise alpacas, and start a yarn shop downtown. Unfortunately, Gabe passed away suddenly last June and I . . . well, I'm not quite sure what, exactly, I'm doing at the moment."

"Oh, I'm so sorry," Clive said before Mavis Anne interrupted him.

"A yarn shop?" She leaned forward in her seat. "You owned a yarn shop?"

I nodded. "Yes, a lovely little shop. I have a degree in textile and fibers so it was really a dream come true. But I'm afraid the dream fell apart, because with this weak economy my partner is going to be closing the shop."

"Oh, what a shame," Yarrow said.

"It is indeed. Well, we'll just have to see what we can do about that, because I have the perfect venue for a yarn shop." Mavis Anne nodded her head emphatically.

I recalled how she'd made some mention of this the first day I'd met her and how she'd been unsuccessful in getting her niece to open one.

I shook my head and smiled. "Oh, I don't think so. Financially, I'm not in a position to take on a new business."

"Pish posh," Mavis Anne declared while waving a hand in the air. "We need to discuss this more after dinner."

"Uh-oh!" Yarrow said. "My aunt has that look in her eye, and when Mavis Anne Overby has *that* look in her eye, watch out."

# Chapter 10

I wiped my lips with the rose colored linen napkin. "That was absolutely superb," I said. "You guys should have been chefs rather than interior decorators."

Clive laughed and leaned over to refill my wineglass. "Ah, but see, if we had to cook for a living, I don't think it would be quite the same. We cook for the pure joy of it."

He had a point. "Well, I'm not sure I've ever had duck confit as wonderful as this. And the garlic mashed potatoes and fresh green beans were excellent."

"Thank you," David said. "I'm glad you enjoyed it, but wait until you see what Marta has prepared for dessert."

As if on cue, Marta entered the dining room with a smile on her face and winked at me as she began to remove our plates.

I took a sip of wine and looked around the room. Situated off the kitchen, separated by a small hallway at the back of the house, the dining room had huge windows overlooking the patio area. Beautifully decorated with a mahogany oval table and matching chairs, it looked like a smaller scale version of a formal dining room one might see on the British television series *Downton Abbey*.

I hadn't seen the upstairs rooms yet, but I couldn't help noticing that I had experienced a wonderful calm and tranquility ever since I'd stepped through the front door.

A few minutes later Marta entered the dining room carrying a strawberry torte on a pedestal crystal dish. The sight of it did make me gasp out loud. She placed it at one end of the table, left the room and returned with small serving plates.

"Oh, my goodness!" I said. "That looks like something from an exquisite French bakery."

"It's even better," David said, jumping up to assist with the servings that Marta was slicing.

After each of us had a plate, Marta returned with a carafe of coffee and began filling our cups.

One bite of the torte and I thought I was in heaven. David was right. I didn't see how a French bakery could possibly be better than this.

Conversation was minimal as all of us enjoyed the dessert.

When Marta returned to clear the plates, I felt like I was gushing but such a work of art certainly deserves the highest of compliments.

"Thank you," she said and didn't seem aware of her extraordinary talent.

After we finished our coffee, Mavis Anne said, "Yarrow, why don't you show Chloe around upstairs. I'm going to retire to the patio and then we'll show her the gardens."

"Sounds good," Yarrow said and I followed her down the passageways, back through the sitting area and formal living room to the front staircase.

"So you've lived here since the age of ten?" I asked, as we climbed the stairs.

"Actually, I feel like I've lived here all my life. Even when my mom was alive, I spent more time here than with her, but when she died, I came here permanently. She had a cottage nearby on Orchard Lane—which is where I live now. It stayed empty for years but when I got out of college, I decided that was where I wanted to live."

I noticed that no mention at all had been made of Yarrow's father and, even though I was curious, I thought it better not to ask.

We reached the top of the stairs, where a long hallway ran the length of the house. Like the downstairs, the area had a warm feeling. I saw a highly polished wood floor, more antique tables with vases of fresh flowers, and wall hangings.

I followed Yarrow to the back of the house and a bedroom at the far end.

"This used to be my grandfather's room," she explained. "But when he died, Aunt Mavis decided to switch rooms and take this one."

Another beautifully appointed room with antique furniture, lots of bold floral prints, and a sense of calm.

"It's gorgeous," I said, walking to the window, which overlooked the back garden. It was then that I saw the fishpond. There it was. Behind the stone wall. With brightly colored fish swimming around. Just like in my dream. How could this be possible? How could I dream about a place that I'd never been?

"Are you okay?" I heard Yarrow ask.

I swung around to face her and smiled. "Yeah, I'm fine. I think I was just captivated by the fishpond."

Yarrow joined me at the window and nodded. "That's been there ever since I can remember. Actually, I think some of the fish in there are over sixty years old. Koi are known for their longevity. But I'll let Aunt Mavis tell you the story behind the fishpond."

I followed her into two more bedrooms. Like Mavis Anne's room, each one had an attached bathroom and each one was furnished in Victorian décor with antiques, beauty, and calm.

Until we got to the last bedroom, which overlooked the front of the house. This was the room that jutted out with the turret. As we stepped over the threshold, a different sensation came over me. Not the calm I'd felt in the rest of the house—but melancholy.

"This was my mother's room when she was growing up," I heard Yarrow say, as I looked around to see a beautifully carved sleigh bed, matching bureaus, pale yellow-and-white-striped wallpaper, lace curtains, and a sitting area at the far end of the room with French doors.

"Rumor has it that my mother would sneak out over her balcony when she was a teenager," Yarrow said as I followed her.

She opened the French doors and we stepped out onto a roofed balcony with a small table and two chairs. I looked across the side garden and could just make out another house through the leafy tree branches. I assumed this was where David and Clive lived.

I looked over the edge of the half wall and laughed. "Are you serious? Your mother jumped to the ground from here to sneak out?"

Yarrow laughed. "Oh, no. She was too clever for that. When she had plans to go out at night, she made sure she propped a ladder against the balcony. She'd climb down and then back up when she returned and made sure she got rid of the ladder in the morning. But it wasn't a secret. My aunt knew exactly what she was doing and I think my grandfather did too. But as my aunt said—my mother was spoiled rotten and it was never discussed."

Mavis Anne was right: Emmalyn Overby was a wild one. As I stepped back inside, a sense of unease came over me and, silly though it sounds, I had a feeling that Yarrow and I weren't the only ones in the room.

I followed Yarrow back downstairs and saw her grab a set of keys from a hook on the kitchen wall. "Come on," she said, "We'll show you the garden and the schoolhouse."

Schoolhouse? "There was a school here?"

Yarrow laughed and shook her head. "Not really. Aunt Mavis will tell you about it."

It looked like Mavis Anne had been dozing but when she heard our voices, her eyes popped open and she sat up straighter in her chair.

"So what did you think of your tour of Koi House?" she asked.

"It's a magnificent home. My aunt Maude had an old house in Brunswick, Georgia, and my sister and I spent a lot of time there. I think that's where I developed my love and passion for older homes. She always told me that I was just like her—drawn to the mystique of old houses."

"Your aunt was a wise woman," Mavis Anne said. "Because older homes do have a mystique. Many things are woven into the soul of a house—good and bad. And over time they become so ingrained, they will remain there for eternity. That's why I could never sell this house to a stranger. It would be like giving away a part of myself." She slid to the edge of the chair and reached for her cane. "Do you have the keys for the schoolhouse?"

Yarrow jangled them in the air. "Right here."

With the assistance of her cane, Mavis Anne made her way across the patio toward the fishpond and we followed.

A stone archway led into the pond area and as I walked through it, a sense of tranquility came over me. Stone benches surrounded the circular pond, with huge tubs of orange and yellow lantana, violet pentas, and milkweed placed between the benches. I detected a hint of lavender and mint in the air. And there in the water were brightly colored red and white koi fish happily swimming around.

I let out a deep sigh. "This is just beautiful," I said, allowing the peace to envelope me.

"It is," Mavis Anne said, sitting on the one of the benches. "And it's been my sanctuary for most of my life. In 1952, when I was ten, I contracted the polio virus. I was fortunate that my father was a doctor and understood the disease. I did have a mild case of it compared to some, but I wasn't able to walk for a few months. After a stay in the hospital, my father hired a private nurse and I recuperated here at home, but I was a terrible patient and wasn't making any attempt to walk. My father told me about koi fish and how legend has it that they can climb the falls of the Yellow River to become dragons. They symbolize personal strength or perseverance as one goes through difficult situations. He said they had become a symbol for people struggling to make it through tough times and overcome obstacles."

I sat beside her on the bench and shook my head as my eyes continued to watch the fish. "I never knew that. What wonderful symbolism."

Mavis Anne nodded. "It is and so, my father told me that if I began to make an attempt to walk, if I faithfully did my daily exercises with my nurse, he would have a koi pond built just for me."

I smiled. "And so you did."

"I did, but it was much harder than I thought it would be. There were days I just didn't think my muscles would ever work well enough for me to walk. But while I was attempting to make this happen, my father had hired a crew to dig the pond, make the wall, and follow through on his promise. He had the utmost faith in me. And finally, almost a year later, with the assistance of crutches at first, I was walking. I'll never forget the day my father and I walked out here for the first time and I saw the fish. That was over sixty years ago, and some of those fish you see today are the original ones."

"That's an amazing story," I said. I couldn't help but admire the fortitude it must have taken to get through such a very difficult time.

"I have a strong feeling that it helped to form the person I would become. There were more disappointments, heartache, and sadness over the years, combined with much joy, but I always found that coming here to my fishpond diminished the bad times and enhanced the good ones."

I glanced up to see a swarm of butterflies hovering over one of the plants. I recalled that butterflies symbolized change and growth and couldn't help but wonder if all that had happened in the past year had been meant to bring me right here, in the company of Mavis Anne Overby, to this moment.

She patted my knee. "Okay," she said, leaning on her cane to get up. "And now we shall show you the schoolhouse.

"It wasn't really a schoolhouse," she explained as we walked across the garden toward the medium-size, honey-colored, stone structure.

"My father had this built as a playhouse for David, Emmalyn, and me when we were kids. I can't even remember why, but somehow we began calling it the schoolhouse."

Yarrow unlocked the wooden, oval-shaped door, which reminded me of a thatched cottage in the English countryside, and we stepped into a large, empty room. Light flooded the area from two rectangular skylights in the peaked ceiling, with additional light streaming through a bay window in front and French doors to my right, which led back out to a garden area. Wide white paneling covered the walls and above me I could see white beams between the skylights. At the far end, in the center of the room, was a stone fireplace that acted as a divider from another room behind it.

"Oh, wow!" I exclaimed. "How beautiful!"

Mavis Anne smiled and nodded. "Much like my fishpond, this cottage has given me many hours of solace."

I followed her and Yarrow toward the fireplace. Two arched doorways flanked either side and we walked into a kitchen area, complete with small sink, cabinets, and stove. More French doors on the right led out to a small brick patio area with towering oaks providing shade.

I shook my head. "This was some playhouse. What lucky kids you were."

Mavis Anne let out a chuckle. "As kids, I don't think we realized just how fortunate we were. But now—oh, yes, I'm very grateful for what I was given. My life has been blessed and I certainly have no regrets. There's just been one thing missing—one dream that was never fulfilled."

Somehow I had a very strong feeling I knew exactly what she was going to say. "Owning your own yarn shop," I blurted out.

She threw her head back and laughed. "Chloe Radcliffe, you are a very intuitive woman."

# Chapter 11

I had been surprised that following the tour of Koi House with Mavis Anne's revelation, she made no further mention of possibly turning the schoolhouse into a yarn shop—with me at the helm. Which was fine with me. Although I had to agree that the space would be an ideal location for a shop, I was in no position to take a business risk. Hell, I wasn't even sure if I'd be staying in the area permanently.

I answered my cell on Wednesday morning to hear my sister's voice.

"Are you busy?" she asked.

"Not at all," I said, grabbing my mug of coffee and heading out to the balcony with Basil. "What's up?"

"I'm just wondering what you've been up to. Haven't heard from you since Saturday. How'd the dinner go at Koi House?"

I brought Grace up to date on all of my news and heard a deep breath come across the line when I finished.

"Wow," she said. "That house sounds fantastic. And you're as bad as Aunt Maude and me when it comes to the connection with old houses, but Mavis Anne sounds like an impressive woman. She's had quite a life. Seems to me that she's trying to tempt you into opening that yarn shop for her."

I chuckled. "Yeah, I think you could be right."

"Well, would that be so bad? You did love being a partner with Dora and you're not the type to sit around doing nothing."

True. "I know that. It's just . . . I'm still not sure if I'm going to stay here permanently. I think I could be very happy here, but . . . I just don't know."

"You will in time. Let it go and just enjoy the moments. You felt the same way before you came to Cedar Key, remember? And that turned out to be a good thing, even if it wasn't meant to be forever."

I knew Grace was right. "I do know one thing. I'm glad I agreed to stay here longer than two weeks. That wouldn't have been enough time to make a decision. As a matter of fact, I'm meeting with a Realtor this afternoon to look at a few places to rent."

"Oh, that's great, Chloe. I'm hoping you'll find exactly what you want. I have to run, but I'll talk to you on Friday. You haven't forgotten it's your birthday, have you?"

I let out a chuckle. "Hardly, but I think it'll be a pretty quiet one this year. Love you and talk to you later."

The fact that I had a birthday on Friday had come out in the conversation at the Sunday dinner, but I hoped it had been quickly forgotten.

After viewing two townhouses and one detached home, I was feeling a letdown. Though I couldn't say what it was, exactly, that I didn't like, I just knew none of the three places was for me. It suddenly struck me that it had more to do with how I *felt* walking through the various rooms, rather than the physical sight of them. What was lacking was that spark, that burst of energy or what some called vibes. That precise feeling I had from the moment I entered Koi House.

I needed a pick-me-up and headed to the tea shop. I was surprised to only see Yarrow and Mavis Anne when I walked in.

"Quiet day?" I asked, heading to the counter.

"I was busy this morning, but I think bad news has a way of making people scatter," Yarrow said. "What can I get you?"

"I'll let you decide. What's going on?"

She began to prepare my tea and before she had a chance to answer, Mavis Anne placed her knitting in her lap and said, "What's going on is my niece is about to be forced to close this shop. The owner has informed her that the building has sold and the new owner doesn't want a tea shop here. He has other plans."

"Oh, no," I said. Just when I was feeling I had found my niche, the place that would provide friendship and bonding, it could all be falling apart? "This is terrible. I'm so sorry, Yarrow. Geez, your day doesn't sound much better than mine."

We all fell silent while my tea brewed.

"What's wrong with your day?" Mavis Anne questioned as I sat on the sofa with my tea.

I proceeded to tell them about my property viewings. "They just didn't *hit* me. I can't explain it. The price was okay, the location was fine . . . I don't know what it was, but if I'm going to stay in this area, I need to find the right place to live."

Mavis Anne banged her cane on the floor, causing both Yarrow and me to jump. "Indeed you do," she said. "And I have the solution."

I felt a skeptical expression cross my face as I looked at her.

"You will move into Koi House. Lord knows there's plenty of room, and now that I'm staying with David and Clive, it's almost sinful that poor house is sitting alone and empty."

Was she serious? There was no way I could afford the rent that house would command. "Oh, well, thank you, Mavis Anne, but . . . I don't think so. I just don't see—"

She cut me off and waved her hand in the air. "Now look . . . the way I see it, you need a place to stay, a place to call home. My home is empty. Just sitting there, being tended to by Marta, but with nobody to give it the love and attention it needs. Of course I'm aware of the rent I could get from that house, but honey, there comes a point in life where it just isn't about money anymore. Not at all. Answer me a question."

I looked at her and waited.

"If I came up with a fair and equitable price that you could afford, would you consider it then?"

"I guess I'd be a fool not to," I blurted out, which caused Mavis Anne to throw her head back laughing and stamp the floor with her cane again.

"Then it's settled. We will discuss a price and you will move in. Now . . . I only have a few rules."

I saw Yarrow roll her eyes as she mumbled, "Oh, God."

"Hush," Mavis Anne hissed. "Of course you must bring that dog of yours, Basil, and by the way, I still haven't had the chance to meet him. You have full run of the house and by that I mean you are to feel free to invite friends over and do anything you would do in any other rental. Also, while I'm sure you'll clean up after yourself, I will still retain Marta to do the bulk of the cleaning. First of all, it's a large house and I certainly don't want to put her out of a job. It will be up to you if you'd also like Marta to prepare any meals for you. You can talk it over with her and you'll be responsible for paying her accordingly for any extras. Any questions?"

"No," I stammered. This was all too good to be true. "It sounds more than fair to me."

Mavis Anne nodded her head emphatically. "Okay. A few more things. You must sign a lease for one year and if possible, I'd like you to use the furniture in the house rather than moving in your own things, and secondly, you will take the front bedroom. The one with the turret and balcony."

I felt a shiver go through me at the same time my heart fell. Emmalyn's old room? The one room in the house that made me feel uneasy? Damn. I let out a deep breath.

"I have no problem with signing the lease or using your furniture, but . . . is there any particular reason why I couldn't have one of the other two bedrooms?" I knew one was Mavis Anne's but that still left two empty rooms.

"Yes, there is, but it doesn't warrant an explanation. At least not right now. Take it or leave it."

This woman drove a hard bargain.

"I'll take it," I hastened to say before she could change her mind.

"Good," she said as a smile crossed her face. "Now on to Yarrow's problem. You have two choices, my dear. You can either attempt to find another location downtown or . . . you can just close the tea shop completely. And I stay abreast of real estate in the historic district, so I feel quite justified in saying there are no empty shops at the moment that you could either afford or that would be conducive to a tea shop."

Yarrow rolled her eyes again and took a sip of her tea before folding her legs beneath her and leaning forward. "And I just *bet* you have another solution, Aunt Mavis?"

Mavis Anne let out a sniff. "As a matter of fact, I do."

I looked from one to the other and began to feel I was watching a television drama.

When Mavis Anne remained silent, Yarrow said, "Well?"

"Well, like I've always said . . . with some refurbishing and decorating, the schoolhouse would make an ideal tea shop."

"And finally . . . you'll get your way," Yarrow stated, as a look of annoyance crossed her face.

"Call it what you will. I'm simply being practical. You'll pay rent to me, so don't worry about that, and if it makes you happy, I'll charge you what you're paying here. But you know yourself it's a wonderful spot for a tea room. My goodness, you even have the French doors leading out to the garden and you could place some tables and chairs out there for the good weather."

What Mavis Anne was saying certainly sounded logical to me, and I waited to see how this would play out, but Yarrow remained silent, sipping her tea and looking off to the side, avoiding eye contact with her aunt. After a few minutes, she banged her mug on the table and jumped up.

"Okay," she said. "I'll consider it with a provision."

These women were proficient in dealing with provisions.

"And what might the provision be?" Mavis Anne questioned.

"I will open my tea shop in the schoolhouse if Chloe will open a yarn shop in the front part of the building. If Chloe decides to rent your house and stay here, she'll need a job. You've always wanted to own a yarn shop, and combining both my tea shop and a yarn shop makes perfect sense to me. It's a win-win situation."

I felt two pairs of eyes glued to my face.

# Chapter 12

When I awoke on Friday morning, turning fifty-two wasn't the first thought to cross my mind. My first thought was the fact that in a little over two weeks I'd be moving into Koi House. And it wasn't a dream.

I was surprised that following our discussion two days before, neither Mavis Anne nor Yarrow had pressured me for a commitment. It had been agreed that I would take the time needed to make a decision on the yarn shop. And no matter what my decision was, it would be completely separate from our rental agreement.

I rolled over in bed and smiled. I was quickly forming a deep affection for both of these women. I couldn't help but agree with Yarrow that opening a yarn shop in conjunction with her tea shop was a win-win idea. So many women enjoyed tea and just as many enjoyed knitting, as evidenced by those who gathered at Yarrow's shop. Combining both in one venue would provide a warm and welcoming place for women in the community to come together to share their lives and themselves.

Getting up, I gave Basil a hug, threw on shorts and a T-shirt, clipped on his leash and headed out for our walk on the beach. The sun had just popped above the horizon, turning the sky a soft pink. I loved these morning walks and wondered if I'd miss them when I left the condo. But I smiled as I realized it wasn't like living in Cedar Key, where one had to drive almost an hour to get anywhere. I could put Basil in the car, drive over the bridge, and we'd be at the ocean in five minutes.

When I returned to the condo an hour later, I noticed I had a message on my cell phone, and answered to hear Isabelle and Haley singing me a rendition of "Happy Birthday." I smiled as I filled a mug with coffee and dialed Isabelle's number.

"Thank you for the lovely birthday greetings," I told her.

"It was our pleasure. Do you have an exciting day planned?"

"Not really. Just going to the tea shop later this afternoon. The group usually gathers there around two. But I have some news for you," I told her and brought Isabelle up to date on my move to Koi House.

"That's really great, Chloe, and I'm happy for you. The house sounds amazing and it sounds like the perfect place to begin a new chapter for yourself."

"I think so, too, and hey, Mavis Anne was very insistent on letting me know I'm free to invite guests to visit. So I'd love to have you and Haley come stay with me."

"Really? Gosh, that would be great. School finishes at the end of the month and I think we both could use a change. Thanks, Chloe. I'll keep you posted, but maybe we'll take a trip down there this summer."

I received more birthday phone calls throughout the morning from Grace, Dora, and Berkley. Although Isabelle had called, I experienced a twinge of sadness once again on the loss of Gabe. To perk myself up I decided to treat myself to a birthday lunch at LuLu's. It was located in Ormond Beach, not far from the condo, and I'd been told that patrons could dine outside and the restaurant was pet friendly.

"What do you think, Basil? Wanna help me celebrate my birthday with lunch out?"

A bark and jumping in circles told me it was a good idea.

Since LuLu's was located a short distance from the condo, I thought Basil and I would walk over. It was a perfect May day with low humidity and a breeze off the ocean. We were seated at a table outside and Basil settled down by my feet as I looked the menu over.

"How's that tire of yours?" I heard a male voice say. I looked up into the extremely handsome face of Chadwick Price.

"Oh . . . hi. The . . . um . . . tire is just fine," I stammered.

Chadwick bent down to give Basil a scratch between his ears as the dog danced in circles with happiness. I knew he loved me, but he also missed male companionship.

Chadwick smiled at Basil. "Good to see you again, buddy. Glad to hear you got that tire taken care of. So you're settling in okay?"

Before I could answer, the waitress came back, spotted Chadwick, and a huge smile crossed her face. "Mr. Price, so nice to see you again. Are you joining this woman for lunch?"

"Hi, Whitney. Actually, she does owe me a drink," he said, pulling out the chair across from me and sitting down.

I looked from him to the waitress and back to him again and saw his raised eyebrows and smirk.

"Ah, right. Sure . . . that would be . . . fine. I'm having lunch. Would you like to join me?" I was certain this was the first time I'd ever been in such an awkward position over lunch.

"That would be great," he said as if it was all my idea. "A glass of wine first?"

I simply nodded as he took control and ordered for both of us.

When Whitney walked inside, Chadwick let out a laugh. "Sorry if I made you feel uncomfortable, but I couldn't resist the chance to cash in on that drink for services rendered. By the way . . . I almost didn't recognize you." A smile crossed his face. "You look a bit different from the day you had the flat."

I was glad I'd taken extra care with my hair and makeup that morning and chosen to wear a nice pair of cropped pants and knitted top. "Right," I said. "As opposed to looking like a drowned rat."

He laughed again. "So . . . are you settling in okay? Do you like it here?"

"I do like it here a lot. As a matter of fact, I've made a commitment to stay for a year."

"That's great, but I'm not surprised. It's a wonderful area and a great community. So you're able to have the condo you rented for a year?"

I shook my head. "No, I'm only there till the end of the month. I've been very fortunate to meet a wonderful woman, and she's going to rent me her house, but I have to sign a lease for one year, which is fine. You might know her. Mavis Anne Overby."

Chadwick threw his head back laughing. "Oh, yes. I think everybody knows Mavis. She's a real character. Ah, so you'll be living at Koi House?"

I nodded. "Yeah, and it was really odd how it all happened. I went to the tea shop, met both Yarrow and Mavis, we connected, and here I am . . . renting her house."

"That's wonderful. I have no doubt you'll love it there."

Whitney brought our wine and said, “Ready to order?”

With no hesitation, Chadwick said, “Yes, I’ll have the cobb salad.”

I guess I was also treating him to lunch. “I’ll have the same,” I told her.

He lifted his glass and said, “Well, let me officially welcome you to Ormond Beach. I think you’ll be very happy here.”

“Thank you,” I said and took a sip of the red wine. “Hmm, this is good.”

“Glad you like it. It’s one of my favorites here.” He took a sip and then reached down to pat Basil, who was relishing the newfound attention. “He’s really cute. What’s his name?”

“This is Basil,” I told him. “He belonged to my significant other, but Gabe passed away last year, so I inherited his dog.”

“Oh, I’m sorry for your loss, but how nice you and Basil have each other. Losing a loved one is never easy.”

I saw a sad expression cross his face, making me think he’d probably also experienced a loss.

“So if you’re going to be living here, are you also looking for a job?” he asked.

I nodded. “I am but I’m not sure yet exactly what I’ll be doing. I was a partner in a yarn shop on Cedar Key and I have a degree in textile and fiber, so I’ll probably do something in that area again.”

“That would be great. I’m sure the town could use a yarn shop. Have you thought of opening one here?”

I felt a smile cross my face. “I’ve given it a little thought, but nothing definite yet.”

“I own a real estate office in the area, so if you need any help finding space, just let me know. Do you come to LuLu’s often?”

“My first time. But since it’s my birthday, I thought I’d treat myself to lunch,” I said and then regretted the mention of my birthday.

“Oh, well happy birthday to you,” Chadwick said, lifting his wineglass. “I’m glad I bumped into you to help you celebrate.”

Actually, so was I. There are worse things than having lunch with a good looking and pleasant guy. Looking at him more closely across the table, I realized there was something familiar about him. I had sensed it the first time we met in the pouring rain but didn’t give it much thought. But now I could see he looked vaguely familiar, even though I was pretty sure we’d never met before two weeks ago.

“Thank you,” I said. “So are you from Florida originally?”

"No, I'm from the Atlanta area. But when I hit the big three-oh, I decided to relocate down here. My life seemed to be going nowhere. I did have a real estate business up there that was doing fairly well, but then my brother passed away and I thought maybe it was time for a whole new start. I found the house in Ormond-by-the-Sea, opened a business here, and twenty-five years later, I've never looked back. It was the right choice for me."

I was pretty sure that the loss of his brother accounted for his earlier expression of sadness.

"And hopefully, this area will prove to be the right choice for you as well," he said.

By the time we finished lunch, I was shocked to see it was going on three and we'd been sitting there talking for more than two hours.

"Oh, gosh," I said, glancing at my watch. "I guess I'd better get going. I have to take Basil back home and get over to the tea shop. I told Mavis Anne and Yarrow I'd stop by around three."

Chadwick lifted his hand in the air to signal the waitress. When Whitney approached, passing him the check, he said, "Well, thank you for a delightful lunch. I really enjoyed it and I hope you'll enjoy the rest of your day."

"But that check is mine," I told him. "I want to repay you for helping me."

"Absolutely not," he said. "Consider it my birthday lunch to you."

"Well, thank you. That's really nice but I still have to do something to repay you."

"I agree," he said and I saw a sexy grin cross his face. "You should give me your number so I can call you to make arrangements to take you to dinner some evening."

It had been a long time since a guy had flirted with me and it took a moment to realize he was doing exactly that. I laughed before saying, "You're a tough businessman."

# Chapter 13

I arrived at the tea shop about thirty minutes later to find a large gathering of women, birthday balloons, and a huge cake decorated with my name.

When I walked inside, everyone yelled, "Happy birthday, Chloe!"

I instantly felt a sense of acceptance and friendship as a huge smile crossed my face.

My gaze flew to Mavis and Yarrow and I shook my head. "You guys should *not* have done this, but thank you."

"Any excuse to eat cake," Louise hollered, causing me to laugh.

"Come on," Mavis said, patting the chair beside her. "Come sit down and let Yarrow wait on us."

Yarrow walked over and gave me a hug. "Happy birthday, Chloe. I don't think you've met Paige yet," she said and pointed to a young woman on the sofa who appeared to be in her early thirties. "Paige owns the dog grooming shop in town."

"Nice to meet you," she said and I noticed she was working on a gorgeous lace shawl.

"Same here. That shawl is beautiful."

"Thanks. It's the knit-along pattern for *Downton Abbey*. The pattern is on Ravelry and I'm using the Lorna's Laces yarn."

"The colors are spectacular."

"I know. One skein is Edith's Secret and I chose Old Rose for the other one."

"I think I might have to get that pattern and yarn," I told her.

"We're all *Downton Abbey* fans here," Yarrow said. "Do you watch the show?"

I laughed and nodded. "Definitely."

"I would have loved living in England during that era," Mavis said. "But of course I'd only live upstairs."

The women laughed and Maddie said, "Oh, I don't know. Some of those maids seem to be pretty happy."

"I'll start slicing the cake," Yarrow said, heading back to the counter. "It'll go great with tea."

I sat down and removed the socks I was working on from my bag.

"Oh, pretty color," Paige said.

"Thanks. Yeah, I liked the mulberry. This is the fairly new CoBaSi yarn by HiKoo. It's a blend of cotton, bamboo, and silk. Perfect for socks in Florida and it has a bit of elastic in it, which makes it really nice."

"Oh, I'd heard about that yarn," Maddie said, getting up to take a closer look. "And you'll carry this when you open our new yarn shop, right?"

My head snapped up to see the crowd of women staring at me. "What?" I said.

Mavis Anne waved her hand in the air. "Now, now, women. Give Chloe a break. She hasn't actually agreed to this plan."

I let out a chuckle and shook my head. These women were no different from the ones in Cedar Key. Gossip traveled at lightning speed and apparently the topic of the new tea shop and possible yarn shop had already been discussed.

"Yes," I blurted out. "I will definitely be carrying this yarn." Although until I'd just said the words, I hadn't been certain. But I was now. "I've made my decision. I'm very fortunate to have met Mavis Anne and Yarrow and be given this opportunity. So yes . . . I'm confirming the fact that I'd love to open a yarn shop here in Ormond Beach."

A round of applause filled the shop.

"Yay for you."

"Yay for us."

"Oh, I'm so happy—it's such a great location for the new business."

The excited comments from the women spilled forth until Mavis stamped the floor with her cane, demanding attention.

"Well, a very wise decision indeed," she stated and shot me a huge smile. "I'm very happy to hear this, Chloe. We'll get together over the next few days to work out the details."

"So how much longer will you have the tea shop open?" Maddie questioned.

"Now that Chloe has committed, I'll give my notice that I'm vacating. If possible, I'd like to stay here another month or so. And plan to close on July first."

Louise put the sweater she was working on in her lap and looked up. "And how long will we have to wait for the new tea and yarn shop to open?" She looked at Mavis, waiting for an answer.

"I'm not sure," Mavis said. "I have to call in a contractor to do some work on the schoolhouse and then of course stock for both yarn and tea will have to be ordered. We'll have to decorate and get everything in order. I would think we should be up and fully operational by late September."

A collective groan filled the room.

"Oh, no," Louise said. "We have to wait till then to gather for our knitting?"

"Not exactly," Mavis explained. "Chloe and I will discuss it, but I was thinking we might be able to meet at least once a week at Koi House. Of course, this will be entirely up to Chloe, since it will be her home."

"Oh, absolutely," I said. "That's a great idea and I'd love it. Let's do it until the new place is open."

"What a relief," Louise said, causing us to laugh.

Conversation continued as we enjoyed our cake and tea. The women offered some great ideas for the yarn shop and suggestions for various classes we could do. I found myself getting quite excited about the new path my life was about to take.

"Oh, Paige," I said. "Do you have a business card? Poor Basil is looking a bit shaggy. I'd love to book an appointment for him."

She reached into her bag and passed me a card. "Great. I'd love to meet him."

"And since you're going to be living and working here," Maddie said, "I'd love to be your tour guide and drive you around to learn the area."

"Oh, that sounds like fun," I told her. "I'm free anytime, so whenever is good for you."

"The shop is closed on Mondays. So how about if I pick you up at ten Monday morning?"

"Sounds like a plan. Thanks."

I returned to the condo a little after five, in time to feed Basil, and then we had our walk on the beach.

I looked out to the ocean and sky and let out a deep breath. So much had happened in the less than three weeks I'd been here. I felt so fortunate to have connected with Mavis Anne and Yarrow. There was no doubt I was building more friendships with the women at the tea shop. I had a new and wonderful place to live and once again I would be part owner of a yarn shop. Not to mention that it seemed I'd caught the interest of Chadwick Price.

At the moment, my life appeared to be on track and I was looking forward to the journey ahead of me.

# Chapter 14

I was outside the condo building just before ten Monday morning, waiting for Maddie to pick me up. I'd had a nice, but quiet, weekend. Grace, Lucas, and Solange had flown to Paris Saturday night as planned. We'd had a lengthy phone conversation the day before. By the time we hung up, I wasn't sure who was more excited about my upcoming plans—her or me. It had been decided that after they returned, she'd pack up my personal belongings and, with help from Berkley and Marin, they'd come for a day to see my new place and visit.

Maddie pulled up in front of the building. When I got in the car, she passed me a Styrofoam cup.

"Good morning," she said. "I thought we'd begin our tour with a cup of coffee."

"Thanks. Sounds great."

I noticed we were heading south on A1A toward Daytona Beach.

"The first place I have to introduce you to is the chocolate shop," she said.

"Oh, Angell and Phelps?"

"So you know about it?"

"Yeah. My friend Berkley owns a chocolate shop in Cedar Key. She makes her own signature chocolate clams but she orders a lot of her chocolate from Angell and Phelps."

"Great. So we'll pay a visit there and take care of our chocolate fix."

I took a sip of coffee and nodded. "Perfect plan. You've been in the area for a few years? Where're you from originally?"

"Yeah, I came here about five years ago. No particular reason. Just did some research and it seemed like a nice town right on the Atlantic coast. I'm originally from Philly."

"Oh, Gabe was from Philly too. Do you still have family up there?"

Maddie shook her head. "No. My daughter and her family ended up moving to Tampa a few months after I moved here. Her husband got a transfer with the bank he works for. So I'm fortunate that I get to see them and my grandchildren frequently. Tori is nine and Logan's seven. How about you? I know your sister lives in Cedar Key, but any children?"

"Yes, two sons. Mathis lives and works in Atlanta and he's still single. Eli is married and at the moment he and Treva live in Manhattan, but they're relocating to Jacksonville around late September. He's been offered a nice position with an accounting firm there. Needless to say, I'm thrilled they'll only be a couple hours' drive away."

"I can see why you're excited. That's really great. Any grandchildren?"

"Not yet, but I think they're starting to work on that, so my fingers are crossed."

Maddie laughed. "Yeah, there's something extra special about grandchildren. I often think it's because we're getting a second chance to do the things we didn't do with our kids."

I smiled and nodded. "You could be right."

"And you're also divorced?"

"Yeah, gosh, it's been a few years now. Parker left me for a trophy wife, got her pregnant and married her. They're still in the Savannah area, but I headed to Cedar Key to be with my aunt and my sister where I could lick my wounds."

"Ah and yet one more trophy wife story. Same here. Jim was running around with one of the nurses at the hospital and decided after almost twenty-five years of marriage, a flirty blonde fifteen years his junior was much more appealing than the wife he'd known since college. It was tough at first, especially since I worked at the same hospital, but looking back . . . he really did me a huge favor. I've been able to discover who I was truly meant to be."

"Oh, are you also an RN?"

She nodded. "I am. Jim's a doctor. I got pregnant with Freya in my sophomore year of college, so I dropped out and we got married. But once she went to preschool, I returned to college to complete my nursing degree."

"And you didn't want to work in nursing down here?"

"Not really. Don't get me wrong, I loved my nursing career, but I was pushing fifty and I had always wanted to have a florist shop. Flowers and plants were always my passion. So I thought, well, now's the time. Just *do* it, Maddie. Sometimes life isn't about finding yourself, it's about creating yourself. So I made the choice to open Blooms of Color and become my creative self."

"Wow, great story," I said. I realized that I was doing exactly the same thing by making the commitment to co-own the yarn shop with Mavis Anne.

"Angell and Phelps is just a little farther up on the right. There used to be a yarn shop a little farther down but it closed a few years ago, so it'll be really great when you open yours. Have you thought of a name yet?"

I glanced to my right and saw various shops lining the sidewalk as Maddie found a parking spot and we pulled up in front of the chocolate shop.

"Not yet," I said, "But I'm having dinner with Mavis Anne and Yarrow tomorrow evening. A business meeting of sorts; we have a million things to discuss. A name for the shop is one of them."

After drooling over all the chocolate behind the glass display cases, I finally settled on my favorite, honeybees, and purchased a pound. I also got a pound of truffles to bring to Mavis Anne the next evening.

Getting back in the car, Maddie wasted no time fishing for a piece of chocolate from her box and plopping it into her mouth. A groan of ecstasy followed. "Oh, my God. I admit it. I'm a chocoholic. If I wasn't careful, I could easily consume chocolate morning, noon, and night."

I gave a laugh as I bit into my honeybee. "I do love chocolate . . . but maybe not quite as much as you."

After she finished savoring her chocolate, she said, "Okay. Next stop will be the Casements."

As we headed north on A1A, we passed lots of hotels and condos on the beach side and loads of restaurants across the street.

"That's a great pub," she said when we passed The Black Sheep. "And they have great steaks," she added when we drove by Charliehorse.

We drove past my condo and she took a left back onto Granada. Farther up on the left was the Casements, formerly the winter home of John D. Rockefeller.

"We can probably catch a tour," she said as she pulled into the parking lot.

Bordering the house, along the Halifax River, were beautiful gardens. "How pretty," I said.

"Yeah, they have a fair number of weddings there. The perfect romantic venue. But they also hold concerts and cultural events."

We were able to catch one of the tours. By the time we left, I felt I'd gained quite a bit of knowledge about both the house with its beautiful hand-cut casement windows and the man himself. I had been surprised that although Rockefeller was the founder of Standard Oil, and America's richest man, the house itself was more simple than ostentatious. An interesting tidbit was that the house had been a boarding school for girls during World War II and apparently they liked to sunbathe on the roof, drawing the attention of air force pilots flying over. Rockefeller died at his home in 1937 but reached the age of ninety-seven, attaining both wealth and longevity.

"Thank you so much for taking me here," I said as we walked to the parking lot. "I really enjoyed it."

"Great. And one of these days we'll have to drive to Deland and visit the Stetson Mansion, owned by John B. Stetson, maker of the famous hats. You'll love that place."

Maddie pointed out the old Ormond Hotel across the street from the Casements. "It's condos now," she said. "But it still looks much like it did when the rich came to spend winters there. I'm going to take you behind the hotel to Orchard Lane. It's tucked away and even many people who live in Ormond Beach don't know it's there."

We drove down a narrow road flanked on both sides with residential homes. Some were modern but most were adorable, quaint cottages. One was an unusual A-frame home.

Maddie stopped in front of one of the cottages and pointed. "That's the Nathan Cobb Cottage. It's a three-room house built of the timber that was salvaged from the Nathan Cobb shipwreck of 1896. The exterior's constructed from the railroad ties carried as cargo. The historical society does a holiday tour of homes every December. We'll have to go this year and you'll be able to visit a lot of the homes."

"Oh, that sounds like fun."

"And this one," she said, slowing the car and pointing to my left, "is where Yarrow lives."

I leaned over to see a medium-size cottage set back from the road. Grass frontage led up to the side door of the wooden structure with peaked roof and narrow windows.

"It's amazing, but that house is so Yarrow," I said and laughed. "It looks like the perfect place for her."

"There's no printed confirmation, but rumor has it that the house had originally been a chapel for the Ormond Hotel staff. And you probably know that Yarrow's mother lived here before she died."

"Yeah, she told me that."

"And this one," she said, as she slowly turned the corner, bringing us right behind the old Ormond Hotel, "is called Talahloko. It's also a private home and one of the few remaining Florida structures built of palmetto logs."

"Very interesting," I said. "And I'd really love to do that holiday tour of homes to get inside."

"It's a deal," Maddie said. "Okay. That was my tourist tour. Now for the resident tour."

She drove back out to Granada and I saw we were headed over the bridge to the downtown area.

"If you're going to be living here, you have to know the important things. Like where the best hairdresser is."

I laughed and nodded. "Right. I called Paige on Saturday and got Basil an appointment to be groomed next week, so I'll need to find somebody to groom me too."

When we came over the bridge, I saw North Beach Street and the location of my new home on the right. Just a little way down, Maddie pointed.

"That's the shop I go to. Helen has hands of gold. If you go, be sure to tell her that I sent you."

I saw a wooden plaque to the side of the door that said Glam and smiled as I recalled the Curl Up and Dye on Cedar Key, where Polly tended to my hair needs.

"Oh, it's just a few doors down from your shop," I said.

"Yup and just a couple doors down from Helen is Paige's shop. Nice and convenient. So now you can see why the women are so excited that your yarn shop will also be very close."

It was certainly a much larger downtown area than Cedar Key had. But it wasn't so large that you felt you were in a big city. With the center island of the boulevard filled with palm trees and flowers, the town had a homey sense of community. Which I liked a lot. For the first time since I'd announced my decision on Friday, I began to feel excited about the prospect of being not just a resident but also a business owner in this community.

Maddie then pointed out City Hall, the police department, and the library in the downtown area.

"I don't know about you, but I'm starved. Do you like seafood?"

"Love it," I said and glanced at my watch. "Oh, my gosh. It's after one already."

Maddie headed back over the bridge.

"I know. I'm going to take you to Betty's on A1A. Been there a million years and the best around for seafood, especially if you love New England clams."

The clams were every bit as good as Maddie promised. Except for fighting over the check—I won—by the time I returned to the condo in late afternoon, I knew I'd made a very good new friend.

# Chapter 15

I had just finished filling the washing machine the following morning when my cell phone rang. The caller ID told me it was Henry Wagner. I hadn't heard from him since my first week at the condo.

"I hope I'm not bothering you," he said, when I answered.

"Not at all. How are you, Henry?"

"I'm great. I was just calling to make sure everything was still going well for you."

With all the activity of the previous week, I'd neglected to call Henry and let him know that I'd actually be staying on in Ormond Beach.

"Yes, everything is just fine. So much so that I've made the decision to permanently relocate here."

I heard a chuckle come across the line. "That's wonderful but I'm not surprised. Sounds like the town and people worked their magic on you."

I laughed. "Something like that, yes. And . . . I'll also be opening a new yarn shop in town."

"Well, my goodness, you've been quite the busy woman. And again, that's wonderful. Have you found a place to stay?"

"I have," I told him, and went on to explain about Mavis Anne and my connection with her.

"I've met Mavis a few times because she's good friends with my neighbor, Louise. She's quite a character and a delightful person. Well, Chloe, I'm so happy for you."

"Thank you. I'm quite excited about all of it. I'll be staying at the condo until the thirty-first, if that's okay with you."

"Of course it is. You rented it for the month of May. I'm planning to be down there mid-June and I've arranged for the cleaning crew to come in on the first to get things in order for me. Listen . . . ah . . . since you'll be staying permanently, maybe we could get together and actually meet in person."

I laughed as I realized that, although I felt as if I knew Henry, we'd never actually met. "Oh. That's a great idea. I'd love it."

"Terrific. And Basil? How's he doing? I take it he's settling in well?"

"Very well. He also seems to love it here. How's Delilah doing?"

"Oh, she's great," he said and I could almost see a smile cross a face I'd never seen. "I think she's also ready to head south. It's been a miserable spring up here, I'm afraid, so we're both looking forward to the warm temps and the ocean. Well, listen, Chloe, I won't keep you. When I get down there and settled, I'll give you a call. Perhaps we could do dinner some evening?"

"That would be nice," I said. "Have a safe trip down here."

I disconnected the call and stood in Henry Wagner's kitchen with a smile covering my face. *Gee, Chloe*, I thought, *you're not doing so bad for a woman who just turned fifty-two. You've been offered two dinner invitations from men in the past week.*

I spent most of the morning catching up on laundry and doing a bit of housecleaning in the condo. After a walk on the beach with Basil and lunch, I decided to sit on the balcony to enjoy the gorgeous weather with my knitting.

Pulling the socks out of my bag to work on, I recalled Maddie asking about a name for the yarn shop. I let my mind wander, trying out different names, and came up with a few that I'd discuss with Mavis Anne over dinner. I wasn't sure how we were going to work tea and yarn into the names of the combination shop at Koi House. I realized then that I hadn't had any dreams at all since my first night here at the condo. I was never a big dreamer and certainly had never had any odd dreams like the ones about Koi House and the fishpond. It was at that moment the perfect choice for the yarn shop name came to me.

I juggled the tote bag containing Mavis's chocolates in one hand with Basil's leash, as I pushed the doorbell.

Like the first time, David swept open the door, a huge smile on his face, but this time I found myself being scooped into his arms.

"Welcome, welcome. Welcome to *your* new home. I'm *so* delighted that it's you who will be living here."

I laughed as Basil danced in circles for attention.

"Oh, yes, and you too, *mon petit cheri*," David said, bending down to pick up Basil. "I'm so happy to make your acquaintance. I hope you'll like your new home. The ladies are on the patio," he said, before spinning around toward the back of the house.

When we stepped out to the patio, David put Basil down and the dog immediately flew toward Mavis Anne, jumping up in her lap and showering her with kisses.

"Oh, Basil, no," I yelled, running to get him down.

But Mavis Anne had thrown back her head and was laughing. "You flirty boy, you. Well, hello, Master Basil. Very pleased to meet you."

"God, I'm so sorry," I said. "He never does that. Basil, down."

"No, no. He's fine. I think I'm flattered. I also think we're going to get along wonderfully."

I looked at Yarrow, who shrugged and laughed.

Basil curled up in Mavis's lap, looking quite content, but avoiding eye contact with me.

"Welcome to your new home," Clive said, passing me a glass of wine.

"Yes, here's to much happiness for both of you." Mavis Anne lifted her wineglass in a toast.

"Thank you," I said and took a sip, keeping an eye on Basil.

"I had Marta prepare a nice quiche and some pumpkin soup for us. But first we'll have our wine and then we'll go into the schoolhouse before we eat so I can show you what I discussed with the contractor this morning."

I sat down and shook my head. "You've already had the contractor out here?"

Yarrow laughed. "She would have had him here first thing Saturday morning, but he couldn't make it till today."

"You certainly don't waste any time," I said.

"Well, as it is we have to wait about four months before we can open." She scratched Basil between his ears. "And this little guy is so cute. I think we're going to be great friends."

From the way Basil was staring at her with adoring eyes, I thought she was right.

After we finished the wine, the three of us entered the schoolhouse.

"Okay," Mavis said, walking to the center of the room and pointing to the blank wall. "I told the contractor that we'll need him to build us wooden cubbyholes covering the entire wall to hold yarn. What do you think?"

I nodded. "Perfect."

"I'm also thinking that perhaps some tables set up here and there with displays of yarn. And maybe one or two armoires holding the pricey yarn like cashmere and qiviut. What kind of furniture do you think we should have?"

I thought of the carriage house at Yarning Together in Cedar Key and nodded. "Yes, great ideas for displaying the various yarns. Well, maybe two sofas and a few comfy chairs, but we also should have a fairly large table for classes."

"I agree," Mavis Anne said. "We'll go shopping together and make our decisions. Now, back here," she said, walking toward the kitchen area, "I'll let Yarrow tell you what she has in mind."

We walked through one of the arched doorways and Yarrow pointed to her left. "Since the prep area is over here, I thought the contractor could build me a small counter to separate it from the seating area. And on this side, I should be able to fit in about six small round tables with chairs. The rest of the seating will be outside. Of course, the knitters will take their tea into the knitting area."

"Sounds good," I said. I could visualize the welcoming scene.

"Also," she went on, "although tea is my main specialty, I'm thinking of getting a coffee machine. When we open, I'm going to be advertising for the general public, not just for knitters. And I'm going to use those French doors to the garden as my entrance. This way people coming just for tea or coffee won't be traipsing through the yarn area."

"Great idea," I said. "I like it."

"The contractor is also going to give the whole place a new coat of paint. I thought we'd stay with the white since we want brightness and light. But I was thinking maybe a border print at the top to make it feel cozier. What do you think?" Mavis asked.

"Oh, definitely. Yes, we want the shop to be a knitter's home away from home."

"Okay, then," Mavis said, clapping her hands together. "I think we have a good start here. Now let's go eat and see if we can come up with a name."

"I'm going to be so spoiled living here," I said and took the last bite of my quiche. "I may just be employing Marta to cook for me on a full-time basis. The quiche and soup were delicious."

"She's willing to work out any arrangement with you," Mavis Anne said. "I'm glad you enjoyed it."

"It's too bad David and Clive couldn't join us."

"Well, they had dinner plans with friends of theirs, but you'll see quite a lot of them once you move in. Now, let's brainstorm a name for the shop. Any ideas?"

Yarrow laughed. "Since I named my tea shop simply Yarrow's, I think you can see I'm not very creative. Do you have any ideas, Chloe?"

"Well, I do have one for the yarn shop, but how do we want to do it? A separate name for each shop or a combined name?"

"It really doesn't matter to me." Yarrow shrugged. "What do you have in mind for the yarn shop?"

"Dreamweaver," I said.

"Oh, how perfect!" Mavis Anne exclaimed. "I love it. A dreamweaver is something or somebody who creates dreams. And a yarn shop certainly encourages this. I love it, Chloe."

"Nirvana," Yarrow blurted out.

Mavis Anne and I both stared at her, not understanding.

"*Nirvana*," she repeated with emphasis. "That's the name I want for the tea and coffee shop. In Buddhism it means the state of perfect happiness or idyllic place. I want my shop to be *that* place."

I thought it was the perfect name for Yarrow's shop. "I think it's *you*," I said. "Plus, I think the names blend well together—Dreamweaver Yarn Shop and Nirvana Tea and Coffee."

Mavis Anne nodded. "I totally agree. I love both names." She raised her hand for a high five. "Ladies," she said. "Here's to a long and profitable business together."

# Chapter 16

I walked into the tea shop the following Friday to a huge round of applause and began laughing. "What's this all about?" I asked.

"We're thrilled with the name of the yarn shop."

"It's just perfect."

"I can't wait to see all the yummy yarn you'll be carrying."

The comments tumbled out as I made my way to an empty seat on the sofa.

I let out a deep breath. "It *is* rather exciting," I said. "And I'm glad you approve of the name."

"Oh, we do," Louise said. "And we also love Nirvana for the tea shop."

"I agree. It was like kismet the way Yarrow just instantly thought of it."

"We still have to get together and decide which yarns we'll be selling," Mavis Anne said. "Maybe we could discuss it today when the knitting group is over."

"Sounds good," I told her.

"And when this place closes in a month, we'll be meeting at Koi House?" Maddie asked.

"Absolutely," I said. "Friday seems to be a good day for everyone, so we can still meet on Friday afternoons."

"That would be great," Maddie said. "I close the florist shop at one on Fridays. Hey, a woman has her priorities."

Conversation went back and forth while we knitted and enjoyed our tea.

"Has anybody heard how June is doing?" Louise asked.

"I spoke to her the other day on the phone," Maddie said. "It's not easy raising a five-year-old grandson, but she's struggling along."

"Well, she didn't have much choice, did she?" Mavis adjusted the reading glasses on her nose to peer over them. "Poor thing. No father in the picture for Charlie, and June's daughter is in rehab."

"Oh, that does sound like a difficult situation. Is she one of the knitters here?" I asked.

"She used to be," Yarrow said. "But when Charlie came to live with her a few months ago, her life was turned upside down."

"Yeah, but she now has Charlie all settled in a good day program here in town, so she said it won't be much longer till she returns to join us." Maddie looked up from the sweater she was working on and smiled. "Plus, at least she has Tony, her husband, to share everything, and that makes it a little easier."

"Yeah, but still, it certainly can't be easy dealing with a child full-time in your fifties," Louise said. "Although never having had children of my own, I'm only guessing."

"No, I think you're right," I told her. "I'm sure glad I had my boys when I was young. I think that's part of the joy of grandchildren—we can send them home when we're tired. I can't even imagine taking care of children full-time now."

The topic of conversation made me wonder how Parker was really coping. He'd left me five years before to marry his girlfriend, who was three months pregnant; now at age fifty-five, Parker was raising his own daughter, Aubrey. From the news relayed to me by Eli, Kelly wasn't about to give up her job at the real estate company Parker owned, so their daughter had been in day care since she was an infant. But his evenings and weekends were consumed with child care. Although I'd never met Aubrey, Eli and Treva visited Parker once a year in Savannah and Eli was forming a relationship with his half-sister. I never admitted it, but when Eli sent me digital photos of their visits, which included shots of Aubrey, I always felt a twinge of jealousy that Parker got the daughter I'd always wanted.

By four o'clock the women had left the tea shop and Mavis Anne and I were ready to discuss business.

"Any more tea?" Yarrow asked.

"None for me," I said.

"What I'd really enjoy is a glass of wine." Mavis Anne returned her knitting to the leather bag beside her. "In the new shop I think we should keep a stock of wine on hand. You know, for special occasions."

Yarrow laughed. "Oh, you mean like the close of the work day?"

"Precisely," Mavis said. "Okay, we need to decide what types of yarn we'll be carrying and which distributors we'll be using. Any suggestions, Chloe?"

"Well, we have to carry the usual—sock yarn, worsted, fingering yarn. There's so many yarn companies now, but some of my favorites are Universal, Plymouth, Cascade, and Lorna's Laces."

Mavis made notes in the notebook on her lap. "That's a good start. I'll give them a call tomorrow. They'll need to send a rep out so we can pore through their catalogs and get our orders in. And of course we need to order needles and all the accessories." She looked over to Yarrow. "Will you be using the same distributor for your tea?"

"Yes, but I need to find somebody to order the coffee from, so I'll get going on that."

"Great," Mavis said. "And Chloe, you and I should begin working on some items for display in the shop. It always attracts sales when a knitter can see the finished project."

"Good idea," I said. "I have a lot of patterns from various companies, so I'll look through them and my yarn stash. Also, I was thinking of designing maybe a shawl pattern, and we could sell the yarn at the shop and offer a knit-along for the women."

"Oh, I like that idea." Excitement sparkled in Mavis's eyes. "Yes, feel free to begin working on a design. I think the women will enjoy doing something like that together at the shop."

The three of us looked up as the door opened and Chadwick Price walked in. Damn, but that man was handsome.

I felt his eyes connect with mine and a huge smile crossed his face. "I thought I might find you ladies here."

"Chadwick, how nice to see you," Mavis gushed. "Sit down and join us. Yarrow will get you some tea."

He laughed and raised a palm in the air. "I'm afraid I can't stay, but I wanted to drop off the invitations for my Fourth of July fundraiser," he said, passing an embossed invitation to each of us. "I hope you'll be able to join us too, Chloe."

"Oh," I said, surprised that I was included. "Oh . . . well . . . thank you."

"Of course she'll be there," Mavis assured him. "Especially since Chloe is about to join the ranks of business owners in the community."

His eyebrows arched and a smile crossed his face. "Really?"

"Yes," Mavis explained. "Chloe and I are starting a yarn shop together. We're hoping to open late September."

"That's wonderful news. Where's the location?" he asked, directing his gaze toward me.

Before I had a chance to answer, Mavis said, "The old schoolhouse behind Koi House. It's a great central location for downtown and it will be perfect. Yarrow will be in the back half and she'll have a tea and coffee shop."

"Ah, so you finally convinced her, huh?" he said, letting out a chuckle. "You've always wanted to utilize that spot, and it sounds like this will work out perfectly. Congratulations to all of you. With you living in Koi House, Chloe, it really will be ideal."

I saw both Mavis Anne and Yarrow turn to me, waiting for an explanation as to how Chadwick knew this piece of news.

I nodded. "Absolutely ideal," I said.

"Okay, well, it was great to see you and I hope all three of you will make it for the fund-raiser. I have more invitations to drop off in town, so I have to run. And Chloe, I haven't forgotten about that dinner invitation."

The moment he walked out the door, Mavis Anne exclaimed, "What *exactly* is going on that we've not been privy to?"

I shook my head, laughing. "God, you guys remind me of my sister and Aunt Maude." I explained about lunch at LuLu's and the promise that he'd call to take me to dinner.

"Well, my, my," Mavis Anne said. "Sounds to me like you have a very interested beau, and a woman could certainly do worse than Chadwick Price. He's always reminded me a bit of my Jackson. Lots of charm and good looks but a sincere type of man."

"I agree," Yarrow said, a grin covering her face. "Chadwick is quite a catch. You'll be the envy of every woman in Volusia County."

I raised my hand in the air and shook my head again. "Hey, hold on. We had one lunch that he invited himself to and a promise of a dinner. That's it. Besides, I'm not sure I'm ready to get involved with somebody right now. I'll be busy enough with the opening of the shop and my move."

"Right," they said at the same time. I noticed the smirk covering their faces as they nodded.

# Chapter 17

I woke on the last day of May and smiled up at the ceiling. Once again, my life was about to change. I'd be moving into Koi House later in the day and beginning a new chapter. Probably the first of many. Meeting Mavis Anne and Yarrow had started the ball rolling and I felt very grateful.

I still thought of Gabe every single day but after a year, the pain of loss was beginning to heal. I felt quite fortunate that I'd be living in Koi House, and in about three months I'd be co-owner of a yarn shop once again. Life was very good.

Following our walk on the beach, Basil and I returned to the condo. I didn't have much to pack and get together, but I wanted to leave the condo in the same condition I'd found it. Even though Henry assured me a cleaning girl was coming and not to bother, I did a general clean-up.

I didn't want to leave Basil alone in a new house right away, so after lunch I drove to Publix to stock up on food and then drove back to get Basil and our belongings.

I had just finished loading the car in the parking garage when Louise pulled up.

"Is today the day?" she asked, crossing the parking lot toward me.

"Yes, Basil and I are headed to Koi House now."

She leaned over and gave me a hug. "I'm so glad you're moving into that house. As silly as it sounds, over the years Mavis Anne has convinced me that house truly has a soul. She's been moaning about it being empty since she moved in with David and Clive, so I know she's thrilled. She feels you'll stir some love back into that house."

I laughed and shook my head. "I'm not so sure about that, but I'm very happy to be renting it. You'll be there for the knitting group a week from Friday, right?" It had been decided that even though the tea shop was still open for a few more weeks, we'd begin meeting at Koi House.

"Wouldn't miss it for anything," she said and headed to the elevator. "See you then."

I pulled into the driveway of Koi House, shut off the ignition, leaned over the steering wheel, and stared at the house. No doubt about it. It was a gorgeous house. I loved how my bedroom turret jutted out and added character to the structure.

I let out a deep sigh. It was then that I noticed swarms of butterflies floating past the car, over the house, and toward the back garden. I couldn't explain why, but I knew that I was exactly where I was supposed to be.

"Come on, Basil," I said, getting out and reaching for his leash. "Time to get settled in our new home."

I unlatched the gate and walked around to the back door. Fumbling with the keys, I found the correct one and we walked into the kitchen. This room truly was a chef's dream.

"Here ya go," I said, bending down to unclip Basil's leash. "I'll let you go explore."

My eye caught the beautiful vase of fresh flowers on the counter. A note beside it was from Mavis Anne, welcoming me to my new home. Beside the vase was a wooden holder with a stick of incense.

*Here's some sage and cedar to welcome you. Allow your personal energy to envelop your new home*, Yarrow had written on a notecard covered with butterflies.

And next to Yarrow's note was one from Marta telling me she'd prepared a chicken pie for me, which was in the fridge and only needed to be reheated. Her welcome to me.

I let out a deep sigh and smiled. I had felt uncertain when I'd first come to Ormond Beach a month before, but I had no doubt now that I'd done the right thing.

"Where are you, Basil?" I called as I walked through the house to the front room. No Basil. "Where did you go?"

I heard whining coming from upstairs and took the staircase up to the hallway. "Basil?" I called again.

This time he barked—from my bedroom. I walked in to find him curled up on the bed, tail wagging and quietly whining.

"Ah, you found our bedroom, huh?" A smile crossed my face but again, I felt a distinct drop in the temperature in this room. I suppose I might welcome this fact when the temps and humidity climbed, but right now I felt a sense of unease. Damn. I wondered why Mavis Anne had pretty much insisted that I take this bedroom when two others were empty.

"What's up, buddy?" I said, walking over to scratch Basil between his ears.

I walked to the French doors, unlocked them and stepped out onto the covered porch. Turning around, I called, "Come on, Basil. Come see our balcony." But he remained firmly planted on the bed and let out another whine. I inhaled the warm air. This was the perfect time in Florida, with no heat and humidity yet. The slight breeze brought just a hint of salt air off the Atlantic.

"Enough stalling," I said, walking back inside. "I have to start unloading the car. Are you coming, Basil?"

But Basil looked up at me, wagged his tail, and put his chin back on his paws.

"Okay, lazy boy. Stay here. I'll be right back."

I had just begun to unload the trunk of food bags when I heard David call to me. I turned to see him walking up the driveway.

"Welcome," he said, passing me a bottle of wine. "I wanted to get over sooner to leave it in the kitchen for you, but I got caught up working on a flower arrangement for a client and lost track of time." He leaned over to kiss both my cheeks.

"Thank you so much, David," I said, reaching for the wine. "This is so nice of you."

"It looks like I arrived just in time. I'll help you take your stuff inside."

Between the two of us, we managed to make a few trips and empty the car of the food, my luggage, and Basil's bed.

"Where is that little scamp?" he asked, placing the bed on the living room floor.

At that moment Basil came racing down the stairs and over to David, who picked him up for a cuddle.

"There you are, you handsome boy."

"It's really strange. He seems quite enchanted with my bedroom. He wouldn't budge off the bed in there."

"Really?" David said, and I saw an odd expression cross his face.

"Do you know why Mavis wanted me to take that particular room rather than the others?"

He shrugged but I noticed he avoided eye contact with me. "I have no idea," he said, putting Basil back down. "Now, here, let me help you carry these food bags into the kitchen."

When we finished and I had the food put away, I offered him a glass of wine.

"Help me celebrate my new home," I said.

He glanced at his watch and nodded. "Yes, okay. I have a little time before I have to prepare dinner. Clive will be later than normal this evening. He went to meet with a client in New Smyrna Beach."

I uncorked the wine and poured two glasses, passing one to David. "Let's sit outside," I said. "Come on, Basil, come enjoy your new yard."

David touched the rim of my wineglass. "I hope you'll both be very happy here, Chloe. I'm so excited for Mavis. I don't think I've seen her quite this happy in a long time."

I took a sip of the pinot noir as I settled on the patio sofa and nodded. "Yes, I think opening the yarn shop has fulfilled one of her dreams."

"Oh, that too," he said and seemed to hesitate. "Although it might seem foolish, I think she's even happier that this house will be lived in again."

I watched Basil as he ran around the fenced yard, checking out the fishpond area and running back to sniff the outside of the schoolhouse. He seemed delighted to have a yard where he could run loose on his own rather than being leashed.

I recalled what Louise had said that morning. "But she lived here until a few months ago, so it *was* lived in."

David took a sip of wine and nodded. "True. But at one time there was Mavis, Yarrow, and me. And before that my father was alive and of course Emmalyn. I think the house was most alive when Emmalyn was here with us."

"I imagine you both still miss her a lot. I'm sure Mavis and her sister were quite close."

David surprised me by laughing and shaking his head. "Hmm, I'm not so sure about that. I think they had a love/hate relationship. Emmalyn could be pretty difficult. Her beauty and charm were both a blessing and a curse. I think deep down she meant well, but she would do or say things spontaneously that could test the patience of a saint." He took another sip of wine and seemed to be remembering a sister who had left an indelible mark on her siblings. After a pause, he said, "I can still see her so clearly. I was thirty when she died, living in London with Clive. But I still see her in her early twenties, with that long wavy auburn hair and deep green eyes. She could meet somebody once, especially a man, and he would be instantly dazzled by her. Emmalyn could be petulant one minute and truly enchanting the next. She was quite the enigma, and adding to her sense of allure was the scent she always left behind—Chanel Number Five. It wasn't overpowering, but it was almost like a subtle presence once she had been in your company."

"She sounds quite remarkable," I said. "What a shame she died so young. It was a car accident, wasn't it?"

David nodded and let out a deep sigh. "Yes. She was a passenger, and with a married man. Needless to say, it created quite a scandal. They were both killed instantly when the car went over a bridge into the Halifax River."

"How tragic," I said. "And poor Yarrow left with no parents. She was very fortunate to have you and Mavis."

"Oh, yes, Yarrow has been such a joy to us. Well," he said, taking the final gulp of his wine and standing up, "I've kept you long enough. I'm sure you want to get settled in. And if you need anything at all, just give us a call. Mavis has been off with a friend this afternoon and should be home shortly so I'll mosey along and get dinner started."

"Thank you so much for everything, David."

"Oh, and by the way, I'm not sure you noticed, but there's a gate in the fence between our yards. Makes it much easier than walking to the driveway. I hope you don't mind if I use that."

I laughed and shook my head. "Not at all. Come visit me anytime."

# Chapter 18

I opened my eyes the following morning and felt a mound near my feet. Looking to the end of the bed, I saw Basil curled up, sleeping away. So much for using his own bed.

During the course of the evening, he'd scampered up the stairs again, and each time I found him on my bed. Apparently, he'd mapped out this spot as his own. At least he was willing to share it with me.

I had spent a relaxing and quiet evening in my new home. I had the delicious chicken pie for supper along with a healthy salad I'd put together. Then I settled myself on the sofa in the living room with a glass of wine and my knitting. Mavis had called to check on me and then I had a surprise call from Berkley. She brought me up to date on the news from Cedar Key. By ten I was ready to call it a day and fell into a dreamless sleep.

I hadn't bothered to unpack the night before and had just grabbed pajamas from my luggage along with my toiletries, so after breakfast that would be my first chore: getting unpacked. I glanced at the bedside clock and saw it was just after six.

"Come on, lazy boy," I said, as I got up. "Time to get you out in the yard."

I let Basil outside and then prepared a pot of coffee. While I waited for it to drip into the carafe, I gazed out the French doors and thought about the conversation with David the day before. I was intrigued with the story about Emmalyn. I wondered if perhaps the man in the accident might be Yarrow's father, but by the time the accident had happened she was already ten years old. Possible but not likely. David had said there was a scandal and I was sure that hadn't been easy for the family. Despite Emmalyn's behavior, I got the feeling she was still very much loved by both Mavis and David. I thought back to a time, years ago, when I had betrayed my sister, Grace. She had been very angry with me, to the point we hadn't spoken for years, but in the end both she and Aunt Maude had shown me unconditional love when I'd showed up on Cedar Key. Somehow, Grace had found a way to forgive me.

I poured myself a mug of coffee and joined Basil in the yard. It was then I realized it was June first—the start of a whole new month. The sun was shining and it looked like it was going to be a gorgeous day. Beyond unpacking, I had no plans. I thought maybe I'd spend some time working on a design for the knit-along shawl.

Following two mugs of coffee and a bowl of cereal, I headed upstairs to the shower with Basil close at my heels. I lifted one piece of luggage onto the bed to unpack some items, then walked to the bureau to place my underwear. As soon as I opened the top bureau drawer an aroma wafted up to me—sensual and haunting. I shivered as the fragrance seemed to fill the room. I wasn't positive but I could have sworn it was Chanel No. 5. I sniffed the air and noticed that Basil was sitting beside my foot whining as he looked up at me.

"This is silly," I said out loud as I sniffed again. But yes, that was definitely the perfume David said Emmalyn had always worn. Well, of course. This was Emmalyn's bureau. Her clothes had been kept here and the scent had just lingered even all these years later. That *did* make sense, didn't it?

I quickly put my underwear in the drawer, shoved it shut, and headed to the shower.

Later that morning I was sitting at the patio table when I looked up to see Marta coming through the gate from the driveway.

"Good morning," she said. "I hope I'm not bothering you."

"Not at all. Would you like some coffee?"

"No, no, but thank you. I just wanted to make sure you settled in okay and check to see if you needed anything."

"Marta, you've done way too much already, leaving me that delicious chicken pie. I really enjoyed that last night for supper, so thank you."

She smiled and sat down. "I'm glad you enjoyed it. Everything is going well? You slept okay?"

"Yes, very well. I guess I was tired but got a good night's sleep."

"Oh, good. I also wanted to let you know that I arrive on Mondays, Wednesdays, and Fridays around ten to clean. Will that be okay with you? I'm at David and Clive's house the other two days."

"Yes, that'll be fine. And Mavis mentioned that I could hire you to prepare meals for me if I needed that. Would that work for you? Most nights I'll do my own cooking, but once the yarn shop opens, it would be a big help a couple evenings a week."

"Oh, yes, that would be good. Just let me know ahead of time when you'll need me. During the summer, I'm pretty wide open but once school starts in August, I have to be available to drive my daughter to various events."

"Sure. Your daughter is Krystina, right?"

A smile of pure love covered Marta's face and she nodded. "Yes, Krystina is now almost fifteen. She has ballet lessons after school and she plays basketball, so I like to be available to take her. We live with my sister and her husband, and they always offer, but . . . well . . . I am Krystina's mother, so they shouldn't have to do that."

"That's really nice," I said. "You sound like a very involved mom. It's also nice that you have family here. You came from Poland, right? And your daughter was born here?"

Marta nodded but refrained from going into any detail. "Yes," was all she said before standing up. "Well, I won't keep you. I just wanted to let you know I'd see you around ten tomorrow."

"Thanks again, Marta," I said and watched her walk to the driveway. I couldn't help but think everybody has a story and I had a feeling that maybe over time I would learn Marta's.

I had just finished lunch on the patio and resumed working on the shawl pattern when I heard Mavis's voice. I looked to the gate separating the yards and saw her walking in. Basil ran to greet her and she let out a chuckle.

"Well, it looks like this handsome boy is settling in just fine," she said, sitting down to join me at the table. "And how about you?"

"Very well. I had a good night's sleep and I love the house. It has such a warm and cozy feel to it."

Mavis nodded with a satisfied expression on her face. "Good. Well, the house is happy again. I'm certain of that. You and Basil have begun to restore some of its former happiness, and I think in time it will resume the joy it had years ago."

"You really think the house can feel emotions?"

She gave me a look of astonishment. "Yes, of course. Don't you?"

I wasn't sure if my rental lease was contingent on this belief, so I only said, "I'm not sure. I suppose it could be true."

Mavis nodded emphatically. "Oh, it's true enough, honey. I can vouch for that. I know for sure the house was the happiest before Emmalyn moved out."

"When was that?"

"As soon as her pregnancy was confirmed. My father begged her to stay at least until she had the baby . . . but she wouldn't hear of it. Nope. Not Emmalyn. She wanted to be on her own. So of course my father relented and purchased the cottage on Orchard Lane for her. Turns out, that was probably the best thing. It wasn't an easy time here."

When I remained silent, she continued.

"A few weeks before Emmalyn announced that she was pregnant, my Jackson was killed in Vietnam. It was a very difficult and sad time for me and I wasn't the most pleasant person to be around. Actually, I became a bit of a recluse. And then Yarrow was born and convinced me that life does indeed go on."

I reached over to pat Mavis's hand. "I'm sure it wasn't easy for you. So your sister and niece helped you to heal?"

"Oh, I'm not so sure Emmalyn had anything to do with it." She let out a sarcastic chuckle. "Emmalyn was always too wrapped up in her own life to be very concerned about others. But she did share the gift of Yarrow with me and for that, I was grateful. Children have a way of making sense out of life."

"So what do you think accounted for the house being the happiest when your sister lived here?"

"Oh, it was her energy. There's no doubt about it. She had a passion and zest for life that simply overflowed, and it consumed everyone and everything surrounding her. Not always in a good way—and that was her problem. Enough about the past," she said, slapping the table with her palm. "Is that the shawl design you're working on?"

"It is. It's just my first draft but I have a starting point. It will be a lace pattern."

"Oh, nice. Lace knitting is so popular right now. Do you have a name for it yet?"

"Not yet, but I'm sure I'll come up with something once the design is complete."

"Very good," Mavis said, reaching for her cane and standing up. "Well, I won't keep you. Have you spoken to Marta yet?"

"Yes, she stopped by earlier and explained she'll be here tomorrow around ten to clean."

"Right. If you need anything, just give a call or pop over. Oh, the workmen will be here tomorrow working on the shop. They promised to come around eight."

"Great. Thanks for everything, Mavis."

"Believe me, it's my pleasure."

I watched her cross through the gate back to David's house and once again I felt grateful to have met this woman.

# Chapter 19

I awoke the following morning with a sense of unease. Rolling over onto my side, I pulled one of the pillows to my chest as I tried to understand why I felt agitated, and then I remembered—it was the dream.

I dragged bits and pieces together until the dream came back into focus. I was standing outside near the fishpond, looking through the archway. A woman was kneeling to the side, gazing into the water. She had long, wavy auburn hair and was wearing a flame red evening gown, off the shoulders, that fell in folds down her slender body. When she glanced up at me, I saw that sadness covered her face and I also saw the most intense green eyes I'd ever seen. I began to walk toward her to see if I could help, but she put up a hand, shook her head and indicated I shouldn't come closer. That was when I saw the tears rolling down her face. And then I woke up.

*What the hell*, I thought. Was that Emmalyn? Although I'd never seen her, the dream woman certainly matched David's description. Why on earth would I dream of her? I let out a deep sigh. It had to be because of the discussions I'd had about her with both David and Mavis. The subconscious was such a mystery.

I was surprised when I glanced at the clock and saw it was almost seven—later than I normally slept. But I'd been awake till almost midnight working on my design.

Whining drew my attention to Basil, who had leaned over and was kissing my cheek.

"Yes, I know," I told him. "Time to get up and get moving."

* * *

By noontime I'd finished the shawl design and was ready to think about lunch. Stretching and letting out a yawn, I stood up from the patio table and could hear the workmen in the schoolhouse.

They had arrived promptly at eight. I went out to introduce myself, bringing mugs of much appreciated coffee. Ed, John, and Tony appeared to be in their early to midforties and greeted me with friendliness. I complimented the work they'd done so far and found myself getting excited about the day when the space would look like a bona fide yarn and tea shop.

I had just walked into the kitchen to prepare myself a salad for lunch when my cell phone rang..

"Hey, there," Chadwick said when I answered. "Have you got a minute?"

"Sure. What's going on?"

"I wanted to invite you to dinner on Saturday evening. Are you free?"

"I am," I told him.

"Do you like Italian?"

"Love it."

"Great. I'll make a reservation at Genovese's and I'll pick you up at seven. Will that work?"

"Perfectly."

I heard a chuckle come across the line.

"You're an easy woman to please. I'll see you Saturday evening and I look forward to it."

"Same here," I said before we hung up.

I held the cell phone in my hand, smiling. I had a date. Nothing too earth-shattering in the scheme of things, but since my divorce, I'd only dated Cameron and then Gabe.

I could hear Marta running the vacuum upstairs as I prepared my salad. My mind wandered back to my dream. I suppose if your life got snuffed out at twenty-eight that would be something to cry about. Maybe that's why Emmalyn was sad—if the dream woman *was* Emmalyn. And of course she'd probably be sad about leaving behind a ten-year-old daughter.

"It was a dream, Chloe," I said out loud. "And dreams are not part of everyday life."

I gave Basil a treat before settling myself to eat at the lemon yellow table in the breakfast area. I had a feeling that even on a dreary, rainy day this spot would be cheery.

Marta walked into the kitchen just as I finished eating.

"I'm going to have my lunch and then I'll be doing the downstairs. Will that be all right?"

"Absolutely. Oh, I was going to ask you, do you think you could make some cookies or cupcakes for the knitting group? They'll be here a week from Friday."

"Sure. That would be fine. Do you have any particular kind in mind?"

I shook my head. "Nah, I'll leave that up to you. Mavis said there'll probably be about twelve of us."

Marta nodded. "Okay, I'll take care of it. I'll bake them on Friday morning. I'll come around eight, if that's okay. Before I start cleaning."

"That'll be fine. I'll pay you for the cookies and your prep time."

I got up to prepare myself a cup of tea and Marta sat at the table to eat her sandwich.

"How long ago did you come from Poland?" I asked, as I waited for the water to boil.

"About fifteen years ago," was all she said.

"Oh, so did you come when you were pregnant with your daughter?"

"Yes."

I had a feeling this was a touchy subject. "Mavis said your sister owns a hair salon downtown and it's the one that Maddie also goes to. I need to make an appointment with her. My hair could really use a cut and color."

She only nodded.

"Does your brother-in-law also work in the area?" I asked, making an attempt at conversation.

"Yes, he's a dentist and has a practice in Palm Coast."

I was prevented from asking any further questions by the ringing of my cell phone.

I saw the caller ID and smiled. "Marin. How are you?"

"I'm just fine. More to the point, how are you? All settled into your new home?"

"I am and I just love it."

"Berkley gave me a lot of the details. It sounds gorgeous. And imagine! You're going to be a yarn shop owner again. We're all so happy for you."

"Thanks. Yeah, it's pretty exciting." I poured hot water into the tea infuser and waited for it to steep. "The workmen are doing a great job on the refurbishing. The schoolhouse will be the perfect spot for a yarn and tea shop."

"I can't wait to see it. Let me know when you want company and I'll be there."

"I was thinking when Grace gets back from Paris I'd love to have you, Berkley, and Sydney come with her to spend the night."

"Oh, Chloe, that would be great. Count me in. Maybe we can have a gathering like Josie's mom, Shelby, had with her college friends."

I laughed thinking about the party the year before. Shelby had survived uterine cancer, and her closest friends had all come to Cedar Key to help her celebrate. And what a celebration it was.

"I will definitely plan something." I saw Marta get up from the table, whisper she was going back upstairs to clean, and I nodded. "So how's Worth?"

"He's just great. Fiona has finished up her classes at UF for this semester and Andrea . . . can you believe she already turned two years old last month?"

No, I couldn't believe it. It seemed like yesterday that poor Marin had found out about Fiona, her deceased husband's illegitimate daughter, along with the news that Fiona was also unmarried and pregnant. But after much thought, Marin had welcomed Fiona into the family with love. Fiona was now with Greg, the father of her daughter, attending college to complete her nursing degree, and Marin was besotted with her granddaughter, Andrea.

"Impossible!" I exclaimed. "God, it seems like yesterday that Fiona gave birth. I bet Andrea's growing so fast."

"Oh, she is, and don't worry, I'll bring plenty of photos to show you when I come visit. I've become a knitting fanatic. It's so much fun to finally be able to make things for a little girl."

I smiled. Like me, Marin had two sons. A girl in the family was pure joy for a knitting grandmother.

"So you're making lots of friends over there?" Marin asked.

"I am. I've met all of them at the tea shop where the knitting group meets on Fridays. You know how friendly knitters are. I've become the closest to Yarrow and Maddie, but they're all wonderful. Until the new shop opens, we're going to meet here at Koi House on

Friday afternoons, so that'll give me a chance to get to know the others better."

"That's just great, Chloe. I'm really happy for you but we miss you."

"I miss you too," I said. "Oh, and guess what? I have a date. Actually, I have two dates."

I heard Marin's laugh come across the line. "Are you serious? Well, you go, girl! Who are they?"

My laughter joined hers. "Oh, don't get too excited. One is the guy who helped me with the flat tire the day I came here. I think Grace told you about him. He's taking me to dinner Saturday evening. And the other is Henry Wagner. He owns the condo that I rented. He's due down here this week, but we've never met. He hinted he'd like to take me to dinner after he gets settled in."

"Well, you're on a roll. That's really great, Chloe. I'm extra happy for you now. It's a year this month that you lost Gabe and . . . well . . . maybe it's time to begin healing."

"You could be right," I said.

# Chapter 20

By the time Saturday arrived, I'd worked myself into a frenzy. You'd think I was a high school girl going on my first date. Most of my clothes were still in Cedar Key and none of the ones I had brought appealed to me. There was only one solution—why, shopping, of course.

Following directions from Mavis, I found my way to the Volusia Mall in Daytona Beach. Two hours later I was heading back home quite satisfied with my selections. Nothing fancy, but I thought the white cropped pants, black silk blouse, and new sandals were appropriate. Besides, new clothes always made a woman feel confident.

I passed the hair salon on Granada and on a whim decided to see if Helen could possibly give me a trim.

I walked in and saw four stylists busy at work.

The woman in the first booth looked over. "Can I help you?"

"Yes, I was looking for Helen and wondering if it was possible to get a trim today."

"I'm Helen," she said and walked to the front counter to consult an appointment book. "Yes, I could do you in about ten minutes."

"Great. My name is Chloe."

A smile crossed her face. "Oh, are you the Chloe who recently moved into Koi House?"

"Yes, and I know you're Marta's sister."

"I am. Have a seat and I'll be with you shortly."

By the time I finished leafing through the current issue of *People* magazine, Helen called me over to her chair.

"It's nice to meet you," she said. "Marta said you might be stopping by. What do you have in mind?"

I ran my hands through my light brunette hair. "I need a trim today but I'd also like to book time for some highlights."

"Okay. Shampoo bowl first."

When we returned to her chair, she said. "So do you enjoy living at your new place?"

I nodded. "I do. It's a beautiful house and I'm looking forward to the yarn shop opening."

"So am I. I'm a knitter but I don't get much of a chance to go to the knitters' group. But it'll be nice to have a shop where I can purchase my yarn."

"Right. It's always great to have a local yarn shop within an easy drive. By the way, I really like your sister. She's such a nice person and an excellent worker."

"Yes, Marta is very special. My husband and I have loved having her and Krystina with us. It wasn't always so easy for Marta when she first arrived here, but she's done very well."

I assumed she meant the difficulty of settling into a new country, not speaking the language and about to become a single parent.

By the time Helen finished my hair, I knew I'd found the perfect hair stylist. She had changed the style just a bit, making the back shorter and the sides chin length, and I now had a part on the side.

"I just love it," I told her. "Gosh, I feel like a new woman."

Helen laughed. "That's what I always hope to achieve, so that's great."

When I walked to the parking lot behind the shop, I could feel my hair bouncing against my cheek. The new clothes and different hair style accounted for the bounce in my step.

At precisely seven the doorbell rang. Chadwick Price was waiting on the front porch.

"Hey," I said, opening the door. "Come on in. I just need to get my purse and a sweater."

Chadwick stepped into the foyer as Basil came hurtling down the staircase to welcome whoever had come to visit.

"Well, hello, little guy," Chadwick said, bending over to give Basil a pat. "Looks like you're enjoying your new home."

"Oh, I think he is." I pointed a finger at my dog. "Now you be a good boy and take care of the house while I'm gone."

As we walked to the driveway, I noticed Chadwick was wearing a light blue short-sleeved sport shirt along with khaki slacks. *Very nice*, I thought, unsure whether I meant the clothes or the man wearing them.

I saw the black BMW and recalled the day I had seen this car drive past me on a rainy road and then turn around and come to my rescue.

He opened the passenger door and I slid in onto the gray leather seat.

"Okay," he said, starting the ignition. "Ready for some great Italian food?"

"I am."

"You look very nice. Is that a new hairdo?"

Ten points for noticing. "Yes, it is."

"Very becoming."

"Thank you."

He pulled the car onto Granada, and we headed east toward the bridge.

"You didn't RSVP yet," he said, "but I'm hoping you'll be able to attend my fund-raiser next month."

"Oh, definitely. I'll be coming with Mavis and Yarrow, and thank you so much for inviting me. Raising money for the local hospital is such a worthy cause. From what I hear, you're quite the philanthropist in the community."

He kept his eyes straight ahead as we drove onto the bridge over the Halifax River. "It's part of giving back," was all he said.

Farther down on the left, Chadwick pulled into the large parking lot of a strip mall with Starbucks and other various shops. About halfway down I saw the sign for Genovese's.

"Here we are," he said.

We were seated at a booth in the back. Not a fancy restaurant but if the aromas drifting from the kitchen were any indication, chances were very good that the food was great.

Both Chadwick and I ordered a glass of Chianti and the waiter placed menus in front of us.

"What's good?" I asked.

Chadwick laughed. "Everything, but do you mind if we enjoy the wine before ordering?"

"Not at all."

"So tell me more about yourself," he said. "You'd mentioned you're originally from Brunswick, Georgia. Any family still up there?"

"No, none. My parents passed away when I was in college, but they had traveled a lot with their antique business. And then Aunt Maude relocated to Cedar Key. After my divorce I followed her there. My sister, Grace, is my only sibling and she owned a coffee shop on the island."

He took a sip of wine and nodded. "That's nice. I'm sure they were a great support while you were going through a difficult time."

"My aunt was, yes. But my sister and I had had a falling-out and hadn't spoken or been in touch for ten years."

An expression of understanding crossed his face and he nodded again. "Yeah, siblings can be difficult. But it sounds like whatever it was is now behind you."

"Yeah, and I'm grateful for that. Actually, though, it wasn't Grace who created the rift. That was all my doing. I had experienced a damaging situation in college and even though I didn't realize it at the time, it had turned me into a very bitter and resentful person. I wasn't able to work through it until many years later, and when I finally opened up and discussed it with Grace, it allowed us to reconnect, and now . . . we couldn't be any closer as sisters."

"Sounds like she's a very forgiving person."

"She is," I said, and wondered if I'd ever truly forgiven the person who'd caused me such anguish in college. "To be honest, I'm not sure I would have been as understanding as Grace was. What I did was the ultimate betrayal of a sister." I let out a deep sigh. "It's all in the past now. Thank God."

I recalled how I'd seen my sister leaving a hotel in Jacksonville with a married man. It still tore me apart to admit that due to jealousy and unhappiness, I was the person who'd relayed this information to Beau Hamilton's wife, setting in motion terrible sadness and chaos in my sister's life—and yet she had forgiven me.

"How about you?" I said, changing the subject. "Did you just have the one brother?"

"Yes, just Aaron. He was two years older than I was. He was the golden boy and had it all—good looks, good marks all through school, and, of course, our family money. Aaron was my idol, even though maybe he didn't always deserve my loyalty."

I took a sip of wine and waited for him to go on.

"He excelled in sports as well, so he had no end of girls begging for his attention."

"Was he married with a family when he passed away?"

Chadwick shook his head. "No, he was single. He was the type of guy who always got what he wanted—no matter what. When he graduated college, he joined our father's law firm, and he was ruthless in court, which I guess could be an advantage. But as I got older, I came to see that Aaron wasn't always a nice person. He was diagnosed with cancer of the pancreas and he was gone within six months."

I let out a gasp. "God, how terrible. I'm so sorry."

"I spent a lot of time with him at the end and we talked a lot. I think it was the first time my brother ever really opened up and shared things with me. I have to say, I do think he was sorry for some of the things he'd done in his life. I like to think that had he been given more time, he would have made amends to many people."

I had a strong feeling that Chadwick's humanitarian efforts had a lot to do with the brother he'd lost.

"Family ties," I said, quietly. "No matter what, they have a way of binding us together."

He let out a deep sigh. "They do. Now let's decide on some food."

By the time Chadwick walked me to my door, I knew I liked him. A lot. I wasn't sure if it was in a romantic way but I did know I very much enjoyed spending the evening with him and getting to know him better. I was still pretty certain we'd never met, but he continued to have a familiarity that I couldn't explain.

"Thank you so much for a lovely evening," I said.

"My pleasure. It was fun and I enjoyed getting to know you."

He leaned over to kiss my cheek. "I was wondering if you'd like to come out on the boat with me sometime. I have a pontoon docked at my house and I like to get out on the river in the good weather."

"That sounds like fun," I said, recalling the boating I'd done in Cedar Key. "Sure."

"Great. I'll give you a call."

This time when he leaned toward me, his lips brushed mine, causing me to rethink the romantic aspect of our relationship.

# Chapter 21

I woke a couple of days later to hear rain pelting the roof and windows. I could also hear the whipping of the wind. We were now officially into hurricane season but the weather forecast the day before had said only rain and high winds.

Basil followed me downstairs. I opened the French doors, attempting to coax him outside. He looked out at the yard and then up at me.

"Go on," I said. "Don't be a wimp. I'll wait right here for you."

Basil moved hesitantly out the door, stood under the sheltered overhang of the house, lifted his leg, did his thing, and raced back inside.

"Good boy," I said, bending down to dry him off with a towel.

Since it was Tuesday, Marta wouldn't be coming and I had the house to myself.

After two mugs of coffee I decided to do some laundry. It was definitely going to be a stay-at-home day.

I had just finished filling the washing machine when a dream from the night before flitted into my mind. Again, it was about the woman in the red gown, and again I was standing at the entrance to the fishpond watching her.

This time she was standing at the far end of the pond, looking across the water at me, and butterflies fluttered above her. Her face looked sad and I heard her say, "It's hard. It's so hard."

"What's so hard?" I asked her. But that was the end of the dream. I woke up.

The ringing of my cell phone brought me back. I answered to hear Mavis's voice.

"Nasty day out there," she said. "David's running to Publix. Do you need anything?"

"Oh, thanks. But no, I'm all set. I think I'll just have a quiet day here. Work some more on my pattern and get some knitting done. How's everything with you?"

"Very well. Yarrow is right on track finishing up her orders with the tea reps and I've heard back from all the yarn reps. I spoke to Ed yesterday—according to him the work in the schoolhouse is going very well. He now thinks they'll be finished by late August."

"Oh, that *is* good news. Do we know yet when we might be opening?"

"I think we can bump it up a bit. I was thinking the week of Labor Day might be good."

"I agree, and whatever you decide will be fine with me."

"Okay, well, stay dry and if you need anything just give a call."

I had just settled down to work on my design at the kitchen table when my phone rang again.

I checked the caller ID and smiled when I saw Isabelle's name.

"How are you?" I asked.

"Good. Am I interrupting anything?"

"Not at all. What's going on with you? Is Haley finished school for the summer?"

"Yes. A couple of weeks ago. After the year she's had, needless to say she's happy to be away from there."

"That's a shame. So nothing improved with her classmates?"

"Not at all." A deep sigh came across the line. "I'm not sure I remember girls being quite so mean when I was in school. And unfortunately, the sadder she got, the more her weight increased. I'm at my wit's end. I've suggested Weight Watchers to her, maybe joining a gym—but nothing seems to work. She's just not interested."

"I'm so sorry about this. For both of you. I wish I could help."

"Well, you might be able to. The one thing that seemed to perk her up was when I mentioned going down there to visit with you."

"Oh, Isabelle, I told you before. Absolutely. I have two spare bedrooms here and I'd love to have you. Any idea when you might come?"

"I was thinking in about six weeks. The end of July. Would that work for you?"

"That would be perfect. I spoke to Mavis earlier and it seems the refurbishing of the schoolhouse is ahead of schedule, so we'll be opening the week of Labor Day. But I'll be free the end of July."

"That's great and I know it'll make Haley happy. We'll come for a week or so if that's all right with you."

"Come for two weeks, Isabelle. There's so much to see and do here."

"Really?" she said. Her tone sounded as if I was giving her a life-line.

"Definitely. It'll be so much fun having you guys here. I've missed you both a lot, and we have a lot of catching up to do."

"I know, and thanks. Can you believe it's one year tomorrow that Dad's been gone?"

"No, I can't. It seems like yesterday we were arriving at your home to visit. I still think of Gabe every day, and I miss him a lot. He was a good man."

"He was. Okay, no sadness. Haley will be thrilled to hear we're confirmed to visit. She really likes you a lot and I know she's dying to spend some time with Basil."

I laughed. "Oh, Basil will love that. Okay, well, keep in touch and give Haley a kiss and hug from me."

I hung up and returned to the table to resume working on my design.

Poor Haley. I felt bad that she was going through a tough time. Being a teenager was tough enough without mean girls making it worse. I hoped her visit here would bring her some happiness. She was such a caring and giving young woman and certainly didn't deserve to be treated this way at school.

I felt my stomach grumble and was surprised to see it was almost one. I had been totally engrossed working on the shawl pattern, and except for a bit of tweaking, I think I had it completed. Now I had to test it and do a sample to see how the repeat lace pattern would work out.

I got up from the table, stretched, glanced out the window and saw it was still raining. Maybe not quite as hard as earlier but still coming down. Time for lunch, and then I'd look through the stash of yarn I'd brought with me and begin working on the shawl.

"Basil," I called, looking around the kitchen. I should let him outside while the rain was less intense. "Basil?" I called again. The last I'd seen of him, he was curled up on the kitchen floor, but he wasn't there now.

I walked through the passageway to the living room and called his name again. I heard whimpering coming from the top of the staircase.

"What are you doing up there? Are you sleeping on my bed again?"

I got a whine in reply. What *was* it about that room that enticed him so much?

"Come on," I hollered, heading to the back of the house. "Let's go outside." I could hear him coming down the stairs and turned around to see him following me.

After Basil came back inside, I heated up some pumpkin soup I'd made the day before and decided to have a grilled cheese sandwich with it. Soup was always good on a dreary day.

As I sat there eating my lunch I thought of my dream again. Actually, both dreams of the same woman. In the same location. It's said that everybody dreams every night, but many of us have no recall in the morning, and I certainly could not remember ever having repeat dreams about the same person or situation. I didn't believe in ghosts, unlike my sister, who had insisted our mother had visited her during the night shortly before she married Lucas. At the time, I had brushed it off as wedding tension on Grace's part.

But now I wondered. Dreams were one thing, but could Emmalyn's sprit still be hanging around this house? Her bedroom never had warmed up and was always a few degrees colder than the rest of the house. And Basil seemed to have a fixation on being in that room. He didn't appear to be frightened of the room or anything in it—he just enjoyed being in there.

I had just finished filling the dishwasher when my cell rang again. It was Chadwick.

"Hey," he said. "Keeping dry today?"

I glanced out the window and saw the rain had picked up again. "I am. It's a wet one. That's for sure."

His laugh came across the line. "Yeah, but the good news is the rest of the week will be sunny and near eighty. So I was wondering if you might be interested in going out on the boat with me Saturday."

"Saturday? Yeah, that sounds like fun."

"Great. If you don't mind, do you want to come over to my house? We can leave from here around three. I was thinking we could cruise up the Halifax over to the Tomoka River and go to the River Grille in Ormond Beach for dinner. They have a dock right there for boats."

"Oh, that does sound like fun. Sure, I don't have a problem driving over to your house. You're just farther up North Beach, right?"

"Yes, 1505. The brick house on the right. You'll see the brick posts out front and a wrought-iron fence. Just pull into the circular driveway. I'll have the gate open."

"Great. See you on Saturday."

I hung up and felt a smile cross my face. It felt good to have a male companion back in my life again.

I prepared myself a cup of tea and curled up on the living room sofa to begin working on the shawl. After I had casted on and had a few rows finished, it occurred to me that I'd have to come up with a name for the shawl and decide on colors to be used.

Almost immediately, *Chloe's Dream* came into my head. The perfect name. And I could see the shawl completed in shades of crimson, cranberry, and a hint of pink. For a contrasting color I saw gray and white swirling through it. The image of the woman in my dream flashed in my mind and I felt a shiver go through me. What was the connection between my dream and the design for the shawl? I didn't know, but all of it was starting to feel a bit eerie.

# Chapter 22

True to Chadwick's forecast, it was sunny, high seventies and low humidity on Friday afternoon. So I decided to hold the knitting group outside on the patio. It was the perfect day to be enjoying the great weather.

I had just finished placing the cupcakes that Marta had baked earlier onto a platter when my cell rang and I heard Louise's voice.

"Chloe, hi. I was just wondering . . . do you think it would be okay . . . if I brought Ramona to the knitting group this afternoon? I'll keep her in her bag. I promise. But she's letting me know she doesn't really want to stay alone."

I laughed and shook my head. More and more, dogs and cats were becoming bona fide family members, which I thought was wonderful. "Of course you can, Louise. As a matter of fact, because it's so nice today, I thought we'd meet outside on the patio. So Ramona can play with Basil in the yard."

"Oh, that's so nice of you, Chloe, and Ramona will be so excited. She adores Basil and enjoys socializing with him. Great. Okay, well then, we'll see you around two."

I hung up and smiled. When I'd initially offered to take Basil, it was because I felt it was the right thing to do. There was no way I could let Gabe's dog go to a pound and sit there till God knows what might have happened. But over the past year, Basil had become so much more than *just* a pet to me. He was my buddy, my confidant, my best friend, and I knew I'd be lost without him.

I filled the glass carafe with water for coffee and had a saucepan ready to boil water for tea. After I stacked the paper plates and napkins on the counter, I walked outside to visit the schoolhouse. The workers had left about an hour ago. I stepped inside to see the latest updates.

The entire wall on my left now held wooden cubbyholes—perfect for stacking various kinds of yarn. A fresh coat of white paint had been applied to the other walls and I could see the border print would probably be ready to go up soon, which meant that Mavis, Yarrow, and I had to make a decision on what we wanted. I walked toward the back, and it looked like some remodeling had been started for the tea shop also. This really would be the ideal yarn and tea shop.

I walked back outside and through the archway to the fishpond. Basil followed me and I sat down on one of the stone benches as I let out a deep sigh. I hadn't had any further dreams in the past few nights, but sitting there watching the brightly colored fish swim gave me a sense of peace, unlike the sadness and turmoil exhibited by the woman in my dream. What did it all mean? Did it mean anything at all?

"Yoo hoo," Mavis hollered. "Are you here, Chloe?"

"Right here," I called and walked out of the fishpond area to see her coming through the gate.

"Oh, good. I'm a tad early."

"That's fine," I said. "I thought we'd sit out on the patio today."

"Very good idea. It's just beautiful out." She headed to one of the padded chairs with the assist of her cane and sat down.

Basil ran over to greet her and she laughed. "I sure do love this little guy," she said, bending over to pat him.

"He's going to have some company today. Louise called to see if she could bring Ramona and I told her it would be fine. Basil will enjoy a canine visitor."

"Oh, that's nice. I have no doubt when we're in the yarn shop she'll bring her all the time since Ramona can safely stay out here with Basil."

"Right. Oh, by the way, I was just in there looking around. It's shaping up so nicely, Mavis."

"Yes, I peeked in yesterday. They're doing a very fine job."

"But it looks like they'll be ready soon to hang the border print, so we have to decide what we want."

"Yes, I was thinking about that and thinking the three of us need to pay a visit to Lowe's. When are you free?"

"Monday would work."

"Great. I'll let Yarrow know."

We both looked toward the driveway gate as female voices filled the air and the knitters began arriving.

An hour later I looked around at the knitters and smiled. I wasn't in Brunswick, Georgia. I wasn't in Cedar Key. I was in an area where I'd only been for a little over five weeks and yet—it *felt* like home. Meeting new women, women with the common love of knitting, had a way of creating this sense of belonging.

"How's the shawl design coming along?" Maddie asked.

"Very well. I finished the design and I've begun to work on a sample. Here," I said, reaching into my knitting bag. "I'll let you see a preview."

*Ohhh*s and *ahhh*s filled the patio area as eight women leaned forward for a better look.

"Pass it around," I said and gave the piece to Maddie.

"I just love it."

"I definitely want to make that."

The comments flowed and Fay, who was fairly new to the group, said, "It's just lovely. Have you thought of a name yet?"

"I'm thinking of calling it Chloe's Dream," I said and withheld any explanation.

Everybody loved the name.

"How about colors?" Paige asked. "Will we be making it in this purple?"

I laughed. "No, that's just part of my stash. I was thinking of various shades of red combined with gray and white."

Again, the agreement was unanimous.

We resumed our knitting and before I knew it, it was going on four. I jumped up to make the coffee and tea. "We'll have snacks as soon as the coffee and tea are ready," I called over my shoulder and headed into the kitchen.

"Need any help?" Maddie asked as I poured the carafe of water into the coffeemaker.

"Yeah, just turn on the stove to boil the water for tea. And then you can take this platter of cupcakes outside. I forgot to find out who wanted coffee or tea."

"I'll ask," Maddie said as she headed back out through the French doors.

I glanced out the window over the sink and saw that Ramona and

Basil were having a great time running around chasing each other. My pooch would be sleeping well tonight.

"Four coffees and four teas," Maddie said.

"Okay, and I'll have coffee." I reached into the cabinet and removed a large wooden tray, setting five mugs on it. "I put the teacups on that tray along with the canister of different flavored tea bags. When the water's boiled, could you pour it into the cups?" I asked as I began pouring coffee.

"So," Maddie said, dragging out the word. "I haven't seen you all week. How'd your dinner with Chadwick go last Saturday night?"

"Oh. Very well. He's a really nice guy. We went to Genovese's and the food was delicious."

"And so? Any romantic feelings forming?"

I was beginning to see that Maddie had a way of getting right to the point. I laughed. "I'm not sure. It's too soon to tell."

She waved a hand in the air. "Hey, it's either there or it isn't. For what it's worth, I bet there's some chemistry going on. Are you seeing him again?"

I hesitated before pouring the final cup of coffee. "Um, yeah. Tomorrow. He invited me to go out on his boat."

Maddie dramatically cleared her throat. "Ah, yup. Definitely some chemistry going on there," she said as I walked outside with the tray of coffee mugs.

"These cupcakes are delicious," Yarrow said, reaching for a second one. "I have to talk to Marta about doing a little bakery business for me on the side. Her baked items would be a bonus for the tea shop."

"Oh, they would," Louise said, picking up her teacup and pursing her lips. "And I'll be so glad to have your shop open so we can have *real* tea again. No offense, Chloe."

I laughed. "None taken."

"Have you heard from your friend Isabelle?" Mavis asked. "Is she still planning to visit?"

"Yes, she called this week and she and Haley will be down here late July for a couple of weeks."

Mavis clapped her hands together. "Oh, that's wonderful. I'm very much looking forward to meeting them, and this house will be so happy to have some young life breathed back into it again."

Louise batted her hand in the air. "Oh, Mavis, you and your silly thoughts about this house."

Before a conflict ensued, I said, "Yeah, I think poor Haley also needs a breather after the rough school year she had. She's gained some weight and the girls in her class have been so mean to her. The poor kid barely wanted to go to school. Young girls can have such a streak of meanness."

"Oh, it's not just young girls," Fay said. We all looked over at her. "Oh, no. Once a mean girl, always a mean girl, I say. They just get older but they don't change. You wouldn't believe what goes on at Dolphin Run."

I recalled hearing that Fay lived in a very upscale assisted living facility in Daytona Beach.

"Problems?" Mavis asked.

"Of a sort, but nothing I can't handle. Since I moved there in January I've been trying to socialize and fit in. For the most part it's worked out. But there was a knitting group that I wanted to join on Monday mornings, so I showed up at the function room where it was being held. There were about twelve women there, but when I introduced myself, I noticed nobody was making a spot for me at the table and there were no extra chairs in the room. When I said I'd go look for another chair, one of them piped up and said there really wasn't any room at the table. That everybody would feel cramped. It was perfectly obvious that with a little arranging, we'd all have plenty of room. So I caught on mighty fast. These women might be over age seventy—but they were mean girls."

Yarrow shook her head. "Fay's right. Women like that never change. When Fay began coming into the tea shop, I saw her knitting there by herself while she was having her tea, so I invited her to join our group."

"And that was very nice of you," Fay said.

"Yes, you're certainly welcome here," Mavis told her.

"Hear, hear," we all chimed in.

I could only hope that eventually Haley would hook up with a welcoming circle of friends like the ones I had found.

# Chapter 23

Grace called Saturday morning just as I stepped out of the shower.

"I've missed you," I said. "How are you doing?"

"Great. We've been in the south of France for the past week, visiting more of Lucas's family. But it's been a wonderful month. We're all fine and I can hardly believe we fly back to the States on Tuesday."

"The month really did go fast," I told her. "But it'll be nice to have you back on this side of the pond again."

"Right and as soon as I get over jet lag, I'll gather up your things and bring them to you in Ormond Beach."

"I really hate to have you do that. I could drive to Cedar Key and get my stuff."

"Don't be silly. Besides, I'm dying to see where you're staying and hopefully meet Mavis and Yarrow."

"Well, if you don't mind, that would be great. We can go over what I need you to bring later. I spoke to Marin and I'd love to have you guys come to spend the night. I have plenty of room and Mavis has encouraged me to have company. She thinks it makes the house happy."

I heard laughter come across the line. "Seriously?"

"Very seriously," I told my sister. "She's a bit like Aunt Maude in that respect. She feels houses have an energy that we can feel if we pay attention."

"After my own experience at Aunt Maude's house, I'm afraid I tend to agree with her. Any ghosts make an appearance yet?"

"Not yet," I said. "But I have been having some interesting dreams since I moved in here."

"Dreams can be messages sent to us also. How's it going with Chadwick Price?"

I let out a deep sigh. "Well, we had dinner together last weekend and I'm going out on his boat with him later today."

"But? I detect some uncertainty in your tone."

Grace had a knack for knowing me better than anyone else.

"But . . . he's a really nice guy. I enjoy his company. He's quite handsome and successful. But I don't know. I'm not sure I even want to get involved with somebody right now."

"Is it just him or would it be anybody who came into your life?"

Good question. "What do you mean?"

"I mean you're really not known for following through on your romantic attachments, Chloe. I realize that Parker left you, but you admitted maybe you should have given more thought to marrying him. Then after your divorce, you dated Cameron. Nothing happened there. Then Gabe came into your life. Yes, you had no control over his leaving you, but—and don't take this the wrong way—I think being with Gabe had a lot to do with the fact that you needed a change, a reason to move on."

She was right. "So are you saying I have a commitment phobia?"

"Maybe. But not intentionally. I think it could have a lot to do with your college experience."

"I've worked through all of that, Grace. Once I opened up and shared it with you, I began to heal."

"Healing has a lot of different levels. It's just something to think about, Chloe."

I changed the subject and we continued talking. But as usual, Grace had nudged me and given me something to consider.

I easily found Chadwick's house and pulled into the circular driveway. Well-maintained landscaping surrounded the one-story brick structure, with all of it enclosed by a black wrought-iron fence.

As I walked up the three front steps, the large oak door was opened by Chadwick.

"Hey," he said. "Come on in. No trouble finding the house?"

"No, none," I told him, taking in the large foyer leading to an open family room overlooking a huge patio area and the river. "What a gorgeous spot."

"Thanks," he said, leading the way into the room. "How about an iced tea before we set sail?"

"Sounds good."

He walked toward a large kitchen to the right off the family room. "Make yourself comfortable. I'll be right back."

I gazed around the room with approval—beautifully furnished but not ostentatious. Two leather sofas, comfy chairs, and cherrywood tables with porcelain ginger jar lamps. I wandered over to a credenza lined with framed family photographs. One was of an older couple, who I assumed were Chadwick's parents, bundled up in ski gear standing at the base of a mountain. One of Chadwick dressed in shorts and polo shirt, holding up a golf club on a fairway. And a third photo that caused a chill to go through my body. I picked up the frame to look closer and saw Chadwick with another fellow, arms around each other's shoulders, huge grins on their handsome faces, and I froze. The other fellow was *him*. I hadn't seen him in thirty-two years, but I *knew* it was him. I had also never even known his name, but I did now—Aaron Price. Chadwick's brother. The man who had date-raped me after a frat party in college. I gripped the frame and felt lightheaded. How could this be possible? After all the years of keeping the secret, of living with the humiliation and anger, of never sharing any of it with anyone until I told my sister a few years before—how could it be possible that because of a flat tire in the rain I'd now come face to face with my attacker?

"Here we go," I heard Chadwick say as if from a distance.

I turned and saw him walking toward me holding out a tall glass, and I panicked.

"Oh . . . I'm so sorry . . . but I'm not going to be able to go," I stammered. "I've changed my mind. I . . . all of a sudden, I don't feel well." I walked toward the door and my feet felt like lead.

"Chloe, are you okay? Can I drive you home?"

I heard the concern in Chadwick's voice but I shook my head. "No, no thanks. I'll be fine," I said, yanking open the front door and racing to my car. With shaking hands I turned the key in the ignition and headed back down North Beach Street, grateful I only had a short drive home—to safety and privacy.

But as I pulled into the driveway, I groaned at the sight of Yarrow coming down the front steps. I was in no mood to talk to anybody but it was too late to back up and escape. She had seen me and was waving. I let out a deep sigh and got out of the car.

"Hey," she called. "I was just dropping off some new bags of tea for you, but since you weren't home I was planning to leave them on the table out here."

I walked up the steps, clutching my key in my hand, and nodded as I unlocked the door. "Thanks," I mumbled.

Basil raced to greet me and I bent down to give him a pat as Yarrow followed me inside.

"Hey, wait a sec. Why *are* you here? I thought you were out on a boat ride with Chadwick. Are you okay?"

*No,* I thought. *I'm not at all okay*. "Sure. I'm fine," I said, heading to the back of the house to let Basil outside.

"Then what happened to the boat ride?" she asked. "You don't look very well, Chloe. You're really pale. Are you sure you're not sick?"

I blew a puff of air between my lips, grasped the edge of the counter, put my head down and shook it slowly from side to side. "No. I'm not sick," I whispered. "At least not physically."

I felt Yarrow's arms go around me as she led me to a chair at the table to sit.

"Okay, I'm not sure what's going on. But whatever it is doesn't call for tea." She walked to the wine rack, grabbed a bottle of white, uncorked it, pulled two wineglasses from the cabinet, poured and placed one in front of me. "You don't have to talk at all if you don't want to. But take a sip of wine and let yourself relax. You are obviously *very* upset."

I nodded and took a gulp of pinot grigio as the shock of what I'd discovered washed over me. What had just happened now seemed more like a dream, but it wasn't. After all these years I had seen his face again. And in the most unlikely of places. That was when it hit me that he was gone. Aaron Price was dead. Chadwick had said his brother passed away about twenty-five years ago—and for that I was grateful. But even in his grave, I knew I had never forgiven him and never would.

# Chapter 24

After a few minutes, Yarrow reached over and patted my hand. "Doing okay?"

I nodded and sighed. "Yeah, better." I took another sip of wine. "You must think I'm nuts."

Yarrow laughed. "Aren't we all? Just a little?"

That brought a smile to my face. "Maybe."

Yarrow sat there quietly, allowing me to attempt to sort things out in my head. But I knew this wasn't good for me. I had attended enough support groups to know that sharing is what helps. Sharing is the first step toward healing.

"I have a story," I said softly and glanced up to see Yarrow nod as if to say again, *don't we all?*

I took a deep breath. "Something happened to me in college. I went to Savannah School of Design and there was a frat party at a house outside of town. A couple of my friends knew some guys there, so we went. It was your typical frat party—lots of beer, loud music, and plenty of flirting. By the time the night was over, my friends had hooked up with guys and left me stranded there. I remember a good-looking guy offering to give me a ride back to the dorm. I had had my share of booze and, being too stupid to know better, I allowed a stranger to take me home. Hell, I didn't even know his name. I'm not sure exactly what the hell I was thinking, but I guess I figured he was also a student and I'd be okay. But I wasn't. Just before we got to my campus, he pulled over and forced me out of the car into the grass . . . where he raped me."

"Oh, my God, Chloe. How awful. Was he arrested?"

I shook my head. "No. Because I didn't report it."

She didn't seem shocked by my admission and I saw her eyebrows arch in understanding.

"When I got back to the dorm, I didn't tell anybody. I was too ashamed. I had been drinking a lot. I'd been stupid enough to allow a strange guy to give me a ride." I could feel the tears sliding down my face. "And I was no longer a virgin."

Yarrow jumped up and pulled me into her arms, rocking me back and forth. "Oh, Chloe. I'm so very sorry."

She allowed me to cry. While I composed myself she went to the counter and brought back a box of tissues.

Swiping at my eyes, I said, "Pretty stupid, huh?"

"No, not stupid. Young and naïve."

We both remained silent for a few moments and then she said, "But what's all of this got to do with Chadwick?"

"Chadwick is his brother."

Her hand flew to her face. "Oh. My. God."

I explained how he had looked familiar to me ever since I'd met him, and about finding the photograph at his house.

"No wonder you're upset," she said, reaching over to give my arm a pat. "Does Chadwick know?"

I shook my head. "No. I told him I was sick and couldn't go on the boat. I'm sure he didn't believe me."

"Wow. So now what? What are you going to do? Gosh, is there a chance you might run into his brother?"

I let out a sarcastic chuckle. "Hardly. Aaron Price is dead."

"Wow," she said again. I explained how Chadwick had told me about the death of his brother.

"His brother was his idol, but he did admit that Aaron wasn't always a nice person, that he had shared some things with him before he died, and Chadwick even said the major reason for his philanthropy is a form of giving back. To make up for the things his brother did."

Yarrow got up to get the bottle of wine and refilled our glasses.

"So, geez," she said, sitting back down. "Will it be tricky now going out with Chadwick? How will that work?"

I almost choked on my wine. "Are you nuts? I can't continue seeing him. I just can't."

"Couldn't you tell him about all of this? I'm sure he'd understand."

I shook my head emphatically. "No, I couldn't. It would be too awkward. Besides, we've only been out together once. It's not like we forged this great relationship."

"What about the fund-raiser at his house?" she asked.

"No. Out of the question. I'm definitely not going. I'll say I'm sick."

"Hmm. Looks like you're going to be sick a lot. This really isn't a very large town, Chloe. You can't avoid him forever."

"I can try."

When Yarrow left a couple of hours later, amid hugs and promises to call if I needed anything, I fed Basil and heated up some casserole for myself. I had just sat down to eat when my cell phone rang. I checked the caller ID, saw it was Chadwick and hit ignore. I had a feeling I'd be doing this a lot until he caught on that I didn't want to see him and he stopped calling.

After I filled the dishwasher and cleaned up, I was going to settle down with my knitting, but I heard a knock on the back door. *Oh, no*, I thought. *Not Chadwick*. But I looked out to see Mavis standing there holding a covered bowl.

"Hi. Come on in," I told her.

"I spoke to Yarrow and she said you weren't feeling well and had to cancel the boat ride. That you might be coming down with a cold, so I brought you some of the chicken noodle soup David made earlier today."

Apparently Yarrow had kept the real reason to herself. "That's so nice of you. Thanks. I've had supper but I'll have it for lunch tomorrow. Be sure to thank David for me. Would you like a cup of tea?"

"Oh, yes, I think I will," she said, bending over to pat Basil before sitting at the table. "One of the deliveries of yarn arrived today from Cascade."

I put a pan of water on the stove to boil. "Oh, great. We're really moving along, aren't we? I can't wait to start filling the shop with yarn and accessories."

Mavis Anne let out a loud sigh.

I spun around from the stove. "Are you okay?"

She waved a hand in the air. "Oh, yes. It's just that my heart's kinda weepy today. It's forty-nine years since I lost my Jackson."

"Oh, Mavis, I'm sorry." I walked over and gave her a hug. "It's always difficult, isn't it? The anniversary date of losing somebody we love."

She nodded and blotted her eyes with a tissue. "Yes, it is. It's hard to believe that I've lived an entire lifetime since the day I got the news."

"Tell me about Jackson," I said, knowing that talking about somebody no longer with us keeps their memory alive. "How did you two meet?"

Mavis Anne let out a chuckle. "Oh, we were at the beach. I was twenty-one and thought the world was my oyster. I had returned home a few weeks before for my summer break from college. And there I was sitting on the blanket with a few of my girlfriends when these fellows walked by. There were four or five of them but one in particular was staring at me. He was quite handsome and he gave me a wink and a smile. I think it was in that very moment that I knew this fellow was the love of my life."

"Wow," I said, getting up to prepare the tea. "So love at first sight is for real?"

"Oh, I can vouch for that. I found out later that I affected Jackson the same way. In one instant, we both just knew."

I brought our tea to the table. "So what happened?"

Mavis brought the teacup to her lips and blew on her tea. "Well, the other fellows spread out a blanket near us and sat down, but not Jackson. Nope. He came right over to me, knelt down beside me, smiled again and said, 'Hi, I'm Jackson Lee Hawkins.' I knew in that moment that we were destined to be together forever. By the time the afternoon was over, he had my phone number. He called me right away that evening. We were inseparable that entire summer. We both returned to college in the fall. I was at the University of Tampa and Jackson was doing his final year at Auburn."

"But you didn't get married after you both graduated?"

"No, and more's the pity. But we didn't see any need to rush. We had our whole life ahead of us—so we thought. The war in Vietnam was raging in 1965 and I think Jackson wanted to do his patriotic duty. Many were dodging the draft and going to Canada, but not my Jackson. No, he enlisted in the Air Force to be trained as an officer. He wanted to fly, and a year later his plane was shot down."

"How very sad," I said. "Like so many casualties of that war, he was so young."

Mavis nodded. "Just twenty-five. And here we are forty-nine years later, yet I remember it like it was yesterday. I had been at the beach all day with my girlfriends, laughing and carefree, but the moment I walked in that front door . . ." She nodded toward the front of the house. "I knew. I knew something bad had happened. My father was there in the foyer and forced me to sit down. He explained that Jackson's father had just left, and the news he'd received about Jackson wasn't good."

I saw the tears slide down Mavis's face and I reached over to pat her hand.

"My father told me that Jackson's family had been notified that morning. He had been killed. His body was flown home. We had a funeral but I barely remember any of the following months. It was a very dark time for me. Then Emmalyn announced her pregnancy but adamantly refused to name the father. Rumor had it that the man she was seeing was married, so my father and I drew our own conclusions. Rather than pressure her, we helped her. Six months later Yarrow was born, and only then did I begin to heal."

"I'm so very sorry," was all I could say.

She nodded. "Yes, all of it was very sad but over the years I've come to see how fortunate I was. To have that one great love come into my life. Even though it was never meant to last forever, I treasure the time that we did have." She sipped the last of her tea. "And I'm sorry for burdening you with all of this."

"Don't be silly. I only wish it could have all ended differently for you."

Mavis Anne stood up. "Yes, but that's life, isn't it? We just never know where our paths will take us. Thank you for listening to me ramble. Now I'll leave you to rest." She walked toward the back door. "You feel better tomorrow, hear?"

When I got into bed later that evening, thoughts of Mavis Anne and Jackson filled my mind. She had been right when she spoke about that one great love. Not everybody is so fortunate to have it. I certainly wasn't. I couldn't help but wonder if that night over thirty years ago, along the side of a road, had shattered all my illusions about ever having that kind of deep and special love in my own life.

# Chapter 25

The following day Mavis, Yarrow, and I headed to Lowe's to choose a wallpaper border for the shop. After much deliberation we agreed on a print with butterflies. It was colorful with blues and greens and uplifting splashes of yellow.

"Okay," Mavis said as we headed to the car. "Time for lunch. How's The Gourmet Kitchen sound?"

"Great," Yarrow said, sliding into the driver's seat.

"Fine with me. I've never been there."

"Nothing fancy but excellent food," Mavis told me.

Yarrow headed west on Granada and a few minutes later we were pulling into a strip mall with nail salon, yogurt shop, and various other businesses. She parked the car right in front of the restaurant in a handicap spot.

"Yarrow Lyn, what *do* you think you're doing?" Mavis protested.

I saw a smile cross Yarrow's face. "Well, you *are* handicapped, with that cane of yours, aren't you?"

I heard Mavis snort. "I am no such thing. Now move this car right now to a proper space."

Yarrow shrugged as she put the car into reverse and I let out a chuckle. Yarrow always seemed to know how to get a humorous rise out of her aunt.

The restaurant had a cute and cozy feel to it and the waitresses added to that feeling. We sat in a booth and I watched them joking and conversing with the customers.

One walked over, saw Mavis, and smiled. "Well, Miss Mavis. Haven't seen you in a while. How's that leg of yours doing?"

"Just fine. I should be getting rid of this cane soon."

"Maybe," I heard Yarrow whisper under her breath.

"Hey, I heard you're going to be opening a yarn shop in town."

"We are." She pointed across the table. "I'd like you to meet Chloe Radcliffe. She's my partner and we should be opening by early September."

"Nice to meet you. I'm Sally and I look forward to getting my yarn there for crocheting. Now, Miss Mavis, I hate to disappoint you, but we just sold the last of the pheasant under glass."

Mavis laughed and waved her hand in the air. "Stop being such a naughty girl and give us a menu."

Once again I felt the sense of welcome surround me. I was definitely looking forward to becoming a member of the business community and forming more connections and friends. Just as I opened the menu Sally had passed me, my cell phone rang. I glanced down to see Chadwick's name and clicked ignore. I could feel Yarrow's eyes on me but avoided looking up.

I looked over the choices and settled on the egg, cheese, and bacon wrap with macaroni salad on the side.

"Good choice," Yarrow said.

After we gave our order, Mavis said, "Well, have you two girls decided what you're wearing to the fund-raiser? It's two weeks from this Saturday, you know."

When Yarrow remained silent, I mumbled, "Oh, I'll find something."

I looked up to see Yarrow raise her eyebrows as she stared across the table at me. "Same here," she said.

"Well, except for Chadwick's Christmas gala, this is the event of the year. Nothing is too fancy. Beads, glitter, and lots of glam."

Yarrow let out a groan. "I think it would be just as nice with a dress code of jeans and T- shirts."

Mavis Anne shook her head. "Yarrow, you are definitely not your mother's daughter. Emmalyn searched for any excuse to get all dolled up. Oh, how she loved her evening gowns."

"I'm grateful it didn't rub off on me." Yarrow shot me a smile.

The lady from my dream came into my mind. Wearing the red evening gown. Could she be Yarrow's mother?

"How about you?" I asked Mavis. "Didn't you like all the glam?"

She laughed as Sally placed our plates in front of us.

"Anything else?" Sally questioned.

We shook our heads and then Mavis said, "Oh, my, yes. I always loved the fancy dresses, but not to the extent that Emmalyn did. Besides, she always had an escort to whisk her off to one event or another."

"I remember," Yarrow said. "I was always getting shuffled off to your house for sleepovers so my mother would have the night to herself."

For the first time I detected a note of irritation in her comment about her mother, but I recalled my own feelings as a child when my parents would be setting off on yet another trip to acquire antiques, and Grace and I would stay with Aunt Maude.

I saw Mavis pat Yarrow's hand. "Yes, that's true but, oh, how David and I loved having you. You were the most delightful child. Full of curiosity and so precocious."

This brought a smile to Yarrow's face. "Those *were* fun days."

I had taken a couple bites of my wrap. "This is delicious. I'm glad we came here."

"Yes, they have a varied menu and the food is good. Only open for breakfast and lunch, though. By the way, is your sister back from France yet?"

"They arrive back tomorrow and Grace and the others will be here a week from Friday. I've missed all of them, so I'm looking forward to the get-together."

"Do you think your sister will end up moving to France permanently?" Mavis asked.

"I think there's a very good chance of that. I'm pretty sure they did a fair amount of research and maybe even some house hunting on this trip. I hope they do go. Sure, I'll miss them, but I think living in France and raising Solange there is what they both want. And besides, I can fly over any time to visit."

"If you need a companion, count me in," Yarrow said.

"Really?"

"Definitely. I backpacked through France with a girlfriend when I was in my twenties. I always swore I'd get back there and never did."

"Well, it's a deal then. If they move there, we'll both go over for a visit. Mavis, would you like to join us?"

She let out a chuckle. "No, thank you. I've never flown on a plane in my life and I don't intend to start now. I'll babysit Basil."

It was hard to believe that in this day and age there were still people who had no interest in flying in a commercial aircraft.

I smiled. "You're hired," I told her.

When I got home, I decided to sit out on the patio with an iced tea and continue working on the shawl. I glanced up to see Maddie coming through the gate from the driveway.

"Hey," I said. "How about an iced tea?"

"Sounds great. Just thought I'd pop by and see what you're up to. It's nice to have the shop closed on Mondays and have the day to myself."

Basil came running out of the house when he heard a new voice and ran to greet Maddie.

"Hey, little guy," she said, bending to pat him.

"Be right back," I told her and headed to the kitchen.

When I returned, I saw she was holding the sample shawl in her hand.

"This is turning out so pretty, but when are you going to get the yarn colors you settled on?"

"Well, I need to either get to a yarn shop or order it online."

Maddie glanced at her watch. "It's only going on two. I could drive you to the shop in Longwood. It's just north of Orlando and we could be at Knit in just about an hour. They're open till five."

"Really? Gee, I really would love to get the proper yarn. If you don't mind, that would be great."

"I don't mind at all. I never turn down a chance to visit a yarn shop."

Just after three we walked into Knit, a fully stocked and pretty shop. Located in a shopping area with trees and flowers, the shop had a welcoming feel to it. Maddie introduced me to Marney and Ruth, the owners, and it was obvious Maddie had frequented this shop a lot. She rattled off the names of about six women knitting at the table in front and then she began to point out the various fibers and names of yarn lining the walls.

"Oh, hey," one of the women at the table said. "Are we ever going to see you again here? We heard a new yarn shop is opening in Ormond Beach."

Maddie laughed. "Of course you will. The new one will become my local yarn shop, but what knitter can resist a trip to visit someplace different? And actually, Chloe is one of the new owners of Dreamweaver."

"Dreamweaver?" one of the women gasped. "Oh, I love the name."

"Thanks," I said feeling a sense of pride much like when my boys were small and people commented on how handsome or smart they were.

"Yes," Marney said. "We heard Mavis Anne Overby is the other owner, so you be sure to tell her that if we can help with anything, just give us a call."

"Oh, that's really nice of you. I appreciate it." Yarn shops are an extremely competitive business but I've always found that in the knitting community, people are always ready to lend a hand. Whether it's with instruction, decisions on yarn, or finishing projects, women always come forward to help and support one another.

"Okay," Maddie said. "Start browsing."

I considered Lorna's Laces, Patons, Malabrigo, and a few others, but in the end I decided on Universal Yarns Angora Lace. It was a fine merino superwash, angora, and nylon. As usually happens in choosing yarn, it was the colors that attracted me first. For the main color I chose Heartfelt—shades of crimson, pale pink, and cranberry. And for the contrasting color I chose a yarn called Foghorn with grays and whites. The red reminded me of the evening gown in my dream and the grays would symbolize the misty quality of a dream. Perfect.

Maddie dropped me off back home around six and I decided to stir-fry some shrimp to mix in a salad for supper. I'd just poured myself a glass of wine to go with it when my cell rang. The caller ID confirmed it was Chadwick. Again. God, I knew I couldn't go forever without taking his calls so I decided to let it go to voice mail; I'd return the call after I ate.

An hour later I was dialing his number.

"Chloe," he said and I heard the concern in his voice. "Are you okay? I've been trying to reach you for a couple days."

"Oh, yeah. Fine. Much better. Just busy."

"Well, I'm sorry it didn't work out for the boat ride but we can reschedule."

"Right," was all I said.

"I'm glad you're feeling better, though. Maybe we can get together this weekend for dinner or a drink."

"Gee, I'm really busy right now. I have company arriving next week and a lot going on with opening the yarn shop."

There was a pause before he said. "Sure. I understand. Okay, then, I'll be in touch soon."

I hung up feeling the slightest twinge of guilt. He *was* a nice guy. He really was. But I wasn't able to separate him from his brother. And I wasn't sure I'd ever be able to.

# Chapter 26

The following week I received a call from Henry Wagner. He explained he was very disappointed but something had come up. He'd been offered a photo assignment in the Blue Ridge Mountains of North Carolina and his trip to Florida would be delayed until probably mid-September. But we had a very nice chat and he asked if it would be okay to call me now and then over the next few months.

"Of course," I told him because I found that I really did enjoy talking to him, even though he was somebody I'd never met in person.

"Great," he said. "Then I'll give you a call next week."

I hung up, shook my head and smiled. "Feast or famine," I said out loud. For a brief period I'd had two men interested and the possibility of dating. Now—not so much.

I decided to give Grace a call because we still needed to discuss what she'd be bringing to me on Friday.

"Just tell me what you want," she said. "I'm going to make a list and between both cars we won't have any problem bringing you what you need. This house hasn't sold yet, so whatever isn't necessary right now can stay here."

"Okay, that sounds great. Well, I need the rest of the clothes in my closet. And empty out the bureau drawers too. I have books and CDs, but those can wait. I think the only other things I need are the bins of my yarn stash."

Grace laughed. "I see you have your priorities straight. They're in your bedroom closet, right?"

"Ah . . . yeah. And in the guest room closet. And there's some in the hall closet too."

"Good thing we have two cars to transport them. Do you think maybe we should hire a moving van for the yarn stash?"

"Very funny. No, you won't need that. At least I don't think so. Oh, and could you please bring my Daylight Magnifying Lamp? It's clipped to the end table in the living room. I'm really missing that for my nighttime knitting."

"Okay, got it. I wrote it all down. I can't wait to see you on Friday. I know you said the spare bedrooms each have twin beds and I could bunk in with Berkley, but I'm bringing my Aerobed. I thought I could put it in your room and we could have our own private slumber party. Would that be okay?"

"Oh, that would be wonderful. How are Lucas and Solange? I'm sure they also enjoyed France."

"They're fine. Yes, it was a wonderful trip. We'll talk about it when I see you. How's it going with Chadwick?"

"Hmm, we'll talk about that when I see you too."

"Okay. We should be there around noon on Friday. See you then. Love you."

The humidity was beginning to climb, which was normal for late June, so after lunch I decided to turn on the air conditioning and begin working on the shawl while I enjoyed a glass of iced tea in the living room.

Basil and I had enjoyed a long walk on the beach after breakfast so he was ready to curl up next to me on the sofa for his afternoon nap. I began casting on the required stitches with the Heartfelt yarn and my mind wandered to Henry Wagner. I really didn't know that much about him. I knew he said he dabbled in photography but getting a photo assignment seemed to be more than *dabbling.* He had a Golden named Delilah and he stayed part of the year in Vermont. Beyond that, I really didn't know much more. Our brief phone conversations had been superficial. I knew he wasn't married now but wondered if he had ever been, and if so, was he divorced or a widower? From hearing his voice on the phone, I thought he seemed like a very nice person and realized that I was curious as to what he looked like.

My mind then strayed to Chadwick. Was I being unfairly harsh? He hadn't done a thing to me except go out of his way to be kind. I knew I was blaming him for what his brother had done and yet I couldn't help myself. Aaron Price didn't deserve one ounce of forgiveness. What kind of fellow violates a young college girl? What kind of fellow goes through life taking what he wants, never paying the price, never being a responsible human being? But maybe ultimately he did pay the price—by losing his life so young.

I realized I had dozed off and woke to find my knitting in my lap and Basil whining at the top of the stairs. I stood up and stretched.

"What's going on, Basil?" I called up to him. More whining.

"Okay, I'm coming," I said climbing up the stairs.

The moment I stepped into my bedroom I felt the drop in temp and saw Basil curled up at the foot of my bed. It was then I remembered the dream I had just had.

Once again, the woman in the red evening gown was standing near the fishpond. But this time, she was wearing the finished shawl I was working on—Chloe's Dream. She pulled it more tightly around her shoulders and when she lifted her face, she nodded in my direction and I saw a hint of a smile cross her lips. *Love is forgiveness,* I remembered her saying, and in a mist of grays and whites, she disappeared, and I woke up.

I felt a chill go through me. This was getting downright crazy. And what the hell was that supposed to mean? Love is forgiveness? The only person I couldn't forgive was Aaron Price, and I certainly had never loved *him*.

I needed to be outside in the bright sunshine. I was beginning to feel stifled in this room. "Come on," I told Basil, clapping my hands together. "Let's go out in the yard."

He followed me through the French doors out to the patio. The sun was beginning its slow descent and there was a nice breeze coming from the ocean. As Basil sniffed around the yard, I walked into the fishpond area—almost expecting to see a woman wearing a red evening gown standing at the far end.

I sat on one of the stone benches, watched the fish make lazy circles in the water, and let out a sigh. Could this woman in my dream be Emmalyn Overby? And if she was, how could that be possible? I'd never even seen a photo of her and certainly had never met her. There was something different about this dream, though. Although far from happy, she didn't appear as distraught and sad as she did in my first dreams.

The chill and unease I'd felt a few moments before had disappeared and been replaced with a sense of tranquility. Once again, I discovered that sitting near the fishpond allowed me to feel calm. I had no idea what any of this was about—why I kept having the same dream, why being near the fishpond restored my sense of contentment, or even why I had dreamed of both Koi House and the fishpond before I'd ever even seen them.

But one thing I did know for certain: I was in my element. I was precisely where I was supposed to be.

# Chapter 27

I saw the two cars pull into the driveway shortly after noon. Like an excited kid I went running outside to greet Grace, Berkley, Marin, and Sydney.

"Oh, my God! You're here!" I exclaimed.

There we were, five grown women, jumping up and down, hugging and kissing like college kids.

"We are," Grace said, laughing.

"Did you have a good drive?"

"Very good," Marin said. "It took just under three hours."

Basil had followed me outside and was now dancing in circles. Everybody bent down to greet him and Grace scooped him up to carry him back into the house.

"Oh, Chloe, this is just gorgeous," Sydney said as we stepped into the foyer.

"Come on, I'll give you the downstairs tour to the kitchen. I have a bottle of white wine chilling and Marta prepared a delicious lunch for us."

They followed me to the back of the house and I heard Marin exclaim, "Look at this designer kitchen. It's to die for."

I laughed as I reached for the bottle of wine. "Make yourselves comfortable," I said, pointing to the table and chairs.

"No wonder you wanted to stay here," Berkley said. "What a great house."

"It is," I replied as I filled their wineglasses. "I'll show you around the grounds and the schoolhouse after we have a toast."

Grace reached for her glass and then touched the rim of ours before lifting it in the air. "Here's to the best sister and friend in the world. We're wishing you a lifetime of happiness, Chloe."

"To friendship and new chapters," Sydney said.

All of us took sips and I said, "Come on, bring your glasses. I want to show you the schoolhouse and the fishpond."

With Basil leading the way, we walked outside. I reached into my pocket for the key and unlocked the door of the old schoolhouse. "Welcome to Dreamweaver," I said, gesturing with my hand as we stepped inside. I walked toward the back and told them, "And also welcome to Nirvana Tea and Coffee."

"Oh, Chloe," Marin exclaimed. "This is absolutely perfect."

"It is," Sydney agreed, looking around.

"It's exactly as you described it." Grace shot me a huge smile.

"Wow, I love it," Berkley said and then I saw an odd expression cross her face.

"What? What is it?"

She waved a hand in the air. "Nothing to be alarmed about, but I feel a presence in the air."

"What?" I gasped. "Like a ghost?"

Berkley laughed. "Could be. But it's friendly energy. Almost playful."

"There she goes again," Marin said. "Your metaphysical side is showing."

I recalled that Berkley also sold crystals and gemstones at her chocolate shop; she had a firm belief in energy or anything paranormal.

"Hey, nothing to be worried about. Really."

That might well be, but Berkley had no knowledge of my dreams or the woman in red.

"Okay, enough hocus pocus," Grace said. "I absolutely love this shop. And how nice that customers will be able to enter from that gate in the driveway." She walked over to the French doors and looked out. "Oh, is that where Mavis Anne lives now?"

I nodded. "Yes, she lives there with her brother, David, and his partner, Clive. You'll get to meet everybody while you're here. Come on, I'll show you the fishpond."

We walked back outside and through the archway, where exclamations of appreciation filled the air.

"How beautiful."

"What a tranquil place to sit and chill out."

"Oh, look at the butterflies," Berkley said, pointing toward the far end of the water. "And I just love koi fish."

We were heading back to the patio when I heard Mavis Anne

holler, "Yoo hoo, Chloe?" and looked over to see her coming through the gate. "Am I interrupting?"

"Not at all," I said, walking over to give her a hug and lead her toward the patio. "Come and meet everyone."

I got her situated in a chair and put my hand on her shoulder. "I'd like you all to meet the illustrious Mavis Anne Overby—my friend, my benefactor, and my business partner. This is my sister, Grace, and my friends Sydney, Marin, and Berkley."

"Welcome to Koi House," Mavis Anne said with a huge smile on her face. "We are so delighted to have you here."

Her use of the pronoun *we* wasn't lost on me.

Greetings were exchanged. I ran into the house to get the bottle of wine and another wineglass.

"I hope you'll all have a wonderful visit," I heard Mavis Anne say when I walked back outside.

"Oh, I know we will," Sydney said. "We've certainly missed Chloe on the island, but I can see she's very happy here."

Mavis Anne shot me a wink. "Yes, it took a bit of convincing, but I think Chloe feels at home here. Thanks," she said, reaching for her wineglass. "So what do you gals have planned for the rest of the day?"

"Well, we'll have lunch and then get the car unloaded," I told her. "And then, we're just going to chill out and catch up on news. Yarrow is planning to come by, isn't she?"

Mavis Anne laughed. "Oh, yes, she's quite eager to meet everybody. She said to tell you she'll stop by around four after she closes the tea shop."

"It's so nice that she'll be opening her new place right in the yarn shop," Marin said.

Mavis took a sip of wine and nodded. "Yes, if not for Chloe, I'm not sure that would have ever happened. I've been trying to convince her for years to open her tea shop in the old schoolhouse, but it took Chloe committing to the yarn shop before my niece would agree."

"And this is the house you grew up in?" Sydney asked.

"Yes. Chloe probably told you that my father was the doctor in town and he bought this house shortly after my parents were married. It was a wonderful place to grow up. David and I have such fond memories of our childhoods here."

"But you're living next door now? You must miss your own house."

Mavis Anne looked at Berkley. "Yes, I moved in with my brother in February when I had a nasty fall that required knee surgery. It was difficult to navigate the stairs here and I have a very nice bedroom on the first floor at his house. Besides, I must admit that between David and Clive, they've managed to spoil me quite lavishly." She let out a chuckle. "So no, I really don't miss Koi House, and having Chloe here makes me miss it even less. I plan to stay put because David and Clive insist I'm no bother and they love having me there. They could be fibbing, but that's okay."

All of us laughed. Mavis said, "Well, I don't want to intrude on your visit, Chloe, but I wanted to come over and say hello. If I don't see you before you leave, all of you have a wonderful stay."

We watched Mavis Anne walk toward the gate with the assist of her cane.

"Oh, she's a true gem," Sydney said. "No wonder you love her."

"She really is," Grace agreed. "Such a sweet woman. She reminds me a bit of Aunt Maude."

Berkley and Marin nodded.

"Yes," I said. "She's a keeper." I slapped the side of my thigh. "Okay, ladies, we've had our wine. Time for lunch."

# Chapter 28

Everybody raved about the shrimp salad lunch that Marta had prepared that morning. Served with rice pilaf and followed by Marta's famous Polish paczki for dessert, the food was a hit.

"Oh, my God," Sydney said. "The paczki are similar to a jelly donut, but yet they're not even close."

"I know," I told her. "They're unique. She made them for the knitting group last week and I thought I died and went to heaven."

"Cripes, if I lived here and had Marta available, I would have put on twenty pounds by now," Berkley said. "But you look like you've lost weight."

I laughed and told her I was sure it was due to all the walking I'd been doing.

When we finished up our coffee, I said, "I hate to bring up the subject of work, but we really do have to get the cars unloaded."

I heard a collective groan before Marin said, "Yup, you're right. We have to work off those calories anyway. Let's go."

An hour later we had managed to get everything inside and up to my room. Since I planned to store the bins of yarn in my large walk-in closet, I told everybody just to stack them in the hallway for now. I needed to do some rearranging of the closet and my yarn stash before I got the bins put away properly.

"Now it's time to relax and play," I said as we trooped into the kitchen. "You guys grab your knitting projects and I'll get the wine. We can sit on the patio. You need to catch me up on all the Cedar Key news."

Once the wine was poured and everybody settled, I said, "Okay, so what's happened since I left?"

Marin laughed. "You're kidding, right? Nothing ever happens on Cedar Key."

"Oh, but that's not true," Grace said. "Shelby Sullivan has a new book coming out in the fall and there's a rumor that Polly might be closing the Curl Up And Dye."

I let out a gasp. "No! Polly's owned that hair salon for ages. What's going on?"

"Well, I heard that business is way down. The bulk of her clientele have either died or they're getting up there in age. The young kids do their hair themselves or they go to Chiefland, so she's really slow. But Polly's in her late sixties now and has been having some knee problems. Looks like she could end up with a knee replacement."

"What a shame," I said. "And Dora? How's she doing?"

"Fit as a fiddle," Marin said. "Nothing can keep my mother down. The yarn shop is now officially closed but she seems fine about it. Since she lost Oliver . . ."

"Oliver's gone?" He seemed fine the last time I saw him and I'd thought he was doing well for an older dog.

"Oh, I'm sorry. I thought you knew. Yeah, he passed away in his sleep just after you left the island. I guess my mom didn't want to say anything on the phone. She took it pretty bad. But now with the yarn shop closed, she's giving some serious thought to getting another dog."

"What a shame. Oliver was a legend. Going to the school for the reading program with the kids. And spending time at the yarn shop. Everybody loved him."

Marin nodded. "Yeah, she misses him a lot, so I'm hoping she'll get another dog."

I felt a wave of sadness wash over me and Sydney confirmed it when she said, "I know it's the life cycle, but so many are now gone who were there when I first moved to Cedar Key. Both Sybile and Saren are gone, Mr. Al, Maybelle Brewster, your aunt Maude." She let out a deep sigh.

We were silent for a few moments, lost in our own thoughts.

"How's Monica doing?" I asked. "It's a shame she couldn't make it over here too."

Sydney nodded. "I know. She really wanted to come but she and Adam have had this family vacation planned all year. Oh, she's doing great. The triplets are getting so big and Clarissa Jo—she's as delightful as ever. She's thirteen, but so far she's not exhibiting any of those nasty teenage traits."

We all laughed and I asked Grace about Suellen. "Do you think she'll stay in Gainesville?"

"I'm not sure. I forgot to tell you on the phone, she's met somebody. He's a professor at the university and they've really hit it off, but he's taking a new position at the University of North Carolina. However, he has asked her to join him there and I think she might do it."

"Oh, that's great," I said and felt a twinge of regret on the emptiness of my own love life. "I'm really happy for her."

"Well, I have some news," Grace said and a smile lit up her face.

"You're pregnant," Berkley blurted out.

Grace laughed. "No, but it's not for lack of trying. Lucas has decided to close the bookshop right after Christmas."

"Oh, we thought that might be coming," Marin said.

I nodded. "So does this mean you're going to be relocating to France?"

"Yes, we made our decision while we were over there. Paris is wonderful but we think we'd like to be in the country to raise Solange. So we did research on a lot of villages in the south near Lucas's family and found one we like a lot. We also found the perfect home, a restored farmhouse just outside town. Making our decision final is the fact that the owner of the local bookshop is selling and it would be perfect for Lucas."

I jumped up to run and hug my sister. "Oh, Grace! I'm so happy for you. I know how much you and Lucas have wanted this."

"That *is* exciting news, Grace," Sydney said. "But we'll miss you."

"I know, but we'll have lots of spare bedrooms in the house so all of you must come to visit. You can fly right into Toulouse airport and it's only about a one-hour drive to where we'll be living."

"I'll book a flight for Saxton and me next week," Berkley said and we laughed.

Sydney let out a deep sigh. "Gosh, all of a sudden I'm starting to feel so old. So much has happened and so much has changed since I first arrived on Cedar Key to stay with Ali at the B and B. Marriages and births and deaths, people coming to the island, people leaving the island. I never could have realized when Stephen died and I made the decision to go to Cedar Key all the patterns of change that would follow."

I heard the melancholy tone in her voice and I nodded. "Yeah, I think you said it a little while ago—it's called the cycle of life."

"Right," Sydney said, holding her wineglass in the air. "And here's to life."

"I'll drink to that," I heard Yarrow say as she came walking through the gate.

"Hey," I said. "I'm glad you could make it." I made the introductions and told her to pull up a chair. "I'll get another bottle and another wineglass."

When I returned, Berkley and Yarrow were talking about the old schoolhouse.

I poured wine into a glass and said, "Berkley thinks there could be a presence in there."

"Thanks," Yarrow said, reaching for the glass. "And I'm not at all surprised."

Yup, she definitely did have strands of hippie running through her.

"You're not?" I asked.

She shook her head. "Not at all. First of all, so much of the land around here was once owned by the Indians. Some of the burial places have been preserved, but one can't know where they all are."

"Right," Marin said. "Same thing in Cedar Key."

Yarrow nodded. "So who knows what energy has remained. But Berkley said it's a lighthearted energy, so I don't think we need to worry."

I laughed. "Okay, I'll trust both of you on that one. I guess time will tell."

# Chapter 29

It had been such a fun afternoon. Yarrow stayed for a couple of hours, and even though I tried to convince her to have dinner with us, she declined. I knew everybody loved meeting her and enjoyed her company.

We took a vote on whether to go out for dinner, cook, or order a pizza delivery. Pizza won.

"That was really delicious," Berkley said. "I'm glad we chose the pizza."

"Right, plus with a little wine in us we didn't have to drive," Grace said.

"A little?" I questioned.

"Oh, hey, you only get four glasses out of one bottle and there's five of us, so going through a couple bottles sounds about right," Berkley said and we laughed.

I got up to clear the patio table. "More wine or tea?" I asked.

I heard a chorus of tea.

Grace jumped up. "I'll help."

I stacked the dishwasher while she prepared the tea.

"I'm so happy for you, Chloe. I can see you just love it here and you've found some good friends in Mavis Anne and Yarrow."

I nodded. "I agree and you haven't even met Maddie yet. She said she'd try to get by tomorrow before you leave. But I'm also very happy for you and Lucas. Gosh, who would have thought when we lived in Brunswick that you'd end up moving to France."

Grace nodded. "Yeah, Beau and all of that now seem like a lifetime ago, and in many ways I guess it was."

Once again I marveled at how Grace had forgiven me for what I'd done to her concerning Beau Hamilton.

After we enjoyed tea and homemade cookies, courtesy of Marta, we produced our knitting projects once again. We sat outside on the patio until darkness forced us into the living room and we'd changed into our comfy nightclothes. I turned on some soft jazz on the radio and everyone settled back for more knitting and gossip.

All of a sudden Berkley started laughing. "Geez, I just thought of something. We really are old fuddy-duds. We're so low key compared to Shelby's gathering last year with her friends."

We joined her laughter and agreed. "Oh, I don't think we'd have one bit of trouble pulling off a gathering like that, but I think the day we had was perfect for us."

"Right," Grace said. "Besides, we didn't want to be too rowdy and have poor Chloe dealing with the Ormond Beach police on a disturbance call."

This brought forth another round of laughter.

It was past eleven when we all trooped upstairs to bed. Grace had done up her Aerobed with the linens I gave her and was sitting cross-legged while I dangled over the edge of my bed so we could talk.

In the privacy of the bedroom, with just the two of us, she said, "Okay. So what gives with this Chadwick Price?"

I let out a deep sigh. "Well, you know how they say truth is stranger than fiction. I'm here to say, trust me, it *is*."

"What do you mean?"

"Chadwick Price is the brother of Aaron Price."

"Okay, and who is he?"

"The bastard that date-raped me back in college."

Grace leaned forward as her hand flew to her mouth. "No! How on earth did you find this out?"

"The day we were going on that boat ride, I saw an older photo of both of them in Chadwick's living room. I may not have ever known his name—but I never forgot his face."

Grace jumped up to curl beside me on the bed and flung her arm over my shoulder, pulling me close. "Oh, God. I'm so sorry. Does Chadwick know?"

"No. And I don't plan to tell him."

"Wow," was all she said.

"Yeah, wow is right."

"Geez, who would ever think you'd come face to face with his photo over thirty years later."

"Yup."

"So where is he now? Oh, God, don't tell me he lives in this area too?"

"No. He's dead. Passed away from cancer of the pancreas about twenty-five years ago." I went on to explain how Chadwick had come to see his brother wasn't the idol he'd grown up thinking he was.

Grace nodded. "So it sounds like he learned a lot about him—and not good things—before his brother died."

"Yeah, but when all is said and done. Aaron was his *brother*. Blood ties are strong."

"Is that why you don't want to tell him what happened?"

I blew air out my lips. "To be honest, I'm not really sure why I don't want to tell him. I just know I want nothing to do with Chadwick."

"Hmm," was all Grace said.

I sat up to face her. "Hmm? What does that mean?"

"Well, don't get mad at me, Chloe. But it sounds like you're taking your anger over what happened out on Chadwick. Don't you think it might be a little misplaced?"

"I have thought about that and you could be right. All I know is I could never forgive Aaron Price for what he did."

"And you can't forgive Chadwick because of association."

"Something like that."

"That's a shame because he sounds like a really nice guy and you seemed to be enjoying his company."

"He is and I was."

"And your plan is to avoid him forever? Ormond Beach isn't as small as Cedar Key, but that might not be possible."

I remained silent and then she hit her palm along the side of her head. "Oh, geez. Weren't you supposed to go to a fund-raiser at his house on the Fourth?"

"Yeah. I'm not going. I already told Yarrow."

"So she knows what happened?"

I nodded. "I told her the whole story but she didn't voice an opinion one way or the other. Although I got the feeling she feels pretty much like you do. I'm blaming the wrong person."

"What does Mavis Anne have to say about it?"

"She doesn't know. She also doesn't know yet that I'm not going to the fund-raiser. I can only claim to be sick so many times. So I have no clue what I'm going to tell her."

"It seems that you're unable to separate Chadwick from Aaron."

"I'd say that's exactly what the problem is. And while I might realize this up here"—I pointed to my head—"there's no way I feel it in here," I said, pointing to my heart.

Grace nodded. "I understand. I remember once when Aunt Maude told me it's one thing to logically know something in your head, but if you don't feel it in your heart, you can't go forward."

I couldn't help but wonder if Aunt Maude had said that to Grace when she was trying to get her to reconcile with me.

"Damn. Life is tough," I told my sister.

"That it is," she said, pulling me into an embrace.

# Chapter 30

Despite the conversation of the night before, I woke Saturday morning from a dreamless sleep feeling refreshed and rested. I heard Grace snoring lightly and looked down to see her sprawled across the entire length of the queen-size Aerobed. I smiled. Poor Lucas. I wondered if he was able to get any room in bed.

I glanced at the bedside clock and saw it was just going on seven. Later than I usually slept but Grace and I had been awake till after midnight talking. Basil woke and walked from the end of the bed to come up and greet me at the same time I heard Grace stirring.

She yawned and sat up, hair going every which way, and rubbed her eyes. Giving a stretch of her arms and getting up, she said, " 'Morning. Bathroom." And headed that way.

I went downstairs to start the coffee and saw the guest room doors were still closed. After using the bathroom on the first floor, I headed to the kitchen. I removed banana bread and cranberry bread from the fridge and filled the coffeemaker.

"Gosh, I slept so well," I heard Grace say and turned around to see her in her Hello Kitty pajamas. I smiled, knowing that Solange had a matching set.

"Oh, that's good. Coffee will be ready shortly."

"Yeah . . . the only thing is . . . I had the strangest dream. Well . . . at least I *think* it was a dream."

I hadn't confided in Grace about my dreams since arriving in Ormond Beach and felt a shiver go through me. "Really? About what?"

She leaned against the counter, crossing her arms, and I could see she was pulling on her memory to reconstruct it. "Well, there was a woman. Actually, it seemed like she was in our room. Standing in front of the French doors. It was the craziest thing because she was wearing a red evening gown."

I gripped the side of the sink. "What did she do?"

"Nothing. She just nodded to me and gave me the most beautiful smile. She was a knockout. Really beautiful but I have no idea who she was."

What the hell was going on?

"Did she say anything?" I heard myself whisper.

"No. Nothing. Chloe, are you okay? You look pale."

I let out a deep breath. "I need to tell you about the dreams I've been having since I moved here." I went on to share with her my own dreams about the lady in the red evening gown.

"Wow, that's amazing, Chloe. So do you think it really could be Emmalyn? Mavis Anne's sister?"

"I have no idea. You tell *me*. You're the one who believes in this stuff."

"I'm as stumped as you are. And see, there's a difference. Yours were bona fide dreams. Mine . . . I'm not so sure."

"What are you saying? That she was actually in our room? That's nuts!"

"I'm not sure what I'm saying, Chloe. Didn't you tell me that Mavis or David had told you how much Emmalyn loved this house? That she had said she'd never leave it?"

"Yeah."

"Well, maybe she never did. But no matter what's going on . . . I seriously doubt that she's here to hurt you. Most likely—she's trying to help you."

Following a breakfast of coffee with some of the baked breads, we took turns showering and getting dressed. It had been decided that I'd drive the four of them around the Ormond Beach area so they could see my new hometown, and then we'd stop at LuLu's for a late brunch.

Just before we were ready to leave, my cell rang and I saw it was Maddie.

"Hey," I said. "Are you going to be able to get away this afternoon before everyone leaves?"

"No, I'm afraid not. That's why I'm calling. I just got a few emergency orders and I'm going to be stuck here. But I was thinking if you guys are out and about, maybe you could pop into the florist shop and I can at least meet your sister and friends."

"Sounds great," I told her. "We're heading out now and can stop by before we begin our little sightseeing tour."

"Terrific," Maddie said. "I really *do* have to hire a helper. See you soon."

We stopped by the florist shop, drove north, then south on A1A, drove all around town and by one o'clock we were seated outside at LuLu's enjoying a delicious brunch.

"This has been so much fun, Chloe," Sydney said. "Thank you for inviting us."

"I agree," Berkley said.

"It was nice to see where you're living and how you've settled in. If I didn't know better, I'd say you've lived here forever." Marin gave me a big smile.

Grace leaned over to give me a hug. "It really is like this place was meant to be for you. And once the yarn shop opens, you'll really be in your element."

"It was my pleasure having you, but you have to promise to come back over when the shop opens. I want you to see it all decorated and functioning."

Sydney laughed. "You're kidding, right? Keep us away from a yarn shop? Never!"

By the time we drove back to my house and they loaded their cars with luggage, it was three o'clock. Amid hugs and promises to call and email, I could feel moisture stinging my eyes. I stood on the porch, feeling all weepy, with Basil in my arms, waving good-bye as they pulled out of the driveway.

I put Basil down on the porch. "Come on, fella. It's just the two of us again."

He followed me into the house and I headed to the kitchen to prepare a cup of tea. I had just settled down on the patio with my mug and my knitting when my cell rang. I saw Henry Wagner's name and a smile crossed my face.

"Hi, Henry. How are you?"

"I'm good. And you? I'm not interrupting anything, am I?"

"No, not at all. Just sitting on the patio with my knitting and feeling a bit sad because my sister and friends left a little while ago."

"I'm sure you enjoyed their visit but I'm sorry you're feeling sad. The house always seems empty after company, though, doesn't it?"

"Yeah. So what are you up to? Are you in the Blue Ridge Mountains now?"

"No, I'm heading down there tomorrow. So today I'll be packing up and getting things together. I've rented a cabin in the area. I thought that would be better than a hotel room since I'll be there for a couple months."

"Will Delilah be going with you?"

I heard a chuckle come across the line. "Oh, yes, she'll be with me. That's the nice thing about freelance photography. I can make my own schedule and have my girl with me on most of the shoots."

"Oh, I thought you said you just dabbled in photography. I didn't realize you have a career taking pictures. So do you work for a company or a magazine?"

I heard a slight hesitation before he said, "Yes, I'm contracted with *National Geographic*."

"Oh, wow." I really didn't know much about this man at all. "That's impressive and you're quite modest about it. Gosh, I bet that's interesting work. Does it involve a lot of travel?"

"It did years ago, but I've cut way back on my assignments. After Lilian passed away about ten years ago, I realized that life really was too short. Unfortunately, I was forced to travel a lot during most of our married years. But when she was diagnosed with cancer, I began to cut back more and more so we could enjoy what time she had left together."

I detected wistfulness in his tone. "I'm sorry about your wife. Any children?"

"Unfortunately, no. We did try but it wasn't meant to be. How about you? Were you married?"

"Yes, married for almost thirty years and then Parker decided to trade me in for a younger model. He's remarried, lives in Savannah and has a young daughter, but we had two sons together. One lives and works in Atlanta and my other son, Eli, is married and moving from the Boston area to Jacksonville at the end of September for a position with an accounting firm."

"I'm sure you'll enjoy having him so much closer. Are you a grandmother yet?"

I laughed. "Not yet, but fingers crossed it won't be too much longer."

"Well, I suppose I should get moving here and continue with my packing. I'll be down in Georgia by the end of the week, so I'll give you a call then. Have a great week, Chloe. I've enjoyed talking to you."

"Same here," I said. "And have a safe trip."

I disconnected the call and realized this was the first time we'd had a personal conversation, rather than talking about things related to the rental of the condo or Ormond Beach. And I discovered that I rather liked it.

# Chapter 31

I had just finished folding a load of clothes from the dryer when I heard Mavis Anne at the back door.

"Come on in," I called.

"Good morning, Chloe. I just wanted to double-check about the party Saturday and make sure you found something to wear."

I gestured toward the breakfast area. "Sit down and join me. I just brewed a pot of coffee."

"Oh, thanks. So are you all set? Yarrow finally decided what she'll be wearing so I wanted to check with you."

I placed a mug in front of her and joined her at the table. "I'm not going to be attending."

"What do you mean? Why on earth not?"

I let out a deep sigh. "I don't expect you to understand but I have my reasons."

I saw her eyebrows arch before she said, "You're right. I don't understand at all. What's going on?"

I guess I did owe it to Mavis Anne to give her the truth. "Something happened a long time ago. When I was in college." I went on to tell her the story.

"Oh, my. I see." She took a sip of coffee and then shook her head. "No, actually, I don't understand at all. What does any of this have to do with Chadwick?" I could almost see a lightbulb going off in her head as her hand flew to her mouth. "Oh, my word! Was that fellow Chadwick?"

"No, no," I hastened to assure her. "But it was his brother, Aaron."

"Oh. Okay." She continued to stare at me from across the table. "Chloe, I'm really confused. What happened to you was horrific and shouldn't happen to any woman. But I fail to see how Chadwick is connected to this."

Frankly, I was getting a bit annoyed at being told this once again. "You don't have to understand it. It didn't happen to you. But I could never forgive Aaron Price for what he did, and Chadwick is his brother. I'd prefer not to have any contact with him."

After a few moments, she nodded. "I see."

I felt a twinge of guilt. "I'm sorry for snapping at you, but . . ."

"But having any type of relationship with Chadwick would be like forgiving his brother?"

"Something like that. Yes."

"So it seems that you can't separate your feelings for the two men and forgive Chadwick for what his brother did." Mavis Anne nodded and we both remained silent for a few moments.

"Well, I'm glad you shared this with me, Chloe, and I'm so very sorry about what happened to you. I can't say that I agree with your thinking or your decision . . . but I do respect it. Okay," she said, reaching for her cane and standing up. "I guess it's settled then and you're not going. So you will call Chadwick to let him know, right?"

"No, I hadn't planned on it. You can give my regrets when you go."

"No, I won't do that. Where are your manners?"

I felt like I was twelve and being admonished by Aunt Maude.

"Okay," I mumbled. "I'll call him."

"Good," she said before leaving.

I had put some marinated chicken breasts into the oven for supper, poured myself a glass of pinot grigio, and settled on the patio to get a few more rows of the shawl finished when I saw Yarrow coming through the gate from the driveway.

"Hey," she said. "Want some company?"

"Sure. Help yourself to some wine from the fridge."

She returned with her glass and sat down. "So . . . you told Aunt Mavis your story."

I nodded. "She told you?"

"Oh, yeah." She took a sip of wine. "She called me earlier today."

"And?"

"Well, of course she feels terrible about your experience, but she's having a hard time understanding why Chadwick is the one to pay the price."

"Yes, her disapproval was obvious. Does she hate me?"

Yarrow reached over to pat my hand. "Oh, Chloe, don't be silly. Of course she doesn't hate you. She's just having a hard time with the fact that Chadwick is being blamed for something he didn't do."

I could see that opinion was quickly becoming the general consensus but I remained silent.

"So," Yarrow said. "Don't Isabelle and Haley arrive in a few weeks?"

I was grateful she'd changed the subject. "Yes, they do. Haley called me this morning and she's so excited about coming down here. I think it'll be good for her."

"Probably good for both of them. Didn't you say Isabelle's husband left her last year?"

"Yeah, and apparently the latest update is that he plans to be remarried by the end of the year. The divorce will be final next month."

"Makes me happy I'm still single."

"Did you ever have anybody special in your life?" I realized that was something we'd never discussed.

"Oh, sure. The usual relationships that seemed to be growing and then . . . *poof!* For various reasons they just dissolved and went nowhere. But I have to say, I like where I'm at now in my life. No commitments to anybody but myself. I don't even have a pet I'm responsible for. I can do what I want, when I want."

I nodded and took a sip of wine. "Yeah, there's a lot to be said for being independent. Although I have to admit that when I was married, I did enjoy it. I liked that connection to a male partner. It just turned out he wasn't the right male partner."

"Oh, hey, I had an idea about my new tea shop and wanted to run it past you."

"Sure. What is it?"

"Well, I was thinking that it might be fun to set up a delivery service."

"I don't understand."

"I don't think anybody else is doing this in the area. I'd go around beforehand talking to various businesses, and I'd set up an arrangement with employees of dentist offices, hair and nail salons, doctor's offices, that kind of thing. They'd have a choice of various baked goods each day, along with coffee or tea."

"And you'd drive around delivering the items?"

"Right. The deliveries would only be in Ormond Beach and they'd have to be between seven thirty and eleven. So the muffins or breads wouldn't interfere with lunchtime."

"I love it. I can even picture a beautiful large wicker basket carrying the goodies and each item labeled with people's names so there wouldn't be any mix-ups. The only problem is how on earth could you be out doing these deliveries and run the tea shop at the same time?"

Yarrow nodded. "That's my dilemma. I would definitely have to hire somebody to do the deliveries, because you're right, I couldn't do it. But you think the concept is a good one?"

"I do. Gosh, I remember mornings that I had to open the yarn shop on Cedar Key and I was running late with no time for breakfast. I could prepare coffee when I got there, but it would have been so nice to know that within twenty minutes somebody would be dropping me off some yummy banana bread or a muffin. So yes, I think many employees in the area would welcome a service like this."

"Great. I've been giving it a lot of thought and I agree. I think it could work."

"Now you just have to find a reliable delivery person."

"True. Well, I should get going."

"Can you stay for dinner? I have chicken breasts in the oven and rice and a veggie to go with it."

"Oh, that sounds good. Sure, if you don't mind."

"I'd welcome the company. Come on, you can set the table."

"So are you going to call Chadwick to decline the invitation?" she asked as we walked into the house.

"Yeah. I told your aunt that I would."

I didn't call till Saturday morning. And as luck would have it, I got Chadwick's voice mail. So I left a brief message saying I was sorry, but I wouldn't be able to attend the fund-raiser that evening.

Hey, Mavis Anne said to call him. She didn't specify that I had to actually speak to him.

# Chapter 32

The next few weeks flew by. I had gone shopping with Mavis Anne and Yarrow, and the furniture for the yarn shop had been purchased with a delivery date a week before our grand opening. Yarn deliveries were arriving and Mavis and I pored over more catalogs, putting in orders for needles and various accessories. Chloe's Dream was working up beautifully and I was pleased with the results. Henry and I continued our phone conversations, and I felt I was getting to know him better. But I hadn't heard one word from Chadwick. Part of me was relieved but part of me felt guilty for just blowing him off. Still, it seemed he'd taken the hint. Mavis and Yarrow had refrained from mentioning anything about the fund-raiser in my company.

Isabelle and Haley would be arriving later in the afternoon and I was very much looking forward to their visit. I really didn't know Isabelle all that well, and this would give us a chance to bond.

I ran upstairs to check on last-minute details in the spare bedrooms. Everything seemed to be in order. Fresh linens on the beds, vases of brightly colored flowers from Maddie's shop on the bureaus, and the sun streaming through the windows created a cozy feel.

I was in the kitchen preparing a pot of coffee that I thought Isabelle might enjoy when Basil began barking and ran to the front door. I glanced at the wall clock and saw it was just three. It must be them.

I opened the front door and saw an SUV parked in the driveway. Basil went flying out to the gate, barking and dancing in circles. Isabelle emerged from the driver's side, stretched and smiled when she saw me standing on the porch. A few moments later the passenger door opened and Haley got out. My heart fell. She had indeed put on quite a few pounds in the year since I'd seen her. In addition to the extra weight, her overall appearance was sloppy. Limp strands of brunette hair fell to her shoulders. Despite the July heat she was wearing black leggings that only seemed to accentuate her size and a faded, oversize T-shirt dotted with stains. It was hard to believe this was the same girl I'd met in Atlanta a year before.

In contrast, Isabelle looked like she was ready for a fashion magazine photo shoot. She was sporting a short, chic hairstyle with blond highlights catching the sun. Tall and slim, she wore a white tank top and mint green capris that fit her perfectly. Makeup and jewelry completed her alluring look. Poor Haley must feel so inferior next to her mother.

"Hey," I called out, walking down the steps. "Welcome. I hope you had a good drive down."

I opened the gate and walked toward the car with Basil at my heels. He immediately ran to Haley, who reached down and scooped him up. I could hear her murmuring to him as I went to hug Isabelle.

"Yeah. It was pretty good. We would have probably been here a little sooner, but I couldn't resist stopping at the outlets up in St. Augustine on I-95." She stuck out one foot wearing a gold sandal encrusted with gemstones. "And I'm so glad I did. See what I found."

"Pretty," I said, walking toward Haley. "I'm so glad you're here." She was still holding Basil but I pulled her into a hug. "We're going to have a great two weeks. Come on, I'll help you take in your luggage."

"Me too," was all Haley said as she continued to hold Basil.

Isabelle flipped the hatchback open and I reached for a piece of luggage. I couldn't help but notice empty wrappers of candy, crumpled-up chip bags, and crushed Coke cans strewn around the luggage.

"Hey, young lady, when we get inside you are to get a trash bag from Chloe and clean up this mess." Isabelle shook her head in annoyance. "I swear that kid ate her way down here from Atlanta."

"Come on," I said. "Let's get you inside and settled."

"Oh, this house is lovely, Chloe," Isabelle said, following me up the stairs. "No wonder you wanted to stay here."

"Thanks. Yeah, it's pretty special. Here's your room," I told her, pointing to the room on my right. "And Haley, you're right down here."

I walked in behind Haley and deposited her luggage on the deacon bench. "I hope you'll like it."

Still clutching Basil in her arms, she looked around and nodded. "It's pretty," was all she said.

I could see that the extra weight wasn't the only thing that had changed about Haley.

"Okay, then. Well, you can get unpacked and I'll be in the kitchen at the back of the house when you're ready to come down."

"Thanks," she said, flopping on the bed with Basil.

I stuck my head into Isabelle's room. "Everything okay?"

"Oh, gosh, yes. This room is gorgeous, Chloe. Thank you so much for inviting us to spend some time here."

"My pleasure. I'll be in the kitchen. Just go through the living room to the back of the house."

"Okay, thanks."

I pulled mugs from the cabinet and debated whether to put out the lemon squares that Marta had prepared for me. But from the evidence in the car, it didn't appear that Haley was on any healthy food plan. I placed them on a small platter and then flipped the switch on the coffeemaker.

"Chloe, this house is simply gorgeous. You were so fortunate to find it."

I turned around and smiled at Isabelle. "Sometimes I think it was more a case of the house finding me."

"And this kitchen . . . my God, it's every chef's dream."

She walked to the French doors and exclaimed over the patio and garden area. "It's all so pretty. Oh, is that where the yarn shop will be?" She pointed toward the old schoolhouse.

"Yeah, it is. I'll take you out there later and also show you the fishpond. Ready for coffee?"

She waved a hand in the air. "I'd much prefer something stronger, if you have it."

"Sure. How about a glass of wine?"

"Definitely."

I filled two glasses and passed one to her. "Cheers and welcome to Koi House."

"Cheers," she repeated.

"Where's Haley? Is she coming down?"

She took another sip of wine and shook her head. "Who knows about that kid? Honestly, Chloe, I'm at my wits' end with her. Her weight is out of control. She takes no interest in what she looks like.

Her attitude is barely tolerable. You have no idea what I've gone through this past year. Maybe if she paid more attention to her appearance, she'd have some friends and not be bullied."

I was about to reply when I heard Haley say, "I'm sorry if I embarrass you, Mom, but it wouldn't make any difference if I looked like a teen film star. They just don't like me."

I spun around to see Haley and didn't miss the hurt expression on her face.

It didn't appear that Isabelle was going to retract what she'd said, so I walked over to pull Haley into an embrace. "You know what? You're probably very right. Mean girls are simply that. Mean girls. It doesn't have a thing to do with how *you* look, or how *you* act or what *you* do. It's about them, Haley, not you."

I felt her head nod against my shoulder as she returned my hug, and when she pulled away I saw the hint of a smile cross her lips.

"Can Basil go out in the yard?" she asked.

"Sure. But would you like something to eat or drink first?"

"No, thanks."

"The yarn shop is unlocked and the workers have gone for the day, so you can browse in there, and Basil will show you around the fishpond."

"Thanks," she said, following him out the door.

Isabelle let out an exasperated sigh. "She's driving me crazy, Chloe. I'm not sure we'll survive her teen years."

I let out a chuckle. "Trust me, you will. Come on; let's go sit on the patio." I noticed that her wineglass was empty. "A refill?" I asked.

"Sure."

I refilled her glass and we walked outside.

"This is so beautiful."

"I'll show you the yarn and tea shop," I said, and noticed that Haley was sitting on a bench in the fishpond area.

When we stepped inside, Isabelle gasped. "Oh, Chloe. It's perfect." She walked to the back to check out the tea shop. "What a great place for a business. I know you'll enjoy working here. By the way, I saw all the bins of yarn in the hallway upstairs. Is that for the shop?"

I laughed. "No, I'm ashamed to say that's my private stash. Grace brought those to me last week and I haven't had a chance to get the bins put away in my closet yet."

"You know, I've been thinking about learning how to knit. I thought maybe you could teach me while I'm here."

"Absolutely. I'd love to. No knitter ever turns down the chance to recruit a new knitter."

We walked back over to the patio area and Isabelle pointed over the fence. "Is that where Mavis Anne lives with her brother?"

I nodded. "Yes, with David and his partner, Clive. You'll meet all of them while you're here and Yarrow too."

"His partner? Is her brother gay?"

"Yeah, David and Clive have been together for years."

"Oh," was all she said.

"So do you hear anything from Roger?"

Isabelle took another sip of wine. "Well, the divorce will become final in a few weeks, so we got together to go over the details. He's really being quite generous with me financially. He's even agreed to foot the entire bill for Haley's college education."

"That's great. It takes a lot of the burden off of you. So do you think you'll stay in the house till Haley graduates high school?"

"I have no idea what I'm doing. Most days I feel like I'm spinning in circles. Haley is so obviously unhappy and I think she actually blames me for the breakup with her father."

"But that's silly. He's the one who left you for somebody else, right?"

"Yeah, but that doesn't matter to Haley. All she knows is that her life as she knew it is gone forever. Much like mine is."

I thought back to when Parker left me and let out a sigh. "I remember those days well. It's so scary to feel like you're drifting. Nothing solid to hold on to. While your old life is gone, you have to realize that new chapters are waiting for you. You just have to be brave and strong enough to open the book."

Isabelle nodded and a smile crossed her lips. "I'm beginning to see why Dad was attracted to you. You've been through a lot yourself, and yet . . ." She gestured around the garden area. "It seems you've ended up where you're supposed to be."

I smiled and patted her hand. "And I have no doubt that eventually you will too."

# Chapter 33

Over the next week Isabelle and Haley met Mavis Anne, David, Clive, and Yarrow, in addition to Maddie and Marta.

I looked up from the newspaper I was reading with my coffee when Isabelle walked into the kitchen.

"Mornin'," she mumbled.

"Coffee's ready," I told her.

She poured herself a mug and joined me at the table.

"Have you and Haley already had your walk?"

"Oh, yeah. We were both up at six and walking the beach with Basil within an hour."

"I don't know how you do it. I can barely get her to move away from her computer at home."

I wasn't sure how I'd accomplished this feat either. The night they'd arrived I just got the idea of mentioning to Haley that Basil and I loved walking the beach in the morning, hoping to entice her into an exercise regime. And it worked. She jumped at the idea, said she'd set her alarm and would be ready to go shortly after six. So for five days straight we had walked for an hour.

"Where is she now?" Isabelle questioned. "Gone back to bed?"

I laughed. "No. She's next door with Mavis Anne, working on her knitting."

"Good luck to her. I think I'm hopeless," she said, letting out a huge yawn.

Although Isabelle retired to her room by nine most evenings, I had a feeling she wasn't going to sleep, because she never arrived downstairs before ten in the morning.

"You'll catch on," I told her. "But you know the old saying, practice makes perfect."

"Hmm. So what's on the schedule for today?"

"Well, Haley wanted to go to the beach for a couple hours, so I thought I'd pack a picnic lunch for us and we could chill out there for the afternoon."

Isabelle yawned again. "If you don't mind, I think I'll just chill here. I have a bit of a headache."

"Sure, that's fine. There's Tylenol in your bathroom cabinet if you need some."

I got up to prepare a lunch for Haley and me. Having pulled out the wicker basket from the closet, I opened the fridge and began to fill the basket with turkey breast, cheese, rice cakes, and fresh fruit. I added four bottles of water and some napkins.

Then I sliced a couple of tomatoes and cucumbers and put them into a Tupperware container.

"That should do it," I said.

Isabelle was refilling her coffee and peered into the basket. "You don't honestly think Haley will eat that for lunch, do you? She's more a burger and fries kind of girl."

I laughed. "I don't think she is so much. I've only offered her healthy choices since she's been here and she hasn't complained at all."

Isabelle shrugged. "That's all great but I seriously doubt it'll last once we get back home."

It was one of those perfect afternoons to be on the beach. There was a great east wind coming off the Atlantic, which helped to diminish the heat and humidity of the day. The sun was strong and white, puffy clouds dotted the sky. I had parked in the lot at Andy Romano Park and we found a good spot to set up our beach chairs on the sand close to the restrooms and shaded picnic table area. Since it was a weekday, the beach wasn't overly crowded.

I didn't say anything when I noticed that Haley wasn't removing her shorts and T-shirt to reveal her bathing suit underneath. She settled herself in her chair, put on her sunglasses after applying sunscreen, and reclined her head back.

"This is so nice, Chloe. I never get to the beach in Atlanta. I hate living inland and not near the water."

"Yeah, I know what you mean. I've always lived very close to the water and I know I'd miss it terribly. Well, good, then. I'm glad we came today. It's too bad your mother couldn't join us."

"Whatever," was all she said.

After a few minutes, I said, "I hope you're enjoying your stay here."

She sat up straighter in her chair and looked at me. "Oh, I am, Chloe. I love it here. I'd love to stay here forever."

"But you don't have any friends here and—" I started to say.

Haley laughed. "Yeah, right. Like I have so many at home. You have no idea how much I dread going back to school next month."

"That's a shame. School should be fun. Well, at least a little bit."

"It's not for me. I'm not interested in the things the other girls are. Not that they'd invite me to join them."

"What *are* you interested in, Haley?"

She shot me a look of surprise. "Me?" she asked, as if nobody had ever bothered to ask her that question before.

I nodded.

"Well . . . I like music just like they do. But I also love to read, and I think they're lucky to get through a textbook. I love to draw and . . ."

"Really? I had no idea you enjoyed drawing. Anything in particular?"

"You won't laugh?"

"No, of course not."

"I like to draw fashions. Clothes. I know—" She let out a sarcastic chuckle. "I walk around looking like a fat, dowdy loser . . . but I love using my imagination and drawing clothes."

"Wow, Haley, I'm impressed. Are you thinking of becoming a fashion designer someday?"

"Yes, but my mother said if I don't lose some weight and start looking better, nobody will take me seriously."

"I'm not sure that's exactly true, but for health reasons, I do think eating well and exercising is important. You've done super since you've been here, Haley. We've walked every morning and you've been eating healthy food. You just have to continue doing the same when you go home."

"I doubt that will happen."

"Why not?"

She let out a sigh. "Well, I don't like walking alone and I have nobody to walk with. I even asked my mom if I could get a dog. I'd love to have a dog, and we could walk every day just like you do with Basil. And the food? My mom barely cooks anymore."

Now I sat up straighter in my chair. "What do you mean, she barely cooks? She cooked some very nice meals when I was at your house last year with your grandfather."

"I don't know what happened, but most nights we either get take-out or I have leftover pizza. Mom spends a lot of time in her room."

No wonder this poor kid had gained so much weight. What the hell was up with Isabelle being so irresponsible?

"It sounds like she's depressed," I said.

"Could be," Haley replied. "And Chloe? Thanks for being so nice to me. I hope you don't mind, but I consider you like a grandmother to me."

I felt my eyes well up with tears. "Mind?" I reached for her hand and gripped it. "I'm flattered you'd want me as your surrogate grandmother, Haley. I have no grandchildren and I couldn't ask for a better granddaughter."

Haley squeezed my hand and smiled. "Good. I never hear from Mom's mother and my dad's mother passed away when I was really small. And besides, Grandpa loved you and I think he'd be happy about us."

I thought Gabe would be happy too.

A few hours later we were packing up our picnic to go home when my cell rang. I looked at the caller ID to see it was Yarrow.

"Hey, what's up?" I said.

"Please don't worry—everything is fine. Really. I just wanted to let you know that Basil is over at my aunt's house."

"What? Is he okay? What happened?"

"He's fine, Chloe. Well . . . apparently . . . Isabelle had gone out to the store and when she came back, she left open the front door and the gate to the driveway. Basil escaped but thank God, he ran over to my aunt's house. But she refuses to let the little guy go back home and she's keeping him with her till you get back."

"We're on our way," I told her. "We're just packing up."

"I can't believe my mother was so irresponsible," Haley said as I pulled onto A1A.

"Neither can I."

Haley and I walked into David's home to find Mavis Anne sitting on the sofa with Basil curled up in her lap. As soon as he saw us, he jumped down and ran to greet us. Haley picked him up and I leaned over to place a kiss on top of his head.

"What the heck happened?" I said, flopping down in a chair.

"Well, you'll have to get the details from Isabelle, but I guess she went to the store, came back, and neglected to close the driveway gate and the front door. This little rascal ran off. It would have been much worse if he'd run out onto Granada Boulevard. I'm just very grateful he ran over here."

"So am I," I said as relief washed over me.

# Chapter 34

After eight days of Haley's visit, I began to notice a distinct change in her. Her attitude seemed to improve, she seemed perkier, and with Mavis Anne's diligent teaching, she was mastering the skill of knitting very quickly. But while Haley seemed headed in a good direction, I was concerned about Isabelle.

She had apologized profusely for what she called her stupidity concerning Basil. She told me she'd gone to the store to get something for her headache, came back and then went directly to her room to lie down. I thought it odd she'd found it necessary to go to the store since I'd told her there was Tylenol in her bathroom.

And over the past eight days, I'd come to see that wine seemed to be Isabelle's best friend. I certainly enjoyed a few glasses myself some days, but some days none at all. I noticed that not only had Isabelle been drinking every day since she'd arrived, but most days she had her first glass before noon. I also wondered about her retiring to her room so early in the evening, leaving Haley and me to watch a movie together or work on our knitting.

"I'm ready," Haley yelled up the stairs. "Are we going?"

"Yes," I called down. "Be right there."

I walked to Isabelle's room and knocked. "I'm coming," she called through the door.

It was agreed that today would be a shopping day at Volusia Mall.

"I'll be downstairs," I told her.

When I walked into the living room, I saw Haley sitting on the sofa, patiently waiting with Basil curled up beside her.

"Bet she doesn't go," Haley mumbled.

"No, she's going," I reassured her.

But ten minutes later Isabelle descended the stairs wearing no makeup and clothes she clearly would not be caught dead in for shopping.

"I don't think I'm going to . . ." she began to say.

I jumped up from the sofa. "Oh, yes, you are. I'm not sure what's going on, but you're going shopping with us like you promised. Your daughter is looking forward to this and she needs to get her new school clothes. So . . . back upstairs, into the shower, put yourself together, and we'll see you on the patio in one hour."

I wasn't sure if Isabelle realized she would be wrong to disagree or if she was taken aback at my adamant reaction, but no matter what she thought, she turned around and walked back upstairs.

Haley now jumped up from the sofa, raised her palm in the air for a high five and said, "Thanks."

After a successful shopping spree which I'm sure included every single store in the mall, I suggested we have dinner at LuLu's.

We were seated at a table outside. At six in the evening as the sun began to go down, the breeze off the ocean made it just perfect.

Both Isabelle and I ordered a glass of wine as we looked over the menu, and Haley chattered away about the new clothes she'd bought.

I had just decided on the fish selection with a salad when I heard a familiar voice. "Chloe. How nice to see you."

I looked up into the eyes of Chadwick Price and felt heat radiating up my neck.

"Oh . . . same here. How are you, Chadwick?"

"Fine, just fine," he said, but I saw his eyes were fixed on Isabelle.

"Oh . . . ah . . . I'd like you to meet Isabelle Wainwright and her daughter, Haley. Isabelle is Gabe's daughter and this is his granddaughter. They're visiting with me from Atlanta."

He reached across the table to shake Isabelle's hand.

"And this is Chadwick Price . . . a friend of mine."

"Very nice to meet you," he told her. I could be wrong, but I thought I saw a spark of interest fly between them as he held on to her a hand a moment longer than necessary.

"Same here," Isabelle said, a huge smile covering her face. "So do you also live in Ormond Beach?"

He gestured behind him. "Just up A1A in Ormond-by-the-Sea. Not very far from here."

"Chadwick owns a real estate agency," I told her.

"Oh, so if I was thinking about relocating here, then you'd be the guy to see," she said with a flirty tone to her voice.

He laughed and reached into his shirt pocket before passing her a business card. "Yes, that would be me. Here's my number in case you're looking for something in the area."

Isabelle really surprised me by saying, "If you're all alone, why don't you join us?"

His glance flew to me and then back to Isabelle. "I'd love to but I'm just here to pick up something to go. I've been on the road all day and popped in to bring dinner home. But thank you. I hope I'll see you again before you leave."

"That would be nice," she said before he walked inside the restaurant.

Both Haley and I stared at her.

"What?" she said, looking down as she fooled with the napkin in her lap.

"Mom!" Haley exclaimed. "Were you flirting with him?"

Isabelle was obviously flustered. She laughed as she waved a manicured hand in the air. "Don't be silly. He just seems like a nice guy. Right, Chloe?"

I nodded. "Yeah, he is."

We gave the waitress our order and a few minutes later I saw Isabelle smile and wave her hand in the air. I turned to see Chadwick walking toward the parking lot carrying a takeout bag.

*Interesting*, I thought. *Very interesting*.

"Thanks for asking Krystina to come over tomorrow for a sleepover," Haley said as our food arrived. "I don't think I've had a sleepover since I was ten. But . . . I hope she likes me."

"Of course she'll like you," I assured her. "Since she's only two years older than you, I thought it might be nice for you to have some company in your age group. Actually, I've never met her before, but if she's anything like her mother, you'll love her."

When we got home after dinner, I headed to the kitchen to prepare some herbal tea. After a long afternoon of shopping and walking the entire mall, I was ready to settle down to relax and knit.

"Mind if I have some of that?" Isabelle asked.

"Sure," I said and reached for another mug from the cabinet.

"So . . . how do you know this Chadwick?" she asked.

I explained how we'd met the day I drove over here, that he was the one who'd helped with the flat tire.

"Oh, right. I remember that. He's the one who stopped to help you? So . . . ah . . . is there anything special going on between you?"

No doubt about it. She was definitely interested in Chadwick Price.

"No. At least I don't think so. Initially there might have been. We had one dinner together. Strictly platonic. But no . . . nothing going on." And I realized as soon as I said that, it was true. I had no romantic feelings toward Chadwick and never would. I refrained from explaining to her the real reason why I felt this way and said nothing about his brother, Aaron. This was information she didn't need to know.

"Why?" I asked, passing her a mug of tea and heading to the living room.

"Oh, just wondering," she said, curling up in an easy chair. "Nice looking guy."

I smiled. *And you don't know the half of it,* I thought. *One of the wealthiest and most eligible bachelors in Volusia County.*

"He is," I said, before Haley bounded down the stairs to join us with Basil close at her heels.

"Mom?" she said, a few minutes later.

"Hmm?" Isabelle mumbled. Her mind was clearly on Chadwick Price.

"Did you mean what you said tonight?"

"About what?"

"When you told that guy that if you were thinking about relocating here he'd be the one to see? *Are* you really thinking about us moving here?"

Isabelle laughed. "Oh, I seriously doubt that, Haley."

When Haley remained silent, she asked, "Why? Would you like to move here?"

"I don't know. Maybe. It is a nice town. The people are friendly. We have the beach nearby. Lots of shopping and things to do."

"True, but you know I told you when you go back to school next month, I'm going to be looking for a job in the Atlanta area. So once that happens, it might be difficult to just uproot and relocate."

This was news to me. "I thought you were okay financially," I said. "I didn't realize you needed to work."

"I probably don't *need* to. I'm just feeling pretty useless hanging around the house all day. But with my lack of skills, I don't think a lot of employers will be fighting to hire me."

"See, Mom, you can really work anywhere. So why not here?"

It was easy to see that Haley had already warmed to the idea of becoming an Ormond Beach resident.

"I don't know, Haley. Let's drop it for now."

I saw the look of disappointment that crossed Haley's face. "Hey," I said. "Are you up for a game of Scrabble?"

"Definitely," she said, jumping up to get the game.

# Chapter 35

I was making my bed the following morning when I realized I hadn't dreamed about the woman in the red evening gown for a while. Maybe all of it had meant nothing and the dreams had ended.

I threw on a pair of shorts and a T-shirt and headed downstairs to find Haley already waiting for me in the kitchen.

"All set?" I asked, clipping Basil's leash to his collar.

"Yup, ready for our morning walk."

One of the reasons I loved walking the beach before seven was because it was fairly empty. We passed a few other walkers and joggers, but there was plenty of space and quiet.

"Do you think my mom might consider us moving here?" Haley asked as she kept up the brisk pace beside me.

"I don't know, but you'd like that, wouldn't you?"

"I would. I like it here a lot."

"But how about your dad? Wouldn't you miss seeing him?"

She paused a moment before saying, "Well, I don't see him very much anyway. He cancels out a lot of the weekends we're supposed to have together."

I was surprised to hear this. "Oh. Why is that? Is he working?"

"That's what he says."

"But you don't believe him?"

She shrugged. "I don't know. I think he'd rather spend time with his girlfriend."

"Have you met her?"

"No. Never. I've asked Dad if I could, but he always makes an excuse. I think he's ashamed of me and doesn't want her to meet his fat, ugly daughter."

I stopped walking and gripped Haley's shoulders. "Don't you ever think that, Haley. It's just not true. Maybe he thinks you'll resent his girlfriend and blame her for your parents splitting up."

She shrugged again and we resumed walking.

After a few moments, she said, "I'm not even sure that was the reason they did break up. Mom hinted that he left her for somebody else, but I think they had just outgrown each other. You know, like so many other couples. Most of the kids in my class? Their parents are all divorced. So nobody really gets married and stays together."

My heart fell. Though she might be partially correct, it made me sad to think that a young woman of thirteen could have such a jaded attitude toward marriage.

"Oh, Haley. That's just not true. Sure, a lot of couples do get divorced but many others are together for fifty, sixty, and even seventy years. When you find the right person, you're together forever."

"Yeah, that's just it. How on earth do you know beforehand that you *have* found the right person?"

I was beginning to see that Haley Wainwright was extremely mature for her age. And unfortunately, I had no answer for her.

Marta arrived with her daughter shortly after two. I was happy to see that Haley and Krystina seemed to hit it off immediately and surprised to discover that Krystina was also a knitter.

"Did you teach her to knit?" I asked Marta.

"Yes, about five years ago, and she really enjoys it. I don't knit as much I'd like to but I'm glad Krystina does so well. She's eager for your yarn shop to open."

Isabelle walked into the kitchen and instructed the girls to bring Krystina's things upstairs before they headed to the patio.

I offered Marta and Isabelle a glass of sun tea that I'd just brought in from outside.

"Oh, that would be nice. Thanks," Marta said. "But I can't hang around here too long or Krystina will think I'm spying on her."

I laughed and poured two glasses. "Isabelle?"

She shook her head and headed to the fridge to remove a bottle of white wine she'd opened the day before. "Oh, no thanks. I'm going to get a glass of wine and go read on the patio."

I had thought she'd cut back a bit on her wine intake. But maybe not. She had been staying downstairs later in the evening with Haley and me but I was concerned she had a wine stash in her room that she indulged in each night. Certainly nothing wrong with having a glass or two of wine each evening, but hiding it would be cause for concern, so I hoped I was wrong.

The girls came back downstairs and headed outside with their knitting projects.

"Your daughter is beautiful," I said. And she was—tall, slim, with gorgeous long blond hair and fair skin. "She also seems like a very nice girl."

Marta nodded. "Yes. I'm very proud of her. It could have all turned out so differently."

I waited for her to explain.

"My sister knows, of course, and also Mavis and Yarrow. But nobody else." She paused for a moment. "My daughter—she is the result of rape."

I inhaled a breath as a sense of déjà vu came over me and I whispered, "Oh." Suddenly I was a college student checking the calendar and praying I'd get my period on the right day. Luckily, I did.

Marta nodded. "He was the father of the children I cared for. I was a university student and he was a politician in the community. He was involved in many political events in the evenings and on weekends. His wife had died. He needed help and I needed the money. I had always felt a little uncomfortable with him. One night he was very late returning and I knew he had been drinking heavily. The children were asleep and he . . . forced me into his bedroom. Yes, I could have screamed. But I was so scared. I knew he carried a pistol. But most of all, I didn't want to frighten the children. And so . . ."

"And so," I said. "Another man took advantage of a woman. I'm so sorry." I reached across the counter to pat her arm.

"I never went back to his house, and a month later, I knew I was pregnant. I told my parents, and it was decided I would come here to America to be with my sister and her husband. And nobody would know. I would have and keep the baby. That was my choice. Abortion wasn't an option for *me*. Poland has one of the most restrictive abortion laws in the world. However, it is allowed in cases of rape. I think that's a very good thing and I will always strongly support a woman's right to choose. But for me, I knew what *my* choice had to be."

I nodded; I very much agreed on a woman's right to choose. "Does Krystina know?"

Marta shook her head. "No. She thinks her father was my married university professor. That is what I told her and because he was married, she accepts that she cannot contact him."

"How brave of you, coming to a strange country, not speaking the language initially, and giving birth to your daughter. I know you had your sister, but it still had to be very difficult."

"You have no idea," she said as she blew out a breath of air. "I am not here legally. I am one of the undocumented immigrants you hear about on television and read about in the newspaper. Immigration isn't just a Latino issue. Polish immigrants are second only to the undocumented Mexican population."

I let out a gasp. No wonder Marta had seemed uneasy with me at first. "I had no idea."

She let out a sarcastic chuckle. "No. It's not something we advertise. I live under the radar. I would love to return to college and finish my degree, but I can't. I would love to get a driver's license and drive legally. But I can't. Most of the money I make from my jobs has to go into savings because I have no medical coverage."

"Can't you apply for a green card or citizenship now?"

"It's too late. I came here in 2000 on a tourist visa. That was the easiest document to get in Poland and I just needed to get out of there. I was three months pregnant by the time I left. My visa only lasted six months here, which was around the time I gave birth to Krystina. I couldn't take a chance of being deported. I was too scared that I'd be sent back to Poland, and I just couldn't risk that. So . . . I did nothing."

"My God, how sad—your entire story."

Marta nodded. "And I love this country. I would give *anything* to become a citizen, but since 2001 it has only become more and more difficult, especially for people who overstayed their visa. But my daughter? I am so happy because *she* is a citizen of the United States of America. And for that I am grateful."

I let out a deep sigh. The things we don't know about people. The secrets that people live with every single day. And yet—they survive. Human beings are always proving the resilience of their nature.

"Have you forgiven Krystina's father?" I asked

Her eyes locked with mine. "He gave me a precious and cherished gift. How could I not forgive?"

# Chapter 36

I was sad to see Isabelle and Haley leave four days later and head back to Atlanta. Although based on various things Isabelle had said or hinted at, I had a feeling that in time the two of them just might be returning permanently.

It made me happy that Haley wasn't quite the same girl when she left. I think she was committed to healthy eating and an exercise program when she returned home. In just two weeks she morphed from a sulky, unhappy teen to one who was willing to make some changes. A few days before they left she'd asked if Helen could cut and style her hair. That had been a good choice. She'd emerged from the salon sporting a chin-length, sassy, modern cut.

They had just pulled out of the driveway when my cell rang. I was pleased to see Henry's name on the caller ID.

I laughed as I answered. "How is it that you always seem to know the perfect time to call?"

His laughter came across the line. "I'm not sure, but I'm happy that's the case. Did your company leave?"

"Yeah, just a few minutes ago. The house is empty again and Basil is already moping around."

"Aww, poor little guy. I'm sure they'll get back soon for another visit."

"Well, I could be wrong, but it seems that Isabelle is giving some thought to relocating here. Since her divorce, I think she's been looking for ways to make a change in her life. And Haley has already told her she's all for the idea."

"Oh, that would be great. I know you enjoy their company."

"I do. How's it going with you?"

"Pretty good. All of my photo shoots are going well but they're keeping me busy. I figure I should be down there as I'd planned in about six weeks."

I was surprised when I glanced at the clock an hour later. We certainly didn't lag for things to talk about.

"Well, Henry, I really should get going here. Today is the day that I'm finally going to tackle my stash of yarn and get it all properly put away."

I heard his chuckle as he said, "Good luck with that. I'll call again soon."

I headed upstairs to begin sorting the various skeins of yarn first. For once and for all I was going to separate my sock yarn from my worsted from my lace fingering yarn and get everything in order.

Two hours later I had various stacks placed around my bedroom and began filling the plastic bins with cotton, bamboo, silk, and all the other fibers that I had. I was very grateful to have such a large walk-in closet in my bedroom. A very wide U-shaped wooden shelf went around the entire upper perimeter of the closet. This would hold quite a few of the bins, but I'd need a stepladder to reach up there and utilize all of the space.

After finding one in the kitchen closet, I came back upstairs and began the task of placing the bins on the shelf. When I went to place the first bin I gave it a shove in order to push it all the way back on the shelf. That was when a portion of the wall, about a square foot in size, collapsed inward. What the heck? It looked like a small opening had been purposely fitted into the closet wall. I tried to peer inside but it was too dark.

I climbed back down the ladder and went in search of a flashlight. I came back and shined the light inside. There sat a wooden box with a hinged clasp in front. I reached in to remove it and realized it was one of those little keepsake boxes women love to hide.

I brought it over to the bed and sat down staring at it. And that was when I saw the initials *E* and *O* engraved into the top in fancy script. This box belonged to Emmalyn Overby!

I didn't think twice about opening it and lifted the lid. The first thing I saw was a photograph, and I felt a chill go through me as I removed it for a closer look. There was no denying it. The woman in the faded color photo had to be Emmalyn—head thrown back with auburn hair cascading down in waves, a huge smile covering her beautiful face, a champagne glass held in the air, and wearing a beautiful red evening gown. Not only was I positive this was Emmalyn Overby—but she was identical to the woman in my dreams.

"Oh, my God," I said out loud. "How can this be possible?"

I had never met Emmalyn, had never seen her photo, certainly never knew her, and yet she had appeared in my dreams. I felt another shiver go through me.

I let out a deep breath, placed the photo on the bed beside me and reached inside the box to remove the remaining items. Canceled tickets from the Peabody Auditorium in Daytona Beach for a performance of *My Fair Lady*. A cork from a champagne bottle. A peacock feather. A beautiful piece of rose quartz crystal, and at the very bottom, white pages of what appeared to be a letter. They were not in an envelope. I unfolded the crisp sheets and began to read.

*June 1966*

*Dear Emmalyn,*

*Needless to say, I was shocked to receive your news. I am so terribly sorry for something that never should have happened. I don't even know how to respond. What to say or do. You didn't indicate in your letter how you plan to handle this. I only wish that I were there in person to help fix this situation. If that is even possible. I will support you in any way that I can. All I ask—beg—of you is please do not tell Mavis Anne that this baby is mine. You know that one night was my first and only infidelity. You also know that I love Mavis Anne and would never want to hurt her so horribly with this news. Please think of her as you decide. I had my leave in March and you know it's not possible for me to get home right now. But please let me know what you plan to do. Again, I'm so terribly sorry this happened.*

*Jackson*

I lost count of the number of times I read the pages before the words finally began to penetrate. There was no doubt that this letter was meant to be kept private—between only two people. And almost fifty years later it was *I* who'd found it.

Could this even be possible? That Jackson had cheated on Mavis

Anne with her sister, Emmalyn? And compounding that situation—could it be possible that Yarrow was Jackson's daughter? Did Mavis Anne or Yarrow have any knowledge of this?

A million thoughts raced through my mind as I sat there holding the pages in my hand and losing track of time. It was the sound of Basil whining that brought me back to reality.

"Yes, sweetie," I said, standing up and feeling like I'd been in a daze. "Come on. I'll let you out."

I followed Basil down the stairs, through the house to the kitchen, and opened the French doors for him. It was when I glanced across the way that I knew what I had to do. I had to speak with David.

When I called him, I needed to confirm that Mavis Anne wasn't there, that I needed to speak with him in private. When he assured me she was gone for the day with a friend of hers, I told him I'd be over in five minutes.

"Are you sure I can't get you anything?" he asked as I sat on a stool at the counter. "Coffee, tea, a glass of wine?"

"No, thanks. I'm fine."

"So what's the need for privacy?"

I cleared my throat and hoped I was making the right decision by sharing what I'd found with David. "Well . . . I was finally sorting through my yarn stash . . . um . . ." I glanced up to see David giving me a blank stare. "Right. Well, while I was attempting to place the bins on the shelf in my bedroom closet, I found something."

"Okay."

I cleared my throat again. "Did you ever suspect that something might be going on between Emmalyn and Jackson?"

"Going on?"

"Yeah. Like did you ever think maybe Jackson cheated on Mavis Anne with Emmalyn?"

He let out a deep sigh. "The thought did cross my mind." He sighed again. "Oh, not because of Jackson. No. He was very devoted to Mavis Anne. That was obvious. But because of Emmalyn. She was difficult for most men to resist and she seemed determined to turn his head. Why do you ask?"

"I found a letter hidden in a box that had been stashed in a wall space in the closet. Did you ever think that possibly . . ."

"Yarrow is Jackson's daughter?"

I let out a gasp. "You knew?"

"I suspected, but there was no proof."

I removed the letter from my pocket and slid it across the counter.

David reached for a pair of half-moon glasses and began to read.

He removed the glasses and nodded. "So now there is proof."

"Why did you suspect this? And does Mavis Anne know?"

"I guess I suspected because of something that Mavis Anne said years ago. Yarrow was around ten and she was outside playing. Mavis was watching her from the French doors and out of the blue she said to me, 'Don't you think Yarrow resembles Jackson?' and I did. But I had always chalked it up to coincidence."

"Oh, my God, so it probably is true."

David nodded. "I'd say almost certainly, yes, it's true. Jackson had been home on leave three months before he was killed. It's pretty obvious that's when it happened, and I guess this letter is the proof because it's dated in June. He must have written it just before his plane went down."

"But if you think that, Mavis Anne probably also knows . . . how on earth can she still be so in love with him? To this day, she says he was the love of her life."

"Because he was and I have no doubt that Jackson felt the same way about her. I think this letter now also proves that. But Mavis Anne wasn't always so forgiving. Oh, no. As I told you before, she had a love/hate relationship with her sister. I don't think it was until Emmalyn died and Yarrow came to live with us permanently that she truly forgave Emmalyn. I think she considered Yarrow a gift—a gift from Jackson. To this day, she adores Yarrow and would do anything for her. She once told me that part of loving is also forgiving."

A shiver went through me. *Love is forgiveness*. That was what Emmalyn had said in my dream.

"What about Yarrow?" I asked. "Do you think she knows?"

"I honestly can't answer that. She's never seemed curious about who her father was. Not even as a child. It was as if she simply accepted the family she had and that was enough for her."

"What will you do now? Will you show Mavis Anne the letter?"

David remained silent for a few moments. "I don't know. I'm not sure what I'll do. I'll hold on to the letter and give it some thought. Some things are better left unsaid, but maybe after all these years, Mavis Anne has a right to know the truth."

I got up from the stool and placed a kiss on David's cheek. "You're a great brother," I told him. "If I had a brother, I'd want him to be exactly like you."

# Chapter 37

I would never discuss the information I'd found with anybody in Ormond Beach, but the following week I knew I had to share it with Grace. I also knew that Grace would never violate the trust of a secret.

"God, that's really sad," she said. "All of it. The fact that Jackson and Mavis Anne never had the chance to live the life they'd hoped for. It's also sad that Mavis Anne didn't have a child with him, but her sister did. And Yarrow . . . poor Yarrow still doesn't know who her father was."

I agreed. "It is all pretty sad."

"I remember when Berkley came to Cedar Key searching for information about her mother. I guess Yarrow doesn't have that same inquisitiveness about her dad. I wonder what Emmalyn ever told her about him?"

"I don't know. She never mentions him at all. But as David said, she's probably content with the family she does have and that's enough for her. So what's going on there? Any bites on the house?"

"Not a one. Sales on the island are still way down. But we'll keep it listed and see what happens. Lucas is definitely closing the bookshop in December so he's working on discounting the books. What's left over he plans to donate to the library."

"That's a good thing to do. Do you know yet when you'll be leaving for France?"

"Our plan is to go around March. We'll stay with Lucas's sister while we make the final arrangements on the farmhouse. But you'll come here to visit before we go, won't you?"

"Of course I will. I'll definitely be over for a few days around Christmas and I'll bring more of my stuff back here."

"Yeah, we have to arrange to have our furniture and household items shipped to France. That'll be a job."

"If you need any help, I can arrange to come to Cedar Key."

"Thanks, but you have enough to do there with the shop opening in a few weeks. Besides, Sydney, Marin, and Berkley have all insisted they'll be helping me pack."

"I'm so excited for you, Grace. You have a whole new adventure ahead of you."

Her laugh came across the line. "So do you."

After I hung up with Grace, I headed out to get some errands done. Since it was Thursday morning, I made a stop at the farmer's market downtown for fresh produce. Then I drove down Beach Street to Daytona Beach and Angell and Phelps to stock up on chocolate. On the way home, I made a stop at Publix to do some food shopping.

Basil greeted me when I walked in the back door with the groceries. I smiled as I unloaded the bags and watched him dancing in circles, hoping that I'd remembered something for him.

"Yes, I remembered you," I told him, opening a new box of Milkbone biscuits. "Here ya go."

He took the biscuit and ran toward the living room as my cell phone indicated I had a text. I was right in thinking it was from Haley. Most everybody else preferred a live phone conversation to texting. So I was surprised to see she'd written to ask that if I wasn't busy, could I call her.

"Hey, Haley, what's up?"

"Hi, Chloe. Nothing much. I know you prefer talking on the phone rather than texting."

I laughed. "Yeah, I'm from the old school, I guess. How are you and your mom doing?"

I heard a groan. "Okay. School starts next week for me and Mom's been trying to find a job."

"Any luck there?"

"None. I told her if maybe she'd take some college classes and get trained in something, it might be a lot easier."

This kid was pretty mature for thirteen years old.

"I'm happy to see you already understand the value of an education. Hey, don't you have a birthday coming up soon?"

"Yeah, September fourteenth and I turn fourteen this year, so maybe this will be my lucky year."

I laughed. "Could be. How's the exercise and food plan going?"

"Great! I've lost ten pounds since we arrived at your house."

"Oh, Haley, that's super. I'm really proud of you."

"Yeah, and Mom said I could join the local gym, so I've been going there every day to work out."

"I really *am* so proud of you. That's wonderful. Keep up the good work."

"Hey, I wanted to ask you something. Didn't you go to the Savannah School of Design?"

"Yeah, I graduated from there. Why?"

"I think that's where I'd like to go after high school. I gave some thought to what you said about my fashion designs and they have a great program there."

"They do. That would be wonderful. You sure seem to know what you'd like to do for a career."

"It's something I think I'll enjoy, and I remember my dad telling me a few years ago to choose something that I'm passionate about. He said if you're going to work, you may as well be doing something you love."

"Very wise advice. Have you seen your dad lately?"

"Not that much. Only once since we got back. How's Basil doing?"

"He's doing great. In the other room chomping on his biscuit."

Haley laughed. "Well, I have to get going. I'm going to the gym twice a day now and I have a Zumba class in an hour."

"Okay. Say hi to your mom for me and we'll talk again soon."

I hung up and shook my head. That girl really was wise beyond her years. I had no doubt that Gabe would be extremely proud of her.

After I got the bags of food put away, I folded some towels and then decided to sit in the shade on the patio with my knitting. With the breeze off the ocean it was comfortable being outside. I looked up to see Mavis Anne coming through the back gate. I hadn't seen or heard from her since I'd spoken to David.

"Are you busy?" she called out, as she made her way to the patio with the assistance of her cane.

"Not at all. I was just going to do some knitting. Come and join me."

"I don't have my knitting with me, but I'll sit a spell."

"Would you like some coffee or iced tea?"

"Not right now. Thanks. I wanted to let you know that the computer for the yarn shop will be delivered tomorrow. I just got off the phone with Office Depot. I have a doctor's appointment, so I was wondering if you could be here for the delivery. And the next day Brighthouse will be out to install the wifi service."

"Terrific. Yes, I'll be around all day tomorrow. So not a problem. Do you know how much longer the workmen will be in there? I'm anxious to get in and start arranging all the yarn."

Mavis Anne laughed. "I know. I am too. Ed said they should be completely finished by the end of next week. They're waiting for some light fixtures to be delivered and they're finishing up the work in the tea shop. So once that's done, we can get in there and start arranging things. The furniture will be delivered on the third, so that'll give us five days to get everything set up. Oh, and Office Depot is also delivering the cherrywood desk that we got for the computer."

"Wow, it's really all starting to come together. How's Yarrow doing on her end?"

"That's also right on schedule. She has a delivery of all the tea and coffee on the first. I spoke to her this morning and she said she's glad she closed her shop a few weeks ago because she's been really busy trying to get everything in order for Nirvana. Yesterday she went to Sam's and stocked up on paper goods and today she's working on getting somebody from the *Daytona Journal* to come and do a feature on the new yarn and tea shop for the newspaper."

"Gosh, I feel like a slouch. Is there anything at all that I could be doing?"

"You're doing enough working on that shawl. How's it coming?"

I held it up for her inspection.

"Oh, Chloe. It's simply stunning. The women will love that. Oh, you know, there is something you could do when you get a chance."

"What's that?"

"Could you put together some kind of calendar for classes and events? We'll have the computer tomorrow, so maybe you could do it on there and then print it out to hang on the bulletin board we'll put in the shop. I think the very first thing we should plan is the knit-along for Chloe's Dream. What do you think?"

"I agree. Yes, I'll get on that tomorrow after the computer is up and running. What other classes do you think we should schedule? Any ideas?"

"Well, I think for October maybe we could do a class on brioche. That's such a pretty technique and I have some nice patterns for sweaters and other items done in that stitch."

"Great. As soon as I finish up the shawl, I'll begin working on some new things to display in the shop. I also have a lot of my finished pieces that Grace brought to me, and we can display those as well. We're still waiting for the manikins, huh?"

"Yes, but I spoke to the distributor yesterday and she assured me they'd be here by the end of the week."

"Great. I think we're doing very well."

"We are." Mavis shifted in her chair. "Chloe, there's something I'd like to talk to you about."

My head shot up and I put my knitting in my lap. "What is it?"

"David showed me the letter you found."

"Oh."

"I want you to know . . . reading that letter fifty years later . . . well . . . I just don't know how to thank you for finding it."

"Thank me?" I had anticipated various reactions if David chose to give the letter to his sister—but gratitude was not one of them.

She nodded. "Yes. It absolutely confirmed something I always felt in my heart. That Jackson loved me every bit as much as I loved him."

"Yes, that's true, but . . ."

"But he cheated on me? Yes, I guess he did. But, Chloe, nobody is perfect. There isn't one of us alive who doesn't have flaws. My sister was incorrigible, but that's just who she was. Actually, I recall the night it probably occurred quite well. I was home sick with bronchitis and Jackson and I had tickets to attend some fund-raiser in the community. Emmalyn volunteered to go with him and she wouldn't take no for an answer. I trusted Jackson explicitly—my mistake was in trusting my sister. And when Yarrow was born, I counted back the months. I suspected . . . and I hated my sister. I never bothered to force the truth from her, because I knew Emmalyn simply wasn't capable of the truth. But as Yarrow got older . . . the truth became crystal clear to me. She was Jackson's daughter."

"You're a remarkable woman, Mavis Anne."

She let out a deep sigh and shook her head. "No. No, I'm not at all. But just because Jackson made a terrible mistake, it didn't diminish the love he had for me. Not at all. I always knew that in my heart. And this letter? This letter finally proves that to me fifty years later. It's obvious from his words that he was torn apart by a moment of recklessness. An impulsive choice that changed four lives forever. So thank you, Chloe. Thank you for giving the letter to David and for giving me the proof of what I wanted to believe."

I reached across the table and squeezed Mavis Anne's hand. "And Emmalyn? You forgive her?"

"I didn't. For a very long time. But then I came to realize that resentment and anger are toxic. I may have even briefly hated Jackson for a while. But I came to understand that love is so much stronger than any other emotion. I looked at Yarrow as she grew and I saw only *love,* so how could I not forgive Emmalyn and also Jackson?"

I shook my head and squeezed her hand tighter. "As I said . . . you are *one* remarkable woman, Mavis Anne Overby."

# Chapter 38

I had given a lot of thought over the past week to my conversation with Mavis Anne. Despite Jackson's betrayal, it seemed her love for him had never wavered. And the words that he'd written in that letter only strengthened her feelings. So I was glad I'd found the wooden box.

I thought back on all the events of the past four months. Every little step taken that had brought me here. To this moment. Renting Henry's condo. Meeting Mavis Anne and Yarrow. Moving into Koi House. All leading to the moment when I'd find that wooden box that had been hidden in a closet wall for fifty years. Was it fate? Meeting Chadwick Price on a rainy road with a flat tire. How did that play into the overall scheme of things?

I had no answers and I had no explanations. But one thing I knew for certain. I had to call Chadwick.

"I need to discuss something with you," I told him when he answered the phone. "Would it be possible to get together someplace private?"

There was a slight pause before he said, "Sure. But I'm leaving to go out of town this afternoon. I'll be back next Monday evening. Would Tuesday afternoon be okay at my house?"

"That would be fine."

"Okay. Would around three work for you?"

"Yes, and thanks, Chadwick. I'll see you then."

I hung up and let out a breath I hadn't realized I'd been holding.

I had taken the first step on a journey and had no idea where it would end. But for the first time in a long time, I knew in my heart that it was another step closer to a healing process I'd been avoiding for most of my life.

* * *

I headed out to the yarn shop to begin working on the calendar schedule I was setting up in the computer. Basil was close at my heels when we walked inside. Except for the L-shaped cherrywood desk, the place was still empty of furniture. But that would all change next week.

Mavis Ann and I agreed that the desk should be placed just inside the door to the left. It would double as a workstation for the computer and the area where customers would complete their purchases. Sitting down in the leather office chair, I smiled. It was the perfect spot to greet customers and I had an unobstructed view of Koi House, the archway to the fishpond, and the sky.

With the French doors to the side, bay windows in front, and skylights above me, I knew the lighting would be ideal for the knitters to enjoy hours of what they loved doing.

Just as I booted up the computer, my cell phone rang. The caller ID told me it was my son Eli.

"How's it going, sweetheart?" I said.

"Fine, Mom. And how're you doing? Busy with your grand opening in a couple weeks?"

"Yeah, but it's a fun busy. I hate to jinx anything but we're on schedule and Mavis Anne and I are so excited."

"That's great. I'm happy this has all worked out so well for you."

"How's Treva? Anything new on the move?"

"Treva's just fine. And we're right on target with the move too. I think she's getting antsy, though. She's more than ready to move south. Our movers will arrive here on the twenty-seventh of September and we're flying down on the morning of the twenty-eight."

"Do you need a place to stay for a few days? You're more than welcome to stay here at Koi House."

"Thanks, Mom, but we've already booked a hotel in Jacksonville. We want to be close to the house because there are a few things we'd like to get done before the movers arrive."

"Right. That makes sense. But are you sure you won't miss one more winter in Boston?"

I heard Eli's laugh come across the line. "Ah, I think we'll pass on that. After the last winter we had here, which by the way really only ended in June, I think we've had enough New England winter to last a lifetime. Jeez, we really didn't even have any spring here this year."

"Yeah, you have to be tough to live in New England. I think you paid your dues for somebody who was raised in the south."

"I'm glad to hear things are going well. How's Aunt Grace doing? Are they still on track for France in the spring?"

"Yeah, everything is good there too. Have you been in touch with your brother? I haven't heard from him in a while."

"I spoke to Mathis the other day. He's been traveling a lot with his company. He said to say hello if I spoke to you first."

"That boy needs a woman in his life. Any word on that?"

"Nobody serious. You know Mathis, love 'em and leave 'em."

"Hmm. I'm not sure that's such a great philosophy for him anymore. He's twenty-eight now."

"Yeah, but pushing thirty today isn't like in your time."

"*My* time?" I let out a chuckle. "Geez, Eli, you make it sound like I'm ancient."

I heard him laugh. "Aw, Mom. I didn't mean that. You know what I meant. My generation just isn't getting married as young as yours did. If I hadn't met Treva, I'd probably still be single. But the moment I laid eyes on her, I knew she was the one."

I let out a sigh. I'd heard this from Mavis and now my son was saying the same thing. I definitely had gone wrong somewhere. "And you know how happy I am for both of you. You were very fortunate to find each other."

"And we both know it. Listen, I have to get back to work. You take care and I'll be in touch soon. Love you, Mom."

"Okay. Love to both you and Treva."

I had no sooner got back to working on the calendar when my cell rang again. I saw it was Henry.

Before I could even say hello, I heard him say, "What are you doing three weeks from today? That would be Tuesday, September fifteenth."

I laughed. "I have no idea. Why?"

"Because I'm calling to book a date with you. Not coffee at Starbucks. Not a quick chit-chat someplace. An honest to goodness, bona fide date."

I laughed again. "Oh. It seems you're a very decisive sort of man."

"I am and although we've gotten to know each other on the phone, I want to give you a chance to get to know me in person." He paused for a second. "That is . . . if you'd like to."

"Hmm, you were doing great there until you faltered a bit."

He laughed. "Well, I don't want you thinking I'm a control freak. You have a say-so in this date too."

"Oh, that's good to know. And do I get to choose where this date is to take place?"

"Ah, I'm afraid not. No. I can't relinquish all of my control. Besides, I'm the one requesting said date."

"Hmm. I see. Then where might this date be?" I struggled to avoid letting him hear me giggle.

"I was considering Chart House in Daytona Beach. It's on the Halifax River with a scenic view. Would that meet with your approval?"

The giggle squeezed through. "I've never been there but I've heard it's very nice."

"It is. Good. Then it's settled. I'll make a reservation. Oh, wait . . . you didn't actually accept."

Now I was laughing out loud. "You're a very astute man. I didn't. But I do. Accept your date, that is."

Henry's laughter came across the line. "Good. I'm looking forward to it. I will arrive down there the day before. You're probably busy so I'll let you go. I just wanted to get this confirmed. I'll pick you up at seven. I'll talk to you soon, Chloe."

"Sounds good," I told him.

There was a humorous side to Henry Wagner. And I liked it. But even more, I liked the fact that in three weeks I was finally going to get to meet him in person.

The strange thing was I had never given much thought to what he looked like. And I realized I really didn't care. I just liked Henry Wagner—the man.

# Chapter 39

I woke on the first morning of September and instantly recalled my dream from the night before. Again there was Emmalyn wearing her red evening gown. And again I was standing just inside the entrance to the fishpond. But this time Emmalyn was dancing, or maybe she was floating, around the water. Her gown swirled and flowed as it skimmed her ankles. She was swaying her arms back and forth in the air and then suddenly, she stopped, looked straight at me, and gave me the most luminous smile. Her entire beautiful face lit up. She waved at me, drifted down toward the end of the fishpond, and floated up toward the sky. That was it. Then I woke up.

I shook my head and smiled. I had a feeling that might have been the final dream I'd have of Emmalyn Overby. Did she seem happy now because I'd found the box with the letter? Or did it have more to do with me? Was it because I would be meeting with Chadwick Price this afternoon? Again, I had no answers.

"Come on, Basil," I said and got up. "Time to start our day."

I pulled into the circular driveway just before three. I let out a deep breath and gripped the steering wheel. I could do this. I *would* do this.

I rang the bell and Chadwick opened the door almost immediately. Stepping inside, I wasn't sure if my trembling was caused by the chilling air conditioning or my nerves.

"Hey, Chloe. Good to see you. Can I get you something to drink?"

"A glass of water would be good."

I followed him into the kitchen, avoiding the display of framed photographs, and perched on a stool at the counter.

"So your company has left?" he asked before placing a crystal glass of water with a slice of lemon in front of me.

"Yeah, Isabelle and Haley are back in Atlanta."

I took a sip of water and we both remained silent for a few moments.

"So," he said, "what can I do for you? You said you wanted to talk privately."

I nodded and fingered the base of the water glass. "Yes. There's something . . . I wanted to talk to you about." I took another sip of water. "I think you realize that I've been trying to avoid you."

"You've made that pretty obvious. Yes."

"Well . . . I want you to know that it has nothing to do with *you*. At least not directly."

"Oh. Okay. Right. That makes everything crystal clear."

I heard the edge to his tone and I couldn't blame him.

"I like you, Chadwick. I really do." I let out a deep breath. "This is very difficult for me but I need you to know something. When I was a college student thirty years ago, something happened. An incident that I'm only now coming to realize has affected every aspect of my life since then."

Chadwick remained silent while he stared at me across the counter.

I saw him give a slight nod and I continued.

"I was young and extremely stupid. I was at a frat party with some friends. They took off at the end of the night and I found myself stuck, with no way to get back to my dorm. Having had way too much to drink, which is no excuse, I accepted a ride from one of the guys there. A complete stranger. On the drive back to my dorm he—"

"Oh, my God! You were *that* girl," Chadwick exclaimed. "It was *you*."

"You knew about this?" I wasn't sure what I was feeling in that moment—anger, or relief that I wouldn't have to finish telling my story.

He nodded and I saw the sad expression that crossed his face.

"I knew about the incident. Aaron told me before he died. He said he'd done a lot of bad things in his life . . . but that was the worst. He wondered what became of that college student and wished there was a way to make amends. But Chloe, I had no idea it was you."

I tried to digest what he'd just told me.

"How did you know? Did you know Aaron was my brother because of the last name?"

"No. I never even knew his name. But I never forgot his *face.* It was the photograph."

"What photograph?"

I pointed toward the living room. "The one of you with him."

Chadwick looked toward the framed photos and gasped. "*That* was why you flew out of here the day we were going on the boat. That was why you left. And why you've been avoiding me."

I nodded and could feel moisture stinging my eyes.

Chadwick jumped up and pulled me into an embrace. "I'm sorry," he whispered in my ear. "I'm so sorry for what my brother did."

After a few moments I pulled away and swiped at my eyes, attempting to compose myself. Grabbing one of the tissues from the box Chadwick placed in front of me, I said, "I know you are. That's why I had to come and tell you the truth. Once I realized who you were, I put all my anger and blame on you."

"That's understandable," he said.

"I thought it was," I told him. "But it's not. Thirty years of pent-up fury was misdirected. I've allowed one incident to affect my whole life and that was a mistake. I allowed your brother to have the power. But no more. *I'm* the one who now has the power."

He reached for my hand and gave it a squeeze. "You're a strong woman, Chloe. And I can't begin to tell you how sorry I am for what my brother did."

"You're a good and kind person. I knew that the first day I met you when you stopped to help with my tire. And so . . . I need you to know . . . finally . . . after all these years I can honestly say I forgive your brother. I *do* forgive him." I let out a deep breath and felt a sense of lightness wash over me.

"And do you forgive me?" he asked.

"There was never any need to forgive *you*, Chadwick. I just didn't know that. Unfortunately, you were just in the line of fire."

He nodded. "I'm not going to lie to you. I was attracted to you and I had hoped that possibly we might go somewhere. I can see now that won't happen."

I silently agreed.

"But," he said, with the hint of a smile crossing his face, "do you think we could be friends?"

I nodded and raised my hand for a fist bump. “Absolutely. I’d like that. We can never have too many friends.”

Chadwick walked me out to my car about an hour later. I started the ignition and he leaned in the window to kiss my cheek.

“You’re one special woman, Chloe Radcliffe. I’m very glad you had a flat tire that day.”

I laughed. “So am I,” I told him before backing out of his driveway.

And on the short drive down North Beach Street to Koi House, I knew in my heart that another chapter had been concluded in the book we call life.

# Chapter 40

While most people were enjoying boat rides or barbeques on Labor Day weekend, the new owners of Dreamweaver Yarn Shop and Nirvana Tea and Coffee were very busy preparing for their grand opening in a few short days—and we couldn't have been any happier.

"What do you think?" Mavis asked.

I turned around to see that the half-moon–shaped cherrywood table in the corner now held three wicker baskets with pastel colored yarn spilling out.

"Oh, I love it," I told her. "Perfect for that spot."

"Good. I'll start filling the armoire with the cashmeres and qiviut. Oh, those cubbyholes look great, Chloe. Everything is so organized and will be easy to find."

I heard the whistling of a teakettle and looked toward the back of the shop.

"Tea's almost ready," Yarrow hollered to us. "We need to christen our new place."

"That's almost sacrilegious," Mavis Anne told her. "I would think we'd at least pop open a bottle of champagne."

"Not at ten in the morning," Yarrow retorted.

I laughed as I walked toward the tea shop area.

"Oh, Yarrow, this looks great."

Six circular wrought-iron tables and chairs filled one side, and behind the separating counter were a small countertop range and mini fridge. A wooden hutch held an assortment of pastel cups and saucers while a rack on the wall had brightly colored mugs hanging from it. The entire counter next to Yarrow's prep area held glass jars of various teas.

"Thanks," she said. "Here you go. Ginger lemon is the choice for today."

Mavis walked toward us and nodded as she made her way to a chair.

"Very nice, Yarrow. It looks beautiful."

She held up the mug of tea her niece had given her. "Here's to us," she said. "And a very successful business."

"To our business," both Yarrow and I said.

"Anybody here?" we heard a voice call from the walkway outside.

I saw the look of annoyance that crossed Mavis's face.

"Louise Blackstone, you are not supposed to be here. We don't open for three more days."

Louise peeked her head just inside the French doors. "I know that," she said. "But I'm not here as a customer. I'm here as a *friend*. I wanted to help."

Mavis let out a sigh and gestured toward the door. "Oh, all right. Come on in."

Louise stepped inside, her gaze taking in the entire area, and she gasped. "Oh, my goodness. It's just gorgeous. I love it."

"Would you like some tea?" Yarrow asked.

"Oh, that would be great, but . . . I . . . have my little Ramona in the car. I can't leave her out there." She spied Basil, who had run over to greet her. "Do you think . . ."

I laughed. "Sure. Go bring Ramona in. She can play outside with Basil."

"Oh, thank you," she called, as she rushed back through the French doors.

Mavis Anne shook her head. "That woman," she said, but I knew she meant it in the most loving way.

After we finished our tea, the four of us continued working. Mavis Anne sat with Louise, attaching price tags to each skein of yarn. I sorted through the delivery boxes and filled each cubbyhole with various fibers while Yarrow worked on a poster for her price list.

Soft classical music played on the CD player that Mavis insisted we should have. She wanted to provide the most tranquil and relaxing atmosphere possible for our knitters. I looked around and smiled. Women working together, involved in a common love. It was heartwarming how this ritual had gone on for centuries. Yes, there were *mean girls* around. Like the ones who bullied Haley or the ones who excluded Fay. But for the most part, women supported women, through the good and the bad. Women comprised a community that wasn't based on geographical location, but rather a deeply rooted connection—and that's just the way it was.

"Did you finish the shawl?" I heard Louise ask.

"I did," I told her and walked over to a box on the sofa. I reached in and brought out the completed Chloe's Dream, holding it up for her to see.

She jumped up from her chair and rushed over to touch it, causing me to smile. I'm not sure what it was, but most knitters always had an overwhelming need to touch not only skeins of yarn but the finished pieces.

"Oh, Chloe," she gushed. "This is absolutely stunning! You did a wonderful job—I can't wait to begin working on mine."

"Thank you. This knit-along is the first one we'll do. I've posted the September calendar over there on the bulletin board," I said, pointing to the side wall. "I think I can put this on our manikin now."

I walked over and draped the shawl around the upper torso of the form. I put my fingers to my lips and then touched the shawl. *Thank you, Emmalyn*, I whispered. *For everything*.

"You really did an outstanding job designing and knitting that," Mavis Anne told me. "Thank you so much."

"It was my pleasure."

By five we had decided we'd done enough work for the day.

"David and Clive have prepared a nice dinner for us," Mavis Anne said. "They knew we'd be tired after working out here all day. Louise, you're welcome to join us."

"Do I have to go home and change into my glad rags?"

Mavis Anne gave her friend the once-over and snapped, "I guess you'll do," but I saw the grin she tried to hide.

I could already feel the climate slowly beginning to change as we sat on the patio following dinner. There was just a hint of autumn in the air and I welcomed the delightful weather that was on the way.

Louise wiped her mouth with a linen napkin. "I must congratulate you two," she said. "That chicken dish was superb and the pecan pie was exquisite."

"Thank you," they both said and smiled.

I felt a smile cross my face as well. David and Clive were two of the nicest people I'd ever met. Gentle and kind, their love for each other shined through their temperate natures. I envied that kind of love—the kind of love that just *was*. No drama. No lack of trust. And I couldn't help but wonder if I would ever know that in a relationship. *Easy* was the word that came to mind.

"And you must love getting waited on hand and foot," Louise told her friend. "Do you ever plan to return to Koi House?"

"Why would I?" Mavis Anne snapped. "Admit it, you're just jealous."

Louise laughed and I knew it was lighthearted bantering between them.

"You're probably right," she said.

Mavis Anne chuckled. "I know I am. I'm always right. But no, we've discussed it and I think I'm going to make this place my permanent residence. However, I'll be looking for a live-in caregiver for about a month after the first of the year. David and Clive are finally going to take a much-needed holiday to Italy."

"Oh, that's wonderful," I said. "How exciting."

"I agree. You guys work so hard and haven't been away for ages. Will you hire an agency?" Yarrow asked her aunt.

"I'm not sure yet. I have plenty of time to consider that."

After I returned home, I settled down with my knitting. I was now working on a gorgeous twisted cable cardigan we would display in the shop. I was using Cascade Heritage Paint yarn in the Citrus Mix colorway—shades of tangerine, lemon, beige, and white. And it was working into the perfect colors for Florida.

My cell rang and seeing Henry's name brought a smile to my face.

"How are you?" I said.

"Great. I'm finally getting out of here next week and Delilah and I will be quite happy to finally be back in Florida. We're still on for a week from Tuesday, right?"

"I wouldn't dare back out," I told him.

I heard him laugh. "Good girl. So are you on target to open in three days?"

"We are. We spent most of the day in the shop getting organized. The furniture looks great, we'll finish up arranging and pricing the stock tomorrow, and I'm hoping we'll be flooded with customers on Tuesday."

"Oh, I don't think you need to worry about that. I have a feeling this yarn and tea shop will be a huge success."

"Thanks for your vote of confidence."

"How's the weather down there? Still hot and humid?"

"Actually, no, it's beginning to ease up and I could almost feel fall in the air this evening."

"Great. Well, we'll have to take my boat out when I get down there. If you'd like to do that."

I recalled the missed opportunity with Chadwick. "That would be fun, but I didn't realize you had a boat."

"Oh, yeah. Just a little something Delilah and I like to take on the river. Well, I'm sure you're tired from all the work you did today, so I'll let you go. I'll call you again soon. Good night, Chloe. Sweet dreams."

I smiled. For almost a week I hadn't had any dreams. Not one.

# Chapter 41

I awoke on Tuesday morning at five—without the help of an alarm. Today was the day. After four months of indecision and confusion, I knew I had arrived at a good place. I had the opportunity once again to be the owner of a yarn shop. Dreamweaver would open at ten and prove to me that not all dreams happen when we're sleeping.

I lay in bed for a while thinking about the past months and everything that had happened to push me forward on my journey. Gabe crossed my mind, which made me realize that some people come into our lives forever, while others are only meant to stay briefly, but all of them touch us in profound ways. And that included Aaron Price.

When I glanced at the clock again, I saw it was going on six and Basil was beginning to stir. Just as I sat up, my cell phone rang, causing my stomach to drop. Nobody ever called me this early. I saw Henry's name on the caller ID and gripped the phone to my ear.

"Is everything okay?" I blurted.

"Oh, yes. Fine. I'm sorry, Chloe, if I alarmed you and I apologize for calling so early. But I knew you'd be extra busy today . . . and . . . I just wanted to call and wish you the very best of luck with your opening."

I felt a smile cross my face. "Henry Wagner," I said, "you are one of the most thoughtful men I've ever met. Thank you."

"Well, I was thinking of you and I wanted to catch you before you got busy."

Thinking of me at six in the morning? The smile on my face increased.

"You are *so* sweet. Thanks again. I'm hoping for a really great day."

"I have no doubt it will be. I'll talk to you soon."

I disconnected the call and headed to the shower, the smile on my face still intact.

* * *

An hour before we were due to open, I placed the key into the door of what used to be the schoolhouse—and was now Dreamweaver Yarn Shop—and stepped inside.

This was it. As of today, I was a bona fide business owner in Ormond Beach. A community that had welcomed me much as Cedar Key had. I had made very good friends with Mavis Anne, Yarrow, and Maddie, and I had a multitude of acquaintances. I also seemed to have a man in my life who appeared to be quite interested—despite the fact we'd only be meeting in person for the first time one week from today.

I booted up the computer and then walked around straightening skeins of yarn and rearranging lamps on tables. I heard the key in the back door and saw Yarrow coming in with Mavis Anne.

"Good morning," they called.

Yarrow placed platters of baked goods on the counter while Mavis walked toward me. Giving me a hug, she said, "Are you ready for the onslaught?"

I laughed. "From your lips to the customer's ears."

"Now, now, I think we're going to do very well," she assured me.

Fifteen minutes before we were due to open, Mavis Anne jumped up from the sofa, reaching for her cane.

"Oh," she exclaimed. "The gate."

"The gate?" I had no idea what she was talking about.

"We have to unlock the gate in the driveway."

We had decided that for safety reasons, it would be a good idea to keep it locked when we were closed.

"Oh, right," I said. "I'd forgotten. I'll go open it."

"No, no. I'll do it," she said. "Besides, I want to look at our beautiful sign again."

I smiled. The sign displaying the words *Dreamweaver Yarn Shop & Nirvana Tea and Coffee* had been etched onto a bronze plaque that dangled from two chains on the gate. It had been delivered a few days before and the three of us were quite happy with the finished product.

Mavis Anne walked outside just as the phone on the desk rang. The landline had been installed the week before, but this was the first time I'd heard it ring.

"Dreamweaver Yarn Shop," I said and heard the pride in my voice. "How may I help you?"

"Oh, yes, hello. I'm down here visiting for a week and heard you're opening today. What are your hours?"

"We're open ten till five today," I told the caller.

"Great. I'll be over shortly."

I hung up and looked out the window to see Mavis Anne coming back to the shop—followed by about twenty women walking single file behind her. What the heck!

Mavis entered the shop laughing. "Look what I found. These ladies were all waiting in the driveway for us to open. No sense making them wait ten more minutes."

I laughed. "None whatsoever. Welcome."

The yarn shop filled with the excitement of women exclaiming.

"Oh, what a beautiful shop."

"Look at the colors of this cashmere."

"Oh, they carry the interchangeable needles by Knitter's Pride."

"Look at this. The Cascade Paint yarn in such yummy colors."

I had expected our regulars to show up but these women were all strangers to me and apparently they were to Mavis Anne also.

"I swear, it looks like a bus stopped out front," she whispered to me.

I laughed. "I know. Isn't it great?" I walked toward the center of the room. "Ladies, I want you to know that Nirvana Tea and Coffee is also open," I said and gestured toward the back. "Yarrow would be happy to take your orders."

"This is just perfect," I heard one woman say. "I wanted to be here when they opened, so I skipped my coffee this morning."

She headed toward the back of the shop, followed by a few others.

Mavis Anne and I had decided that she'd sit at the desk to ring up orders and I'd cover the floor to answer questions and give assistance.

"Oh, that shawl is simply stunning," one woman said, walking toward the manikin. "Is the yarn available here?"

"It is," I told her. "And we'll be starting a knit-along on Friday to make it."

"I'd love to go to that, but I'm afraid we're heading back to Michigan tomorrow. Do you have the pattern?"

"Yes, and if you purchase the yarn here, the pattern is free." I directed her to where the yarn was located so she could make her choice.

During the next hour I helped women select sock yarn, lace yarn for shawls, alpaca for pullover sweaters, and answered questions about patterns. I glanced up and saw Maddie walk in the door carrying two large flower arrangements.

I ran to give her a hand. "Here, let me help you. Wow, these are gorgeous. For us?"

"For you—and there are two more in the truck."

"Oh, my gosh. Let me help you."

She waved a hand in the air as she walked back outside. "I'm fine. I'm used to deliveries. Open the cards."

Mavis got up to inspect the gorgeous arrangement of yellow spray roses with orange and purple lilies. She removed the card from the envelope, which read "Wishing all of you success. From all of us in Cedar Key." I read the card over her shoulder and saw it had been signed by Grace, Sydney, Marin, Berkley, Dora, and Monica and I felt a lump in my throat.

"How nice," Mavis Anne said.

"It is and they're just beautiful."

"Open the card for that arrangement," she told me.

An arrangement of roses in soft tones of pink, peach, and cream was from Maddie, wishing us all the best.

Maddie walked back into the shop carrying a tall glass vase filled with exquisite white calla lilies. The card revealed they were from Chadwick.

"One more," she said. "I'll be right back."

She returned carrying a large glass bowl, filled with multicolored rocks at the bottom, which supported a beautiful green bamboo plant.

I opened the envelope and read out loud, "May this bamboo bring good fortune and happiness to the yarn and tea shop. Best, Henry Wagner."

"How very thoughtful of him," Mavis Anne said.

Yarrow had joined us and smiled as she sent me a wink. "It certainly is."

We ushered out the last of our customers at five fifteen and the three of us plopped on the sofa.

"Whew," Yarrow said. "I'd say we had an excellent first day, but I'm tired."

I laughed. "Me too. It's going to take a bit of time to get back into the groove of working again. If we continue to be this busy every day, we're going to have to think about hiring another person."

Mavis Anne nodded. I could tell she was weary. "That's not out of the question, but we'll give it a couple weeks and see how it goes. Our regulars did stop by but the majority of the people here today were simply checking out a new yarn shop. They might have their own local shop that they're loyal to."

"True," I said. "And I know a fair number of them were from out of state on vacation."

"Congratulations. Time to celebrate."

I looked up to see David and Clive coming through the door. David was carrying a silver ice bucket with a bottle of champagne peeking out and five flutes in his other hand. Clive had a large platter of appetizers.

"We saw the last of your customers just left. I trust it was a good day?" David began to uncork the bottle.

"This is so nice of you," Yarrow said. "And yes, I'd say opening day was a huge success."

"Well, this is our little gift to you. We thought you might have plenty of flowers," Clive said. He looked around at the four arrangements we'd placed on end tables and the desk. "And from the looks of it, I think we were right."

After David poured the champagne, they toasted us to wish us well. He took a sip and then looked around the shop inspecting the flowers. "Gorgeous," he said. "Simply gorgeous. Oh, and by the way, I'm not sure what you had planned for dinner, but Clive and I have prepared a rack of lamb as the other part of your celebratory gift."

"I won't turn that down," Yarrow said. "I was going home to have a grilled cheese."

I laughed. "I wasn't sure what I was having tonight, so thank you."

"Dinner's at seven," David said. "That'll give you a chance to enjoy the champagne and chill out a little bit."

After we finished the champagne, Mavis went back home with David and Clive. I wanted to feed Basil before joining them for dinner. Yarrow and I did a walk-through, making sure everything was secure till the next morning.

As we walked past the end table that held the bamboo plant, she paused and said, “Your dinner date with Henry is a week from tonight, right?”

“Yeah. Why?”

“This guy is a ten in my book,” was all she said as we walked out the door.

# Chapter 42

The next few days continued to be quite busy at both the yarn and tea shop. Not crazy busy like the first day, but the hours flew by.

On Friday morning we had a lull from the normal rush, which gave us a chance to catch up on things. Mavis Anne had a doctor's appointment and wouldn't be in till around noon. I was going through the receipts from the day before and Yarrow came to perch on the arm of the sofa.

I glanced in her direction. "What's up?"

"So what's he look like?"

"What's who look like?" My concentration had been on tallying numbers.

"Henry Wagner."

"Oh." I laughed. "I have no idea."

"Oh, come on, Chloe. You mean to tell me you haven't Googled him?"

"Googled him?"

Now she was laughing. "Yeah, like in check him out. See if he's who he says he is. And most important, see what he looks like. It's the accepted dating ritual with so many couples first meeting online."

I laughed again and shook my head. "Hmm, I guess I really *am* from the old school. I never considered this for a second."

She nodded toward the PC. "Well . . . go ahead. Type in his name."

I looked at the computer and back to Yarrow. "It doesn't feel right. To be sneaky and see him before he gets to see me. That's kind of like those sonograms that tell parents months ahead of time the sex of their baby. I think I'd rather wait and be surprised."

"The sex of a baby is one thing, but really, Chloe? Aren't you just a little bit curious what he looks like? Besides, how do you know he never checked you out? Your photo is on the Internet from the Yarning Together website."

"Well . . . maybe I'm a little curious . . . but not enough to find out beforehand."

"Then get up and let me do it. I'll check him out."

I laughed and waved my hand. "Get outta here and go make some tea."

David really was spoiling the three of us. Mavis returned from her doctor's appointment shortly after noon. She entered the shop followed by David carrying a large wicker basket.

"I'm back," she called. "And we have lunch."

I looked up from the cowl I was working on to display in the shop.

"Oh, how nice. The knitting group will be here in just over an hour and I wasn't sure I'd get lunch today."

David wagged a finger in my direction. "No, no. We'll have none of that. Skipping meals. It's not healthy. And so—" He whisked a tea towel off the top of the basket in a dramatic gesture and said, "We have crabmeat on croissant with some macaroni salad to go with it and fresh fruit for after."

I walked to the tea shop area and peeked into the basket he'd set on the counter.

"Oh, that looks yummy," Yarrow said.

"It sure does. Thanks," I told him. "But you're spoiling us, David."

He laughed. "Precisely, and it gives me great joy to do so. Now enjoy. I have to run. Clive and I are driving up to Flagler Beach to speak to a potential client."

The three of us sat at a table in the tea shop to eat. Yarrow asked her aunt how her appointment had gone.

"Just fine. I'm as healthy as a horse—well, except for my bum knee. But I'm not sure that will ever be the same again. All the more reason for me to stay with David and Clive."

I caught the wink Yarrow sent in my direction and smiled.

The women began arriving shortly before two. Most of them had already come by on opening day at the beginning of the week, but for some it was their first time in the new yarn shop.

"Oh, wow," I heard somebody say and turned around to see Paige. "This place is gorgeous."

"Thanks," I said, as I continued putting away a new shipment of

Ultra Pima Cotton. "Look around and browse before we start the knit-along."

Fay entered the shop and had the same reaction as Paige. "I'm sorry I couldn't get here before, but I joined the Red Hatters and I've been busy all week."

"Good for you," I told her. "I take it they're a little nicer than the mean girls knitters?"

She laughed. "Much. They're a great group and know how to have a fun time. Minus the dramatics." Her eyes scanned the room and she smiled. "A woman could definitely get lost in here."

By the time we were assembled at the large rectangular table, ten women had joined us for the knit-along. Most of them had already purchased their yarn and had begun working on the shawl.

"This is going to be so beautiful," Louise said.

"I know," Maddie agreed. "I couldn't wait to cast on my stitches the other night."

"I hope I'm not too late," I heard somebody say and looked up to see a woman who appeared to be in her midfifties walk in.

Yarrow jumped up to give her a hug. "Oh, June. I'm so glad you could join us and, no, you're not late at all. Pull up a chair."

"Chloe, this is June. Remember we told you she's been busy caring for her grandson?"

"Right," I said. "It's nice to meet you."

"Same here. I'm so glad you've opened the yarn shop with Mavis Anne."

"Not any more happy than I am," Mavis Anne said, and we all laughed.

"How's it going with Charlie?" Paige asked.

"Very well. I have him all settled in preschool, which gives me a bit more time for myself. So Friday afternoon knitting is back on my schedule."

"I'm happy to hear that," Maddie said. "You deserve some free time and I'm sure socializing is good for Charlie too."

"It is. Oh, Paige, I was going to ask you if you know of anybody with puppies. Since you work with grooming dogs, I thought you might have heard of some that are available."

"Oh, my goodness," Louise exclaimed. "Are you thinking of getting a new dog?"

"Well, with Russ being retired now, he'd like to have a dog again.

We lost our Piper last year and after sixteen years, our house does feel empty without one. Besides, we think it might be good for Charlie."

"Oh, what a great idea," Paige said. "I've always felt every child needs a dog. It teaches them responsibility and compassion. Gee, I don't know of any right now but I'll keep my ears open for you."

"Thanks," June said. "We're going to check out the Humane Society too. So many dogs need a home."

The three hours flew by with the women working away on Chloe's Dream. I jumped up a number of times for customers coming in to purchase yarn and in between I assisted with instruction or questions on the shawl pattern.

We were cleaning up and putting things back in order after the women left when I heard Basil whining outside.

"Where are you, buddy?" I called.

"He's back here outside the French doors," Yarrow said as she washed mugs in the sink.

His whining got louder and I saw Yarrow grab a towel to wipe her hands and head outside. I was walking to the back of the shop when I heard her say, "What on earth is this?"

Mavis Anne followed me outside to investigate. And there in the garden area beside the tea shop was Basil racing back and forth, whining and begging somebody to pay attention to what he had discovered.

A small black-and-white kitten cowered beneath the azalea bush.

"Oh, poor baby," I heard Yarrow say, and then she surprised me by stretching out on the ground and inching her way toward the kitten with hand outstretched. "Come on, sweetie. I won't hurt you."

Pitiful mews came from the cat while Basil seemed beside himself with concern, dancing in circles, looking up at me and then at Mavis Anne.

After a few minutes Yarrow was able to get hold of the kitten and scoop it up into her arms. She stood up and nuzzled her face into its fur.

"Oh, my God," I said. "Where did that kitten come from? He's adorable."

"He certainly is," Mavis Anne said, sitting on a patio chair.

Yarrow also sat down, continuing to murmur endearments into the kitten's ears. Basil immediately scampered over and began licking the kitten's paws. I was concerned he might get scratched for his kindness but the kitten began purring and looked at him with adoring eyes.

"These two already seem to be friends," Yarrow said. She looked around the garden area. "I have no idea where this kitten came from."

"What are we going to do with it?" I asked.

Yarrow and Mavis Anne remained silent and then Yarrow said, "I'm keeping it. He can be the mascot for the shop. I'll take him home with me and bring him back every morning."

"Really?" He was a very sweet kitten but I was surprised at Yarrow's interest. She'd never owned a pet before and she'd even told me that was how she liked it.

"Yup. He's mine. Look, he doesn't even want to leave my arms. I'll bring him to the vet next week and get him checked out."

"You're going to need something to transport him in the car," I said. "You can borrow Basil's carrier."

"Thanks," she said, standing up with the kitten against her chest. "I'll run to Pet Supermarket after I drop him off at my house. I'll get a carrier and food and anything else I might need."

"That's great," Mavis Anne said. "Do you have a name for the little guy yet?"

Yarrow held the kitten up in front of her face and smiled. "He's so soft and silky. Meet Merino. I'm naming him Merino after the yarn."

# Chapter 43

By the time Tuesday arrived, we had the yarn and tea shop open one week, Merino had been to the vet and was settling into his new routine well, and I was finally going to meet Henry Wagner that evening.

A few of the regulars dropped by and were working on their shawls as I unpacked a new shipment of cotton bamboo.

All of us looked toward the door when Louise burst in.

"I've made a mistake," she moaned. "I need help. I'm not sure what I did but . . . well, I'm not sure I'll be able to finish this shawl."

"Calm down, Louise," Mavis Anne said. "Let me see what you have."

I smiled as I saw Louise sit beside Mavis at the table and remove about eight inches of Chloe's Dream from her bag. Non-knitters might not understand, but one mistake was all it took for a knitter to doubt her ability.

"I have no idea what I did wrong. Maybe I should give up on doing the knit-along."

"Louise . . . breathe! And hush. Let me figure out what you've got here," Mavis Anne told her.

I glanced over to see Mavis taking apart a few rows and a few minutes later heard her say, "Okay. You're good to go. I fixed your error. Here. Keep knitting."

Louise let out a sigh of relief. "Oh, thank you. That's what I get for trying to knit when I had one eye on *Downton Abbey*."

The conversation quickly turned to discussing the latest episode of the popular British series.

By the time we closed at five, we'd had another very successful day with sales. We had a group of customers who were visiting from

Canada and about ten women from a Red Hatter group in the Miami area had stopped by, in addition to quite a few others.

"Another good day," I told Mavis Anne. "How'd you do, Yarrow?"

"Very well. I'm glad I decided to also sell coffee. Tea is still my number one seller, but a lot of people like their coffee."

"Well, I think everything is straightened out here," I said. "I'm going to go figure out what I'm wearing tonight."

"Oh, that's right." A smile covered Mavis Anne's face. "You have your date with Henry Wagner. But you mean to tell me he's arriving in two hours and you don't even know what you're wearing yet?"

I shrugged. "Not really."

"Oh, Chloe. Shame on you. In my day, a girl knew weeks ahead of time what she was wearing for a planned date."

Yarrow laughed and said, "Yeah, you might want to give that some serious thought."

"What do you mean?" I asked.

She paused a moment before saying, "Well . . . he *is* pretty hot."

"What? How do you know this? Oh, wait . . . you *did* check him out on Google, didn't you?"

Yarrow laughed again. "Well, of course I did. What are friends for?"

I was dying to ask what he looked like but I wouldn't give her the satisfaction.

"And aren't you just the tiniest bit curious?" she asked.

"No," I stated emphatically. "I am not." I gathered up my purse and knitting bag. "I'll see you guys tomorrow."

"Have a great time," they both called as I headed toward the door.

I walked into the kitchen, poured myself a glass of white wine and went upstairs to go through my wardrobe. I quickly decided on a black sleeveless dress. Simple but stylish. I crawled around the bottom of my closet and finally found my black dressy sandals.

"There," I said to Basil, who was curled up on my bed. "How difficult was that?"

I opened the bureau drawer that held my knitted shawls and chose a black and silver one. It might only be September, but the air conditioning in restaurants could be chilly.

I headed to the bathroom and was going to take a shower when I spied the spa tub I'd never used in the three months I'd lived here. I still had almost two hours before Henry arrived. *Why not?* I thought and turned on the faucets to fill the tub.

A few minutes later I was luxuriating in a lavender scented bubble bath as I sipped my wine and wondered why I didn't do this more often. My thoughts wandered to Henry Wagner. Had Yarrow just been kidding me about him being hot? Probably. And what did it matter anyway? This was a simple dinner date. It only made sense to finally meet each other.

I did find myself taking extra care with my makeup and hair, though. And by the time I slipped the dress over my head and twirled in front of the mirror, I was pleased with the reflection looking back at me.

At precisely seven, the bell rang, causing Basil to race to the front door. I opened it and saw a tall man standing on the porch. In one swift gaze I took in his thick white hair, bronze tan, navy sport jacket, open-collar white shirt, and gray slacks. And with that one gaze I knew Yarrow had been correct.

"Henry, hi. Come on in." For one awkward moment I wasn't sure whether to shake his hand or kiss his cheek.

But he quickly settled the question when he opened his arms for a hug.

A huge smile covered his handsome face when he stepped back and said, "It's so nice to finally meet you, Chloe."

"Same here," I said, and it was then that I noticed he was holding a gorgeous bouquet of flowers.

"These are for you."

"Thank you so much. Come into the kitchen while I put these in water."

Basil was beside himself with joy, jumping in circles trying to get Henry's attention.

"And you must be Basil. What a sweet little guy," he said, bending over to pat him.

"Thanks," I said, heading toward the back of the house. "As you can see, he's not shy."

I heard Henry laugh as he followed behind me. That same laugh I'd heard on the phone a million times.

"This is a lovely house," he said.

I reached into the cabinet for a vase and began to fill it with water. "I know. I just love it here." I arranged the peach roses and baby's breath in the vase. "Thank you again for these flowers. They're just gorgeous."

"My pleasure. Oh, is that the yarn and tea shop back there?" he asked, pointing out the French doors.

"Yes, it is. You'll have to drop by some time for tea or coffee."

"I'll definitely do that," he said. I noticed the emphasis in his tone.

I placed the vase on the table. "Let me get my bag and shawl and I'll be all set."

I was surprised when we walked out to the driveway to see a station wagon parked there. I somehow thought Henry would be a sedan owner, but then I saw it was a luxury Cadillac SRX and I also realized the extra room in back would be for Delilah.

On the drive to the restaurant, Henry talked about his photo assignment in the Blue Ridge Mountains, which allowed me to nod and take sneak peeks at him. I noticed he wore what appeared to be a college ring on his right hand. I also noticed he had a great profile, which made him look distinguished. Dressed in the sport jacket, he could have passed for a college professor or a politician.

Before I knew it, we were at Chart House. Henry gave a fellow his key for valet parking. The hostess led us to a table near the window overlooking the Halifax River. I noticed that Henry had lightly touched the small of my back to guide me and then proceeded to pull out my chair. His manners weren't lost on me.

"The wine list, sir," the hostess told him as she passed him the leather-covered booklet.

"Thank you." He reached into his shirt pocket for a pair of reading glasses and studied the list—as I studied him.

He was quite a handsome man. But in addition to his good looks he had an air of confidence about him. Not in an arrogant way, but natural, as though he was used to bringing any situation to a satisfying outcome. He struck me as a man who made a decision and acted on it.

"How does a bottle of cabernet sound?" he asked, pulling me out of my thoughts.

I nodded. "Great."

He gave the order to the waitress and smiled at me across the table.

"It's so nice to *finally* get to meet you, Chloe," he said, and I realized this was the second time this evening he'd told me that. "It probably sounds silly, but from our phone conversations I feel like I already know you."

I felt the same way. "I agree. Maybe there's something to those Internet dating sites after all."

He laughed and raised his eyebrows. "Could be. So tell me about yourself, Chloe. I'd like to know everything about you."

And over the next two hours, I did. As we enjoyed our wine, then a delicious Atlantic salmon dinner, followed by dessert and coffee, I told him about Grace and Aunt Maude, my previous marriage to Parker, my two sons, relocating to Cedar Key, the loss of Gabe, and about my decision to rent his condo.

He reached across the table and gave my hand a squeeze. "Well, I for one am very happy that you chose my place to stay."

By the time the check arrived, I was shocked to look around and realize we were the last two customers in the restaurant. For the entire two hours I'd felt as if I was in a cocoon. Only Henry and me. I'd learned a little more about his job and life, but I had done the bulk of the talking as he had requested. And now it surprised me that I had shared so much with him—a man I'd only met in person for the first time three hours before. But even more surprising was the realization that all of it had seemed so *right*.

During the drive back to Koi House, we continued talking and by the time we pulled into the driveway I realized I couldn't remember the last time I had enjoyed a date as much as this one with Henry.

He walked me to the porch. "Thank you for a wonderful evening, Chloe. I hope you enjoyed it as much as I did."

"Every bit as much," I told him. I hesitated and then said, "Would you like to come in for coffee?"

"I really would, but I'm afraid I have to get back to let Delilah out. But I'll definitely take a rain check."

"Great," I said and before I knew what was happening he leaned toward me and brushed my lips with his.

As if by instinct, I reached up to put my arms around his neck and he pulled me closer, placing his lips on mine. I lost myself in the deep passion of his kiss, which seemed to go on forever, and yet didn't last nearly long enough.

We were both breathing heavily when we pulled apart.

"That was nice," he whispered in my ear. "Very nice."

"*Very* nice," I repeated as I attempted to regain my equilibrium.

# Chapter 44

Over the next three days Maddie made a floral delivery to the yarn shop every single day—for me. The day after dinner with Henry, Maddie had showed up with a beautiful autumn arrangement of purple, yellow, and orange. The next day it was pink and white star lilies. And on the third day, a stunning bouquet of blood red roses arrived.

It was getting downright embarrassing. Well, almost. I had to admit, I was as delighted as a teenager and very mindful of Henry's thoughtfulness. We had spoken on the phone all three days and he was picking me up at five after we closed the shop. Basil and I were both invited to dinner at Henry's place so we could meet Delilah.

When Maddie walked in on Friday afternoon with the roses, all the women in the shop gasped.

"Pretty soon you're going to have to get rid of some yarn if these flower deliveries continue," she said.

I laughed as I reached for the vase and inhaled the lush scent. "I know. I really have to put a stop to this."

"Are you nuts?" I heard Mavis Anne say. "Honey, a woman never, *ever* turns down flowers. Don't ever forget that."

Everybody laughed and Louise said, "Does this Henry have a brother?"

"Make that two brothers," Fay said.

I shook my head and joined their laughter. "No, 'fraid not. Only a sister in Vermont."

"Figures," Louise said.

"With all these flowers, I'd say we have some serious romance going on here." Fay put the sweater she was knitting in her lap, waiting for my response.

"Oh, well . . . yeah . . . I think it's safe to say we do like each other."

"Oh, please!" I heard Yarrow call from the back. "I think the past three days prove you've gone beyond *like*. A man doesn't send flowers every single day because he *likes* you, silly woman."

The same thought had been crossing my mind each day but I had brushed it aside. What I felt for Henry had happened so fast it had literally taken my breath away. Not only that, but I had a feeling Henry felt the same way.

When he showed up shortly after five, the shop was empty of customers.

He walked in and the moment I saw him something inside of me shifted. What was it about this man that caused me to feel such happiness? I had no control over the smile that I immediately felt on my face. One thing I knew for sure. In that moment I knew no other man had ever made me *feel* the way Henry Wagner did.

I introduced him to Mavis Anne and Yarrow.

"You know my friend, Louise," Mavis Anne told him.

"I do," he said. "We live just down the hall from each other." I saw him glancing around the shop. "What a nice place you have here."

"Thank you." Yarrow came to join us in the yarn area. "It's already proving to be pretty successful."

"That's great. I wish you many years of success. About ready?" His gaze shifted to me and when he smiled, I felt my stomach do a flip-flop. No doubt about it—I was seriously attracted to this man.

"I am. Let's go in the house so I can get Basil's leash and we'll be ready to go. I'll see you in the morning," I told Mavis Anne and Yarrow.

I would have loved to hear the conversation after we walked out of the shop.

Henry pulled into the parking spot at the condo garage and I couldn't help but think back to four months before when Basil and I had arrived. Who could have known the things that would happen in four short months? Life really did change in a heartbeat.

"Here we are," he said, and leaned across the seat to kiss my cheek. "Let's go upstairs so you can meet Delilah."

We stepped from the elevator and Henry unlocked the door of the condo. Unsure what Delilah's reaction might be, I was holding Basil in my arms. The large, beautiful Golden first went to Henry to get her pat and then came to me.

"Meet Miss Delilah," Henry said.

"Well, hello, Delilah," I told her, reaching down so she could sniff my hand. "Aren't you a beautiful girl."

Both Basil and she were whining in excitement. Delilah allowed me to pat her head but she was much more interested in Basil.

I put him on the floor and introduced them. They did the ritual of sniffing each other and then Delilah ran from the foyer and came running back with a ball in her mouth, which she placed in front of Basil, causing both Henry and me to laugh.

"Well, I think it's settled," he said. "She wants to be his friend."

"How cute." I unclipped the leash and Basil grabbed the ball with Delilah chasing after him into the living room.

"I'd say they hit it off as well as you and I have. Would you like a glass of wine?"

"Sounds great. Thanks." I looked around the condo and recalled my first night there. Unsure of where I was going in my life, that feeling of drifting and hoping I'd recover some sense of balance. And over the past four months, I had.

"Here you go," Henry said, interrupting my thoughts. "Here's to our new friendship and to wherever it might lead us."

I accepted the glass of white wine and nodded.

"Let's sit out on the balcony and enjoy the wine, then I'm going to grill some steaks out there."

"Okay," I said and followed him. I leaned on the railing and looked out at the ocean and sky. Calm and peaceful. Which was how I felt. "I really enjoyed this balcony when I was here. I spent a lot of time out here, with my morning coffee and then knitting in the afternoon."

"I'm glad you enjoyed it. The view is exceptional, so it should be enjoyed."

I sat down in the chair beside him and he reached for my hand. Neither one of us said a word; my entire focus was on our two hands entwined. I felt a burst of energy go through me, causing me to let out a contented sigh.

"Can I ask you something?" Henry said.

With my hand still in his, I shifted in my chair to better see his face. "Sure."

"Your plan had been to come here with Gabe and make a life together."

"Right."

"Do you think the two of you would have gotten married?"

Something that surprised me with Henry was that I didn't have to think about what I was going to say before I said it. Without knowing exactly how or why, I found that with Henry I could just *be*. And that meant saying what I truly felt.

"I honestly don't know. We had never discussed marriage. I think we were both comfortable with simply living together. Why?"

"Oh, I was just wondering if you had sworn off marriage after your divorce or if it was something you'd consider again."

"Hmm, good question. I have nothing against marriage. I suppose if I met the right person. How about you?"

"I've dated a few women since Lilian died, but nothing serious. So I agree with you. I have nothing against living together, but nothing against marriage either." He squeezed my hand and stood up. "Just trying to get to know you better. I'm going to start the grill."

"Can I help with anything?"

"Not just yet."

Henry went inside to get the steaks and left me thinking about his question. Since my divorce from Parker, I hadn't given marriage much thought. Not even with Gabe. I realized that the commitment that marriage required depended upon two things: a deep love and trust. Something I wasn't sure I'd shared with a man before. But meeting Henry caused me to reconsider this—because he was different from any other man who had come into my life.

Following a delicious dinner of steak, rice, and salad we cleaned up the kitchen and then took the dogs for a walk on the beach. It was obvious that Basil and Delilah were enjoying each other's company. I walked along holding Basil's leash in one hand while my other hand held Henry's.

"What a beautiful evening," he said. "Full moon next week and nothing beats a full moon over the water. You'll have to come back to see it."

"I think I detect a touch of the romantic in you," I said, and laughed. "All those flowers, and you like a full moon. You could spoil a woman, Henry."

"That wouldn't be such a bad thing, would it?"

I looked up at his smiling face. "Not at all."

After walking for almost an hour, we returned to the condo. Both dogs flopped down on the tile floor and Henry and I settled on the sofa with a glass of wine.

"What else can you tell me about yourself?" he asked.

I took a sip of wine. And before I had time to think about it, I found myself telling him about Aaron Price. And Chadwick.

When I finished, he slipped his arm around my shoulder and pulled me next to him, kissing the top of my head.

"Date rape," he said. "I've read about it and even watched some specials on television but it always seemed so removed from me. I had no children and it isn't something that was made public years ago. It has to be a horrible ordeal for a woman to go through."

"It wasn't easy," I said.

"And you really think that meeting Chadwick and finally having a name for that guy has helped you come to terms with it?"

I nodded. "I do. It might sound silly, but I feel it provided closure for me. I really think that before I could fully embrace my life today, I needed to go back to the past and then let it go forever."

"I don't think it's silly at all. I think that's human nature. So many people are held back in life for various reasons, but most of the time it has something to do with their past. And you've met yours head on, Chloe. You're a pretty special woman."

He leaned over and kissed me and I felt a surge of desire go through my body. Pure, sensual desire. Something I couldn't recall having experienced in a very long time—if ever.

# Chapter 45

Three weeks later, October arrived in Florida in all her glory. Temperatures dropped out of the low nineties into the eighties during the day and sixties overnight, with very little trace of humidity. I had spent almost every day of those three weeks with Henry. There were dinners at various restaurants in the area, we went to a few movies, he took Basil and me on his boat with Delilah. And each one of those days I realized how fortunate I was to have Henry Wagner come into my life.

I came to see what a caring and loving person he was. I came to learn more about him and his life and I came to experience a physical attraction to a man that I was finding quite pleasurable. An attraction that was making it more and more difficult to leave his condo at the end of an evening.

We had plans that night to take the boat out and go for dinner to the River Grille—the place I was supposed to go with Chadwick.

I opened the yarn shop about an hour early that morning to rearrange some yarn. I liked the quiet time because it gave me a chance to think, and my thoughts always went to Henry. It was becoming clear to me that what I felt for him was different from other relationships I'd had—including my marriage to Parker. The word *easy* came to mind. It was easy being with Henry. Our time together lacked anxiety or fear. I felt that for the first time in my life I could truly be the person I was supposed to be. There were no pretenses. Henry allowed me to be my authentic self.

Mavis Anne and Yarrow arrived. Shortly after ten I was bent over emptying a new shipment of yarn from a box when I heard the front door open and somebody say, "Is there a Chloe Radcliffe here?"

I stood up and saw a young fellow standing near the desk holding a bouquet of multicolored helium balloons.

I laughed and nodded. "Yes," I said hesitantly. What on earth was this?

"Then these are for you," he said, a huge grin covering his face.

I walked toward him and saw the logo on his shirt pocket read *Balloons R Us.*

"Well, that's a mighty bunch of balloons," Mavis Anne said.

The fellow nodded. "Three dozen, to be precise." He handed the ribbons attached to the balloons to me. "And here's your card. Have a great day."

I stood in the center of the shop clutching the ribbons and looked up at the balloons bobbing above my head.

Yarrow came to stand beside me. "Well, open the card. Not that we don't already know who they're from."

I slipped the card out of the envelope and read, "Come fly with me. Affectionately, Henry."

"Yup," I said, laughing. "They're from Henry."

"Now that's something my Jackson would have done," Mavis Anne said. "That Henry is a keeper, Chloe."

Yarrow nodded. "I have to admit. You'd be a fool to let him go."

I was beginning to think they were both right.

"Well, now, what do I do with all these balloons?"

"Let them hover up there near the ceiling. All of us can enjoy them today," Mavis Anne said.

And that's exactly what we did. Customers got a chuckle out of so many balloons floating around the shop and every time I glanced up at them, I smiled.

Henry arrived shortly before five to pick me up for our boat ride and dinner.

"Your balloons were a huge hit," I told him when he walked in. "Thank you. We've all enjoyed them."

Henry laughed. "Oh, good, I'm glad you liked them. I was hoping you wouldn't think they were over the top."

I laughed. "Well, they were that too. See you guys in the morning," I told Mavis Anne and Yarrow.

"Have fun," Yarrow said.

"The weather is perfect for a boat ride this evening, so be sure to enjoy it," Mavis Anne told me.

Mavis Anne had been right. The weather was ideal for being out on a boat in the evening. Henry docked at the River Grille and we enjoyed a great fish dinner.

When we got back in the boat, he said, "I was thinking of anchoring for a little while farther down the river."

"Sounds like fun. Sure."

He expertly maneuvered the boat away from the dock and out to the river. I went to stand behind him and placed my hands on his shoulders as I leaned forward to kiss his cheek.

"This is fun," I said.

He reached up to clasp my hand. "Good. I'm glad you're enjoying it."

About twenty minutes later Henry had dropped anchor in a secluded cove area of the river. "Perfect," he said. "Ready for a glass of wine?"

"Sounds great."

I positioned myself on the leather bench seat in the stern of the boat and watched Henry uncork a bottle of red wine, fill two glasses, and come to sit beside me.

"Here's to us," he said, touching the rim of my glass. "To all good things."

I nodded and took a sip. "Oh, by the way, what did the card with the balloons mean? It said come fly with me."

Henry slid an arm around my shoulders and brought me to his chest. "Well, it meant exactly that. Both literally and figuratively."

I pulled away to stare into his deep brown eyes. "I don't understand."

He let out a deep sigh. "I like you, Chloe. A lot. Actually . . . I've fallen in love with you. I know, I know. Some people might think this is crazy . . . hell, *you* probably think this is crazy. We only met three weeks ago. However, we really began meeting back in April when you first called me about the condo. I think I fell in love with your voice long before I met you in person. The moment you opened your door three weeks ago and I saw you for the first time . . . I knew. I knew in my heart I loved you. So I'd like you to fly with me. Fly together side by side through life and also fly with me to Hawaii next May. I've recently accepted a one-week photo assignment there."

Now it was my turn to let out a deep sigh. My head was spinning and I was trying to wrap my mind around all that Henry had just said. He loved me? He'd loved me from the beginning when he first heard my voice? He loved me for who I was? And he wanted to spend the rest of our lives together? I wasn't sure how all of this could be happening so fast. But it was. And in that split second I recalled Mavis Anne and Jackson—how in one brief second she knew he was the one. That *one* great love of her life. And I knew without a doubt that I had found mine with Henry Wagner.

I was trying to let everything he'd said sink in and Henry lifted my hand, brought it to his lips and kissed it.

"I'm sure you're overwhelmed," he said. "I just didn't know how to go about telling you how I feel. I know this all seems to have happened so fast. And it probably did. But I know in my heart what I feel. I love you, Chloe. And what difference would it make if I waited six months to tell you this or a year? My love for you wouldn't change in the least. Hey, we're not in our twenties anymore . . . so if not now, when?"

I edged close to Henry, put my arms around his neck and kissed him. Really kissed him.

"I love you too, Henry," I whispered in his ear. "Maybe I always have. And I want you. I want you to make love to me. Right here. Right now. Like you said, if not now, when?"

# Chapter 46

I opened my eyes the following morning, looked around the bedroom of the condo and smiled. Turning my head, I saw Henry curled up next to me, one arm flung across my body, and still sleeping.

What an evening it had been. We did make love on Henry's boat and he had proved to be a considerate and passionate lover. So much so that I was convinced that sex was wasted on the young. At age sixty, Henry not only knew how to pleasure a woman but he knew how to take her to a place she never wanted to leave.

I gently touched his hair, not wanting to wake him, and I smiled. Henry had insisted that I couldn't spend the night at my house. Alone. He wanted us to spend the night together so he could see my face across the breakfast table in the morning. He was definitely a romantic. So we went to my house, got Basil, packed a small overnight bag, and returned to the condo for more lovemaking before falling asleep in each other's arms.

"Good morning, beautiful," I heard him say.

"You're awake. Good morning. Did you sleep well?"

"The best. How about you?" He leaned over to place a kiss on my lips.

"Better than I have in ages." And I had. A calm and restful sleep.

"Good. What time is it?"

I glanced at my watch. "Just past six thirty."

"Time to walk the dogs."

I smiled. That had such a nice sound to it. "It is. I'll throw on shorts and a T-shirt."

"I'll get dressed and prepare the coffee so it'll be ready when we get back."

When I came out of the bathroom, Basil was beside himself with happiness, running to Delilah and then back to me.

I laughed as I walked into the kitchen. "I think Basil enjoyed his sleepover."

Henry put his arms around my waist. He nuzzled my neck and then kissed me. "Did you enjoy *your* sleepover?" he asked and I heard the huskiness in his voice.

"Hmm, I did," I whispered. "Very much so. But if you keep kissing me, these dogs will never get walked."

He pulled away and let out a sigh. "Ah, true. Come on, let's go. Before I can change my mind."

We returned to the condo an hour later, holding hands, laughing, and bumped right into Louise Blackstone at the entrance.

The look on her face was priceless. She looked at Henry and then at me. Then her gaze went to us holding hands and then to the dogs. In a matter of a couple seconds her expression went from surprise to confusion to understanding and then to happiness.

"Oh . . . well . . . good morning. To . . . ah . . . both of you. Beautiful morning for a walk on the beach. That's where Ramona and I are headed. It's so nice out. Don't you just love this October weather? Doesn't get much nicer than this. Okay . . . well, off I go. You two have a wonderful day."

As soon as she rounded the corner, both Henry and I burst out laughing.

"Oh, my poor neighbor," he said, still chuckling. "She'll never be the same after witnessing the fact that you stayed the night."

"I know. She was so flustered, she was rambling."

The coffee smelled heavenly when we entered the condo. Henry filled two mugs and we sat on the balcony while the dogs settled down for a nap.

Neither of us talked but it was a comfortable silence, each of us lost in our own thoughts. The ocean looked especially beautiful this morning. I glanced up to the blue sky with white clouds moving across it. Life was good.

After a few minutes, Henry reached for my hand. "Any chance you could skip work today?"

"You mean not go in?"

"Yeah. Last night was extra special and I'd like to prolong it by spending the day with you."

That did sound like an enticing idea.

"Well, Tuesdays are usually pretty slow. I guess I could call Mavis Anne to let her know."

I saw the smile that crossed Henry's face and smiled back. I squeezed his hand before getting up. "I'll give her a call."

"Mavis," I said when she answered. "Ah, I'm not at Koi House. I'm at the condo."

"Oh." After a short pause, she said, "Ohh, I see. Got it."

"I was wondering if you could handle the shop today without me. I'd like to spend the day with Henry. If that's okay." I felt like a teenager asking permission.

"Of course it's okay. I'll ask Louise to help out if it gets too busy. She'd be more than happy."

"Great. And thank you, Mavis."

"Not a problem. I'm just happy to hear that you were paying attention last night when we told you to have fun. You did, right?"

I laughed. "Oh, yeah. I did. Thanks again and I'll see you tomorrow."

I walked out to the balcony and stood behind Henry. When I put my arms around his neck, he leaned his head back and I placed a kiss on his lips.

"All set. I'm yours for the entire day."

"Well done."

"I'm going to hit the shower and get dressed."

"And I'm going to cook us breakfast."

"You don't have to do that."

"I know I don't. I want to."

I kissed him again and headed to the shower.

I walked into the kitchen to the aroma of French toast and bacon. Henry had the table set and in the center was a bowl of fresh fruit.

"This looks wonderful. I just realized I'm hungry."

"Good. You have to keep your strength up. All that lovemaking burns up energy. Have a seat."

I laughed and sat down.

"So what do you have planned for today?" I asked. "Or are you going to keep me here in your bed all day?"

Henry laughed and joined me at the table. "Don't tempt me. But I thought we could take the dogs and drive down to New Smyrna Beach. Walk around and find an outside place for lunch where the dogs will be welcome."

"That sounds like fun. Let's do it."

"That was a delicious breakfast," I told him when we finished. "Thank you."

"I'm glad you enjoyed it."

I was helping Henry clean up when I remembered something he'd mentioned the night before.

"You said something about going to Hawaii in May for a photo shoot."

"I did, and I accepted the assignment with the hope that you would join me. I'll have to find a pet sitter for Delilah because I don't board her, and that person could also watch Basil. They get along so well. I'd love it if you'd come with me. The shoot is on the island of Kauai and I'll be renting a beach house there for the week. I'll be working for a few hours each day but there's no reason you couldn't drive around with me. The rest of the time would be completely ours. You don't need to give me an answer right now, Chloe. Things really have moved along fast since yesterday. So think about it. And while you're thinking about Hawaii, I'd also like you to give some thought to our relationship."

"Our relationship?"

"Yeah. Back in the sixties, it was called going steady. Committing to one special person. I have no idea what it's called today. People in our age group who aren't married but live together or have a committed relationship refer to each other as their significant other or partner. So what I'm saying is . . . I'd like to be that person to you. The only man in your life."

We were moving fast. "I'll think about it, Henry. I think the first thing I want to do is tell my sons about you. And Isabelle and Haley have a right to know also. I will definitely think about it—about us and about Hawaii."

"Good."

He walked toward me and pulled me into an embrace before kissing me. "I love you, Chloe," he whispered. "No matter what you decide, I will always love you. That can't change."

I felt the smile that crossed my face. "I love you too, Henry. I think I might have waited my whole life for you."

* * *

I couldn't remember the last time I'd spent such a perfect day. We drove down to New Smyrna Beach, walked around with the dogs, and found a great seafood place for lunch overlooking the water.

By the time we got back to the condo, it was almost five and again I marveled at how quickly time flew when I was with Henry. We never lacked for things to talk about. He was very well read and kept up on political and social issues, which I enjoyed discussing with him.

"Well," I said, after we finished coffee on the balcony, "I hate to say it, but I really have to get going. I need to take Basil home and feed him. This has been the most wonderful twenty-four hours I think I've ever had." And it was true. I really hated the thought of being away from him.

"Same here," he said. "I wish we could spend the night together again, but I guess I have to drive you home."

A thought hit me and I felt a smile cross my face.

Henry laughed. "That's an extremely seductive expression. What are you thinking?"

"I'm thinking that you and Delilah could have a sleepover at my house tonight. I mean, you know, it's only right to have manners and reciprocate."

Henry threw his head back laughing. "Chloe Radcliffe, you're my kind of woman. I love the way you think."

# Chapter 47

By the end of the month we had worked out a routine of spending a few nights a week either at Henry's condo or Koi House—and we continued to fall more and more in love.

I enjoyed having Sundays and Mondays off work when the shop was closed. I had just put a load of laundry into the washer when my cell phone rang.

I smiled when I saw Eli's name on the caller ID. "How are you?" I said. "I've been meaning to call you." I had spoken to my son a few weeks before but had neglected to mention Henry. "Are you and Treva still loving your new house?"

"We are. My job is going well and moving to Jacksonville was a good choice."

"I'm so happy for both of you. Are you planning to get down here to visit soon?"

"We're hoping within the next few weeks. And you'll have to get up here too to see our new place. But the reason I'm calling . . . I have some news for you."

"Oh, good. I have some news for you too. What's yours?"

"Treva's pregnant. You're going to be a grandmother."

"Oh, my God, Eli! Really?" I could feel the moisture in my eyes. "I've waited so long to hear you say those words. How is she? Is she okay?"

Eli laughed. "She's fine. Only about four weeks along but she's already seen the doctor and everything is great. She's due in June."

A grandchild. I was going to be a grandmother. "Eli, I'm so excited for both of you. And for *me* too." Thoughts of knitting baby sweaters and booties and blankets floated through my mind.

"I knew you would be and we wanted you to be the first to know. I plan to call Mathis and let him know he's going to be an uncle."

"I know he'll be thrilled for you."

"So, Mom. What's your news?"

"Oh." I could feel myself hesitating. "Well, it certainly can't compare with your news. But, well . . . I've met somebody."

"That's great. It's about time. Somebody special?"

"Very special, yes."

"This sounds serious," he said.

"It is, Eli. More serious than I would have thought possible. It just kind of . . . happened."

"That's wonderful. Who's the lucky guy?"

"It's Henry. Henry Wagner."

"The guy you rented the condo from?"

"Yes. He came down here about six weeks ago and we met and well . . . it's been a whirlwind, to say the least. But . . . we both know we want each other. It all sounds so high school, I know—"

"Don't be silly, Mom," Eli interrupted. "That's how love is. It just comes along and hits you full force and there's no turning back."

All of a sudden my son sounded like the parent. "That's exactly what happened."

"Well, I look forward to meeting him when we come to visit. And Mom, I'm really happy for you. You deserve to have a great guy in your life. He *is* great, isn't he?"

I laughed. "Oh, yeah. The best."

After my call with Eli, I decided to call Mathis and tell him my news, and his reaction was the same as Eli's. He was very happy for me and said he was planning to come down and spend Christmas with me this year.

My next call was to Henry. "Good morning," I said. "I'm going to be a grandmother!"

Henry's wonderful laugh came across the line. "Oh, Chloe. That's great. I'm so happy for you. I know you've been hoping for this."

"I have, and I wanted you to be the first one I shared it with. Eli called a little while ago to give me the happy news. Treva is due in June. They're planning a trip down here to visit in a few weeks and you'll get to meet them."

"I'm looking forward to that. Are we still on for this evening?"

"We are. Basil and I will be over around four."

"Great. I'll see you then. Oh, and Chloe . . . I love you."

"I love you too, Henry."

Now I wished the yarn shop were open today so I could spread my grandmother news. I saw it was just after ten and knew Mavis Anne would be on the patio enjoying her coffee and the Sunday newspaper.

"Come on, Basil. Let's go visit Mavis Anne."

Both Mavis and Yarrow were sitting on the patio with David and Clive, all four poring over different sections of the paper.

"Good morning," I called.

"Chloe. Good morning," Mavis Anne said. "Come and join us. Would you like some coffee?"

"Thanks, but no. I was in the middle of doing laundry when Eli called, and I have the most exciting news that I wanted to share with you . . . I'm going to be a grandmother."

Yarrow jumped up to give me a hug. "Oh, I'm so happy for you."

David was right behind her, kissing both my cheeks. "Congratulations, Grandma."

"This is *very* exciting news," Mavis Anne said, a huge smile covering her face. "How wonderful—I know you're just thrilled. When is she due?"

"Thanks. The baby is due in June. So it'll be a while."

"That'll give you a lot of time to knit all those baby items I know you've been itching to make," Yarrow said.

I laughed and nodded. "I was thinking the same thing. Gosh, I can hardly believe it. I've looked forward to this day for so long and now, it's finally happening."

"Most things do," Mavis Anne said. "Everything in its own time."

"Very true. Well, I want to go call Isabelle. I wanted to tell her about Henry, but now I have even more news to share."

Basil and I headed back through the gate to the house. I picked up my phone from the counter and dialed Isabelle's number.

"Hello," I heard her say.

Her voice sounded scratchy. "Oh, gosh, did I wake you up? It's Chloe."

"Oh . . . Chloe . . . hi."

"Are you okay, Isabelle? I'm sorry if I woke you."

"No . . . I wasn't sleeping. Just dozing. How are you?"

"I'm good, but you don't sound like yourself. Is everything all right?"

"Yeah . . . fine. What's going on?"

I sensed everything wasn't all right and now I felt awkward telling her about Henry and my grandmother news.

"Well . . . I just wanted to share some news with you. You remember Henry Wagner? The man I rented the condo from?"

"Sure. Didn't you finally meet him and go out for dinner?"

"I did, and that one dinner has evolved into quite a few more. Over these past six weeks . . . well, I know it happened pretty fast, but we're now in a relationship."

"Oh . . . that's great, Chloe. I'm happy for you."

But her voice sounded apathetic—not jealous or angry or even happy, just devoid of emotion. What the hell was going on with Isabelle?

"Where's Haley? How's she doing?"

"Oh . . . she must be at the gym again. Practically lives there now."

Something definitely wasn't right. Was Isabelle depressed? Sick?

"Are you sure you're okay? Any luck finding a job?"

"No luck at all. I can't seem to find anything. But I'm okay. Really."

Her voice perked up a little but I wasn't sure if it was forced to convince me or she really was okay.

"Have you given any more thought to relocating down here? Maybe you'd have better luck finding a job in Ormond Beach."

"I have been thinking about it, but haven't made a decision yet. We'll see. Oh, I have another call. Probably Haley needing me to pick her up at the gym. We'll talk again soon. Love you, Chloe."

"Love you too," I said to the disconnected line and realized we'd hung up before I could give her the baby news.

I made a mental note to call Haley later before I went to Henry's. Something was definitely not right with Isabelle.

I walked upstairs with clothes from the dryer on hangers. Opening my closet door to place them on the rack, my eyes strayed to the spot where Emmalyn's wooden box was still hidden. I had given David the letter, but for some reason I wasn't able to part with the box or the remaining contents. Just as I had suspected, there had been no further dreams of the woman in the red evening gown. Perhaps Grace had been right—the dreams were meant as a message to me. A helpful message.

I pushed aside the clothes and removed the box from its hiding place. Taking it with me, I sat on the bed and traced my finger over the initials on top. Thinking back over the past five months, I felt in many ways I'd experienced a lifetime during that short span. I wondered about the twists of fate that had brought me to where I was now. And I wondered if Emmalyn and my dreams really had anything to do with all of it. Maybe. I'd never know for sure. But I did know I'd always be grateful for my dreams and especially for Emmalyn Overby entering my dream world. I knew now the reason I wanted to keep that box in the closet of Emmalyn's old bedroom was because it belonged there. Just like some form of Emmalyn would always belong in Koi House.

# Chapter 48

I parked in the guest parking spot of the condo garage next to Henry's car. Basil and I took the elevator to the third door and as I slipped the key in the lock, I smiled. Henry had insisted a few weeks before that I have a key. He said ringing the intercom from downstairs made me seem like a guest.

"We're here," I called as Basil and I stepped into the foyer. I unclipped his leash so he could accept Delilah's greeting.

"Hey, there, beautiful," Henry said, coming from the kitchen with a towel slung over his shoulder. "I've missed you."

I laughed. "It's been less than twenty-four hours," I told him and felt his arms go around me.

"Precisely. Much too long."

His lips touched mine and as the pressure increased, desire surged through me. I pulled away and let out a sigh. "Maybe we need to do something about that."

"My thoughts exactly."

He took my hand and led me toward the kitchen, where I saw a bottle of champagne chilling in a silver ice bucket on the counter next to two flutes.

"I thought we'd celebrate your news," he said as he filled the glasses and then passed one to me. "Congratulations on the coming arrival."

I touched the rim of his glass and smiled. "Thanks. I still have to pinch myself."

"Let's go out on the balcony before dinner. I have a casserole in the oven. Nothing fancy but we'll have fresh bread and salad with it."

"Sounds great." I followed him out to the balcony and inhaled the strong aroma of salt air.

"I'm very happy for all of you," Henry said. "And I hope you won't think me presumptuous, but I'm looking forward to sharing these coming months with you and the birth of your grandchild."

Once again I felt my heart skip a beat and knew I loved Henry a little bit more. "That's so sweet of you to say. And you're not being presumptuous at all. There isn't another person in the world that I'd rather share this event with."

He reached for my hand and gave it a squeeze. "Thank you. I'm as excited as you are. I've never had children, so being a part of your happiness means everything to me."

I smiled. "Then I look forward to sharing it together." I took a sip of champagne. "I have some not so great news though."

His eyebrows lifted. "What's going on?"

"Well, I spoke to Isabelle earlier today. She just didn't sound right. At first I thought maybe I'd woken her up, but she said no. She's having a hard time finding a job and I think she's in a slump. I think the breakup of her marriage affected her a lot."

"That's understandable. Anything you can do to help?"

I added another item to my list of why I loved Henry. "Well, I tried asking her to come and stay with me again. I don't think I got very far, though. She said she'd think about it. I did call Haley afterward and she seems to think her mother is depressed. She said her mom spends most of her time in her room. I feel bad for Haley too. That can't be a pleasant house for her right now."

Henry squeezed my hand again and nodded. "No, it doesn't sound like it. But unfortunately, if Isabelle isn't willing to change things, there isn't much more that you can do. Except hope for the best. Relocating here might be the best thing for both of them."

Following dinner we walked the dogs on the beach and then returned to the condo to have coffee on the balcony. It had been another perfect evening and I knew the time had come to tell Henry my decision.

We sat there quietly, holding hands, watching the sky darken over the ocean. My thoughts wandered to all the changes that had occurred in my life. I thought of Dreamweaver and how in many ways it was similar to Yarning Together—but in many ways it differed. I couldn't help but feel that the biggest difference was me. I wasn't the same person who had fled to Cedar Key looking for comfort and healing. I wasn't even the same woman who had arrived in Ormond Beach five months before. That woman was gone forever and that was a good thing—because in her place had emerged a woman who had healed once again, but most important, a woman who had learned to forgive. I had found friendship and a community of people who opened their arms to me and gave me a sense of self. I had come to Ormond Beach to heal and I had found so much more. I had found love. And love was the *most* important thing in life.

"Henry," I said softly, "I've made my decision. About Hawaii. About us."

He turned in his chair and waited.

I looked at his handsome face, saw a wary expression, and gave his hand a squeeze. "I'd love to go to Hawaii with you and I'd love for us to be a couple. Permanently. And right here, right now . . . I'd love to make that permanent commitment to you."

His expression of wariness instantly turned to pure joy. "Oh, Chloe, you have no idea how happy I am to hear that. I didn't want to pressure you and I know what we've found together has moved along very fast . . . but I think when a person finds that one special love . . . there's just no turning back. I knew what I felt. I've just been concerned that maybe all of it was too fast for you."

I thought of Mavis Anne and Jackson and I smiled. "I completely agree with you, Henry. When one has found the love of one's life . . . that one great love . . . there's simply no turning back. At all." Although I'd been privately thinking about it, I had misgivings about voicing my next thought to Henry and then recalled what he'd said to me: "If not now, when?" I let out a deep sigh, took in another breath and said, "And you know what? Hawaii might just be the perfect place for a honeymoon."

I saw the look of astonishment that crossed Henry's face and smiled.

"Are you asking me to marry you, Chloe Radcliffe?"

I laughed. "I think maybe I am."

Without one word, he jumped up and headed into the condo. He returned a few minutes later with something clasped in his hand. He turned his chair to face me directly, opened a black velvet box, removed a ring and reached for my hand.

"I admit that so far our relationship hasn't been the most conventional. However, if there's any proposing to be done, I'll be the one doing it. So . . . will you marry me, Chloe?"

I felt the tears sting my eyes as my heart overflowed with love.

"Yes," I said. "Yes, Henry Wagner, I will marry you."

He slipped the gorgeous oval-shaped diamond onto the third finger of my left hand, then pulled me up into an embrace and kissed me.

He pulled away and held on to both my hands. "It's official," he said. "We're engaged to be married. Do you like the ring?"

I held my hand out in front of me. "I absolutely love it. But how long have you had it? Were you that confident I'd say yes?"

Henry laughed. "Actually, I wasn't confident at all and I wasn't even sure the time would come when I felt it would be appropriate to ask you. I wasn't sure you'd ever really be ready to make the commitment of marriage. But as you know, I've loved you long before I met you and after our first date, I was even more convinced. I hoped that someday you might feel the same. I was in Orlando, happened to pass a jewelry store and I went in. As soon as I saw that ring, I knew it was meant for you, and the sign inside the glass display case sealed it for me."

"What did the sign say?"

"It was written in red script on a gray background and said *What Dreams Are Made Of*. I knew it was the perfect ring for you."

I felt a chill go through me. *Thank you, Emmalyn*, I thought. *Thank you for working your magic again.*

"You have no idea," I said. "You have no idea how much this ring was meant for me."

"Let's finish off that bottle of champagne to celebrate. I'll be right back."

I leaned on the railing and watched the moonglow catching the facets of my ring. I looked out at the ocean bringing in the tide and I smiled. Like the changing tides, our lives continue to change. They form patterns and go through cycles. Some good. Some bad.

Henry came beside me and passed me the glass. "Here's to us, Chloe. I love you with all my heart and I always will. Here's to all our tomorrows."

"I love you too, Henry. To all our tomorrows."

And I knew in my soul that no matter what those tomorrows brought, one thing was certain. Love would always surround us—because love really *was* the most important thing in life.

## Author's Note

A huge thank you to Karin Martinez, who designed and knitted Chloe's Dream, the shawl mentioned in my novel. You were a delight to work with and I appreciate your professionalism and knitting expertise.

I hope my readers will enjoy making the shawl that my characters at Dreamweaver worked on during their knit-along.

Please visit my author website to view a photo of the gorgeous completed shawl!

Although the pattern is here at the back of my novel, I know many of you like to have a hard copy of the pattern to follow. Therefore, you can visit Karin's page on Ravelry to purchase this at http://www.ravelry.com/patterns/library/chloes-dream

The yarn used in the sample was Universal Yarns Angora Lace, colorways Heartfelt and Foghorn, and was purchased at The Ball of Yarn in Ormond Beach. If you would like to purchase your yarn here and have it shipped, please call Sandi at 386-672-2858.

If you have questions on the pattern, please contact the designer, Karin Martinez, at Karin@cloudninedolls.com.

Happy knitting!

# *Chloe's Dream*

**By Karin Martinez**

Chloe's Dream is a two-color lightweight crescent-shaped shawl, featuring texture, eyelets, and an original lace border. Increases occur on each right side row, 3 at the beginning of the row and 3 at the end of the row, to create the crescent shape.

Also available for download at: http://www.ravelry.com/patterns/library/chloes-dream

**Materials Required:**

- Size 5 (3.75mm) circular knitting needles, 32" or longer, or size needed to obtain gauge of approx. 30 rows and 24 stitches per 4 inches in stockinette (after blocking).
- Yarn: fingering or light fingering weight (where 100g = approx. 400 yards)

  Main Color (MC)—approx. 340 yards

  Contrast Color (CC)—approx. 265 yards
- Tapestry needle for weaving in yarn ends
- Blocking pins, mats, and/or wires, as desired

**Key:**

- CO—Cast On
- K—Knit
- P—Purl
- YO—Yarn over
- K2TOG—Knit two stitches together.
- SSK—Slip two stitches, one at a time, knitwise. Pass them back to the left needle, then knit them together through the back loop.

- M1L—Make 1, left leaning. Lift the bar between the stitch last worked and the next stitch by inserting the left needle under the bar, from front to back. Knit into the back loop.
- M1R—Make 1, right leaning. Lift the bar between the stitch last worked and the next stitch by inserting the left needle under the bar, from back to front. Knit into the front loop.
- SL2WYIF—Slip 2 stiches purlwise with the working yarn held in front, between you and your work.
- SL2WYIB—Slip 2 stitches purlwise with the working yarn held in back, behind your work.
- SL1, K2TOG, PSSO—Double decrease. Slip 1 stitch purlwise. Knit the next two stitches together. Pass the slipped stitch over the newly knit stitch and off needles.
- CDD—Centered double decrease. Slip 2 stitches together knitwise. Knit the next stitch. Pass the slipped stitches over the newly knit stitch and off needles.
- [ ] Instructions between brackets are worked as a group for the number of times specified, as indicated by * followed by the number of repeats.
- RS—Right side
- WS—Wrong side

## PATTERN INSTRUCTIONS

### Cast on:

Begin with a garter tab cast on, using MC, as follows:

Cast on 3 stitches (long-tail cast on is recommended).

Knit 24 rows in garter stitch (knit all stitches in row, turn work, repeat). Do not turn work after the last row.

After row 24, turn work 90 degrees. Pick up and knit 12 garter ridges to create 12 new stitches.

Turn work 90 degrees. Pick up and knit the original 3 cast on stitches.

You now have 18 stitches on your needles, 12 body stitches and 6 border stitches (3 on each side of the body).

**Stockinette section:**

Set-up row (WS)—K3, P until 3 stitches remain, K3

Rows 1, 3, 5, 7, 9, 11, & 13—[K1, M1L] * 3, K until 3 stitches remain, [M1R, K1] * 3

Rows 2, 4, 6, 8, 10, 12, & 14—K3, P until 3 stitches remain, K3

Stitch count after row 14 = 60

**Chain Section #1:**

Start with CC. Switch between CC and MC every two rows.

Row 15 (CC)—[K1, M1L] * 3, K until 3 stitches remain, [M1R, K1] * 3

Row 16 (CC)—Knit all

Row 17 (MC)—[K1, M1L] * 3, K5, SL2WYIB, [K6, SL2WYIB] * until 8 stitches remain, K5, [M1R, K1] * 3

Row 18 (MC)—K3, P8, SL2WYIF, [P6, SL2WYIF] * until 11 stitches remain, P8, K 3

Row 19 (CC)—[K1, M1L] * 3, K8, SL2WYIB, [K6, SL2WYIB] * until 11 stitches remain, K8, [M1R, K1] * 3

Row 20 (CC)—Knit all

Row 21 (MC)—[K1, M1L] * 3, K until 3 stitches remain, [M1R, K1] * 3

Row 22 (MC)—K3, P until 3 stitches remain, K3

Rows 23–30—Repeat rows 15-22, continuing to switch colors, as noted.

Rows 30–36—Repeat rows 15-20, continuing to switch colors, as noted.

Stitch count after row 36 = 126

**Eyelet Section #1:**

Switch to MC. All rows in this section are worked in MC.

Rows 37 & 39—[K1, M1L] * 3, K until 3 stitches remain, [M1R, K1] * 3

Rows 38 & 40—K3, P until 3 stitches remain, K3

Row 41—[K1, M1L] * 3, [YO, K2TOG, K8] * until 5 stitches remain, YO, K2TOG, [M1R, K1] * 3

Row 42—K3, P until 3 stitches remain, K3

Rows 43 & 45—[K1, M1L] * 3, K until 3 stitches remain, [M1R, K1] * 3

Rows 44 & 46—K3, P until 3 stitches remain, K3

Row 47—[K1, M1L] * 3, K4, [YO, K2TOG, K8] * until 9 stitches remain, YO, K2TOG, K4, [M1R, K1] * 3

Row 48—K3, P until 3 stitches remain, K3

Rows 49 & 51—[K1, M1L] * 3, K until 3 stitches remain, [M1R, K1] * 3

Rows 50 & 52—K3, P until 3 stitches remain, K3

Row 53—[K1, M1L] * 3, K8, [YO, K2TOG, K8] * until 3 stitches remain, [M1R, K1] * 3

Row 54—K3, P until 3 stitches remain, K3

Rows 55 & 57—[K1, M1L] * 3, K until 3 stitches remain, [M1R, K1] * 3

Rows 56 & 58—K3, P until 3 stitches remain, K3

Row 59—[K1, M1L] * 3, K2, [YO, K2TOG, K8] * until 7 stitches remain, YO, K2TOG, K2, [M1R, K1] * 3

Row 60—K3, P until 3 stitches remain, K3

Row 61—[K1, M1L] * 3, K until 3 stitches remain, [M1R, K1] * 3

Row 62—K3, P until 3 stitches remain, K3

Stitch count after row 62 = 204

**Chain Section #2:**

Start with CC. Switch between CC and MC every two rows.

Row 63 (CC)—[K1, M1L] * 3, K until 3 stitches remain, [M1R, K1] * 3

Row 64 (CC)—Knit all

Row 65 (MC)—[K1, M1L] * 3, K5, SL2WYIB, [K6, SL2WYIB] * until 8 stitches remain, K5, [M1R, K1] * 3

Row 66 (MC)—K3, P8, SL2WYIF, [P6, SL2WYIF] * until 11 stitches remain, P8, K 3

Row 67 (CC)—[K1, M1L] * 3, K8, SL2WYIB, [K6, SL2WYIB] * until 11 stitches remain, K8, [M1R, K1] * 3

Row 68 (CC)—Knit all

Row 69 (MC)—[K1, M1L] * 3, K until 3 stitches remain, [M1R, K1] * 3

Row 70 (MC)—K3, P until 3 stitches remain, K3

Rows 71–78—Repeat rows 63-70, continuing to switch colors, as noted.

Rows 79–86—Repeat rows 63-70, continuing to switch colors, as noted.

Rows 87–92–Repeat rows 63-68, continuing to switch colors, as noted.

Stitch count after row 92 = 294

**Eyelet Section #2:**

Switch to MC. All rows in this section are worked in MC.

Rows 93 & 95—[K1, M1L] * 3, K until 3 stitches remain, [M1R, K1] * 3

Rows 94 & 96—K3, P until 3 stitches remain, K3

Row 97—[K1, M1L] * 3, K4, [YO, K2TOG, K8] * until 9 stitches remain, YO, K2TOG, K4, [M1R, K1] * 3

Row 98—K3, P until 3 stitches remain, K3

Rows 99 & 101—[K1, M1L] * 3, K until 3 stitches remain, [M1R, K1] * 3

Rows 100 & 102—K3, P until 3 stitches remain, K3

Row 103—[K1, M1L] * 3, K8, [YO, K2TOG, K8] * until 3 stitches remain, [M1R, K1] * 3

Row 104—K3, P until 3 stitches remain, K3

Rows 105 & 107—[K1, M1L] * 3, K until 3 stitches remain, [M1R, K1] * 3

Rows 106 & 108—K3, P until 3 stitches remain, K3

Row 109—[K1, M1L] * 3, K2, [YO, K2TOG, K8] * until 7 stitches remain, YO, K2TOG, K2, [M1R, K1] * 3

Row 110—K3, P until 3 stitches remain, K3

Row 111—[K1, M1L] * 3, K until 3 stitches remain, [M1R, K1] * 3

Row 112—K3, P until 3 stitches remain, K3

Stitch count after row 112 = 354

**Lace Section:**

Switch to CC. All rows in this section are worked in CC.

Row 113—[K1, M1L] * 3, K until 3 stitches remain, [M1R, K1] * 3

Row 114—Knit all

Row 115—[K1, M1L] * 3, YO, K2TOG, K1, [SSK, YO, K1, SSK, YO, K1, YO, K2TOG, K1, YO, K2TOG, K1] * until 6 stitches remain, SSK, YO, K1, [M1R, K1] * 3

Row 116 & all even rows: K3, P until 3 stitches remain, K3

Row 117—[K1, M1L] * 3, K1, YO, K2TOG, K1, YO, SL1, K2TOG, PSSO, [YO, K1, SSK, YO, K3, YO, K2TOG, K1, YO, SL1, K2TOG, PSSO] * until 8 stitches remain, YO, K1, K2TOG, YO, K2, [M1R, K1] * 3

Row 119—[K1, M1L] * 3, K5, YO, K2TOG, K2 [K1, SSK, YO, K5, YO, K2TOG, K2] * until 12 stitches remain, K1, SSK, YO, K6, [M1R, K1] * 3

Row 121—[K1, M1L] * 3, [SSK, YO, K1, SSK, YO, K1, YO,

K2TOG, K1, YO, K2TOG, K1] * until 3 stitches remain, [M1R, K1] * 3

Row 123—[K1, M1L] * 3, K1, YO, CDD, [YO, K1, SSK, YO, K3, YO, K2TOG, K1, YO, CDD] * until 5 stitches remain, YO, K2, [M1R, K1] * 3

Row 125—[K1, M1L] * 3, K4, YO, CDD, [YO, K9, YO, CDD] * until 8 stitches remain, YO, K5, [M1R, K1] * 3

Row 127—[K1, M1L] * 3, YO, K2TOG, K1, SSK, YO, K2, YO, CDD, [YO, K2, YO, K2TOG, K1, SSK, YO, K2, YO, CDD] * until 11 stitches remain, YO, K2, YO, K2TOG, K1, SSK, YO, K1, [M1R, K1] * 3

Row 129—[K1, M1L] * 3, [K1, YO, K2TOG, K1, YO, SL1, K2TOG, PSSO, YO, K1, SSK, YO, K2] * until 3 stitches remain, [M1R, K1] * 3

Row 131—[K1, M1L] * 3, K3, [K2, YO, K2TOG, K3, SSK, YO, K3] * until 6 stitches remain, K3, [M1R, K1] * 3

Row 133—[K1, M1L] * 3, SSK, YO, K1, YO, K2TOG, K1, [SSK, YO, K1, YO, K2TOG, K1, SSK, YO, K1, YO, K2TOG, K1] * until 9 stitches remain, SSK, YO, K1, YO, K2TOG, K1, [M1R, K1] * 3

Row 135—[K1, M1L] * 3, K1, YO, SL1, K2TOG, PSSO, YO, K3, YO, SL1, K2TOG, PSSO, [YO, K3, YO, SL1, K2TOG, PSSO, YO, K3, YO, SL1, K2TOG, PSSO] *until 11 stitches remain, YO, K3, YO, SL1, K2TOG, PSSO, YO, K2, [M1R, K1] * 3

Row 136—K3, P until 3 stitches remain, K3

Stitch count after row 136 = 426

**Edging:**

Switch to MC. All rows in this section are worked in MC.

Row 137—[K1, M1L] * 3, K until 3 stitches remain, [M1R, K1] * 3

Row 138—Knit all

Row 139—[K1, M1L] * 3, K until 3 stitches remain, [M1R, K1] * 3

Row 140—Knit all

Stitch count after row 140 = 438

**Finishing:**

Bind off all stitches knitwise, using a larger needle if necessary to keep the bind-off loose. I recommend Jeny's Surprisingly Stretchy Bind Off.

Weave in all yarn ends using tapestry needle.

Block enthusiastically, to achieve a finished size of approx. 18" deep x 58" wide (at top, not including forward arching crescent ends).

Enjoy!

photo credit: Madonna Reda

Born and raised north of Boston, **Terri DuLong** was previously a resident of Cedar Key, Florida. She now resides on the east coast of the state in Ormond Beach with her husband, three dogs, and two cats. A retired registered nurse, she began her writing career as a contributing writer for *Bonjour Paris*, where she shared her travel experiences to France in more than forty articles with a fictional canine narrator. Terri's love of knitting provides quiet time to develop her characters and plots as she works on her new Ormond Beach novels. You can visit her website at www.terridulong.com or at her Facebook fan page, www.facebook.com/TerriDuLongAuthor

"You'll fall instantly in love with Cedar Key and this homespun knitting community."
—Lori Wilde

*Every goodbye holds the promise of a new beginning...*

A NOVEL

# Farewell To Cedar Key

TERRI DULONG

*New York Times* Bestselling Author

Made in the USA
Middletown, DE
08 December 2015